# THE BONES OF DECEIT

A DETECTIVE INSPECTOR KAREN HEATH
CRIME NOVEL

JAY NADAL

Published by 282publishing.com

Copyright @ Jay Nadal 2025

All rights reserved.

Jay Nadal has asserted his right to be identified as the author of this work.

No part of this book may be reproduced, stored in any retrieval system, or transmitted in any form or by any means, electronic, mechanical, photocopying, recording or otherwise, without the prior written permission of the author.

This book is a work of fiction, names, characters, businesses, organizations, places and events other than those clearly in the public domain, are either the product of the author's imagination or used fictitiously. Any resemblance to actual persons, living or dead, events or locales is entirely coincidental.

# 1

THE MAGNIFICENT YORK MINSTER, a masterpiece of Gothic architecture and one of Europe's finest medieval minsters, stands at the heart of York. Its soaring towers dominate the city's skyline and beckon visitors from far and wide.

The crisp March sunlight filtered through the stained-glass windows, casting a kaleidoscope of colours across the ancient stone floors. In a section of the Undercroft, a team of workers grafted away, their voices echoing off the vaulted ceilings while they cleared debris and prepared for the day's renovations.

"I'm tellin' ya, mate, my missus is driving me nuts with this new diet of hers," grumbled Tom, a burly man, thick Yorkshire accent, who was always the loudest in the team. He wiped the sweat from his brow with a grimy hand and leaned on his shovel to take a breather.

"At least she thinks about your health," replied his colleague, Pete, rolling his eyes. He lifted a bucket of rubble. "My wife wouldn't notice if I started eating nothing but crisps and beer."

Their laughter bounced off the centuries-old walls.

They'd been working on the renovations for weeks, excavating and reinforcing the Undercroft to ensure the stability of the massive structure above which had shown signs of hairline stress fractures in recent years.

"Oi, did you lot hear about the ghost sightings last week?" piped up young Danny, the newest member, his eyes wide with excitement while he scraped away more debris. "Some tourists swear they saw a figure in a black robe wandering round one afternoon."

"That's bollocks," Tom tutted. "They had too much booze before wandering in," he added, mimicking the motion of drinking a pint.

The banter continued, Pete, a seasoned worker with wisps of grey running through his dark-brown hair, moved to a corner of the Undercroft not touched in decades. He cleared away layers of dirt and debris, his movements slow, careful, and practiced. Each scrape and each gouge needed care to ensure they didn't damage surrounding structures. It was a slow and challenging process and not for those who lacked patience.

Thirty minutes later, Pete's trowel hit something solid. He frowned, crouching to get a better look. The arc lights offered plenty of illumination for their work. Brushing away the loose soil, his eyes widened forcing him to sit back on his heels.

"Bloody hell," he snapped, his face draining of colour.

"What's the matter, mate? Did you find a Roman treasure? A coin or two," Tom called out, his tone teasing.

Pete didn't respond. He stared at the floor his hands shaking.

"Pete?" Ellen's voice held a note of concern as she downed her tools and approached. She'd been working towards the far end of renovation area. "You all right?"

"I... I think I've found something," Pete managed, his voice shaky.

The team gathered round, curiosity piqued by Pete's unusual behaviour. The sight of the hole he'd dug drew a collective gasp from the onlookers.

"Shit," one muttered.

Nestled in the dark earth were unmistakable human remains—a skull, partially exposed, its empty eye sockets staring up at them accusingly and its mouth wide open as if capturing its last scream.

"No way," Danny's voice cracked, his earlier enthusiasm replaced by shock.

Tom pushed through the crowd, his face grim. "Right, everyone, step back. We need to call the site manager."

Carol gripped her phone, her eyes never leaving the gruesome discovery. "I'll do it."

While dialling the workers exchanged uneasy glances. The jovial atmosphere of moments ago had evaporated, replaced by a tense silence broken only by Carol's hushed conversation.

Within minutes, the site manager, a stern-faced woman named Margaret, strode into the Undercroft. Her sharp eyes took in the scene, narrowing as they fell on the exposed remains.

"Everyone out," she barked, her tone brooking no argument. "What a bloody nightmare. I need to secure the area and contact the authorities."

Margaret approached as the workers gathered. She crouched, careful not to disturb anything, and examined the bones.

"How long do you reckon they've been there?" Pete asked, hovering nearby.

Margaret shook her head. "No idea. A long time going on what's left. We need to let the experts handle this." She stood, brushing off her hands. "I'm going to stop work in this section. No one is to enter this area until further notice. Is that clear?"

A chorus of nods and murmured agreements met her words from those leaving.

"Good. Now, I need to make some calls. Pete, since you made the discovery, I'll need you to stay and give a statement when the police arrive. The rest of you go home. We'll contact you when work can resume."

The workers gathered their things and headed out, their earlier chatter replaced by hushed conversations, Margaret pulled out her phone. She shook her head as she made the call.

"Hello, this is Margaret Thornton, site manager for the York Minster renovation project. I need to report the discovery of human remains during our excavation…"

Margaret's eyes drifted back to the exposed skull. In all her years overseeing historical renovations, she'd encountered nothing like this. The Minster had stood for centuries, bearing witness to countless stories and secrets. Now, it seemed, one of those secrets had come to light.

# 2

THE WEEKS of recovery had felt never ending in Karen's eyes. Following the horrific abduction and torture of both Zac and Jade at the hands of Sally Connell's hired muscle and their daring rescue by the SAS, life had changed for everyone.

Karen watched Zac from the kitchen doorway. He sat on the sofa, both hands wrapped round a steaming mug of tea, his gaze fixed on a distant point beyond the living room window. Manky, her cat, sat curled in a tight ball by his feet. Nine weeks had passed since Zac's abduction and torture, and although he was physically healed, he suffered deep mental scars.

She moved into the room, settling beside him on the sofa. "How are you feeling today?"

Zac blinked, turning to face her. For a moment, his eyes were clouded, unfocused, before recognition dawned. "Sorry, I was miles away. I'm... okay. Just thinking. Again!"

Karen nodded, fighting the urge to press further. She'd

learned over the past weeks that pushing too hard led to Zac retreating further into himself. Instead, she placed a gentle hand on his arm, offering silent support.

The extended leave granted on compassionate grounds had been a blessing, allowing Karen to be there for Zac. But it had also been challenging. The man she loved was there, but changed, altered by the trauma he'd endured. She understood it all. The police psychologist had spoken to her at length about the internal struggles Zac faced and how each person healed in different ways and lengths of time. Yes, it was a waiting game now for her, but it didn't stop her from feeling useless.

"I made some toast. Fancy a bite?"

Zac shook his head. "Not hungry. But thanks."

As if on cue, the doorbell rang. Zac flinched, tea sloshing over the rim of his mug. His breath quickened, eyes darting towards the front door.

"It's alright," Karen squeezed his arm. "It's probably the postman as I ordered a few bits online. I'll check."

She rose and hurried to the door. As expected, it was indeed the postman, dropping off a package. Karen thanked him and returned to the living room, where Zac was attempting to mop up the spilled tea with trembling hands.

"Here, let me," Karen offered, taking the cloth from him. While cleaning up the spill, she noticed Zac's breathing gradually returning to normal.

"Sorry." He rubbed the stubble on his chin. "I don't know why I keep reacting like this."

Karen sat back, taking his hand in hers. "You don't need to apologise, Zac. What you went through... it's going to take time."

He nodded, but she could see the frustration in his eyes. There were moments when the old Zac shone through—a flash of his dry humour, or a spark of interest in a case they'd seen on the news. But they were fleeting, often overshadowed by the anxiety and fear which now seemed to be his constant companions.

The night terrors were the worst. Karen had lost count of the times she'd woken to find Zac thrashing in bed, his clothes soaked with sweat, fighting off invisible assailants. The panic attacks were heart-wrenching to witness.

"I was thinking," Karen began cautiously, "maybe we could go for a walk later when I get back from work? Only to the park and back. The fresh air might do us both good."

Zac hesitated, and nodded. "Yeah, maybe. We'll see."

It wasn't a firm commitment, but it was something. Karen counted it as a victory.

A door slammed upstairs, followed by the sound of hurried footsteps. Summer, Zac's daughter, appeared at the bottom of the stairs, her face pinched with worry.

"Everything okay?" she asked, her eyes darting between Karen and Zac.

Karen forced a smile. "Everything's fine, luv. Just the postman at the door."

Summer nodded, but Karen spotted a hint of tension in her. The girl had been on edge ever since Zac's abduction, the progress she'd made in counselling undone in a single night of terror. But as each week passed, Summer improved, and more of the old Summer was returning.

"I'm heading to Molly's. The Uber will be here in a sec," Summer announced, already moving towards the front door. "I'll be back for dinner, if that's okay?"

"Alright, sweetheart. Have fun," Karen called after her, as she kept her voice light. "Make sure you have your phone with you, and it's charged."

"I have, and it is!"

After Summer closed the front door, Karen turned to Zac. He was staring into his mug again, his expression unreadable.

"She'll be okay," Karen said to reassure him, unsure if she was trying to convince Zac or herself. "We all will be."

Zac met her gaze. For a moment, she saw a flicker of the man she knew—determined, resilient. Then it was gone, replaced by a bone-deep weariness.

"I hope so," he murmured.

Karen glanced at the clock. The thought of leaving for work filled her with a confusing mix of emotions. Part of her dreaded leaving Zac alone for the first time, worried about what state she'd find him in when she returned. But another part of her longed for the familiarity of her job and the sense of purpose it gave her. She hoped perhaps being alone might make Zac stand on his own two feet again.

"I should get ready for work," she said, standing. "Will you be alright?"

Zac nodded. "Go on. I'll be fine. Might try a walk in the grounds later."

Karen leaned in and pressed a kiss to his forehead. "I love you."

"Love you, too," he replied, a smile touching his lips.

Karen readied for work. Her mind swirled with conflicting thoughts. She wanted to be home, to be there for Zac every moment of the day. But she also missed work—the challenges, the camaraderie with her colleagues, the sense of making a difference.

She paused at the front door and glanced over her shoulder. Zac moved to the window, gazing out at the road. The mug of tea sat forgotten on the coffee table.

With a sigh, Karen stepped out into the morning air,

closing the door behind her. Zac still stood there. Staring at her? She wasn't sure. Walking toward her car, she felt a profound sense of duality, torn between the life she was leaving and the one awaiting her return.

# 3

Karen sat in her car, gripping the steering wheel as she stared at the familiar brick facades of the police complex. Her heart raced, a potent mix of anticipation and apprehension swirling in her gut. She drew in a long breath, closing her eyes for a moment, trying to centre herself amidst the storm of emotions.

"You've got this," she said. "One step at a time. That's all you need to do."

With a determined nod to shake off the last dregs of doubt, Karen grabbed her bag and stepped out of the car. The crisp morning air filled her lungs, invigorating her as she strode towards her building, her shoulders squared and chin held high, every inch the confident detective she'd always been.

Upon entering, a chorus of greetings smothered her like a comforting wave. Officers she knew by face called out "hi" or "welcome back" with genuine smiles that misted her eyes. Warmth spread through her chest, as she realised how much she'd missed this camaraderie, this sense of belonging.

"Welcome back, DCI!" called out a constable.

"Good to see you, Karen!" shouted another to her left.

"We've missed you round here!" added a third, raising her coffee mug in salute.

She smiled and nodded, exchanging quick pleasantries as she moved through the bustling corridors, the familiar sights and sounds of the station enveloping her. The first place she needed to stop at was Detective Superintendent Laura Kelly's office, a meeting she'd been both expecting and dreading in equal measure.

A quick rap on the door, and Karen straightened herself up. It had been a while since she'd been in a blouse and trousers. For the last nine weeks, she had worn joggers and oversized hoodies, pulling her hair back and holding it in place with a satin scrunchie. She entered at Kelly's familiar "Come in," the words as crisp and authoritative as ever.

"Karen," Kelly rose from her desk with a smile which felt genuine as she came round to greet Karen with an awkward hug. "It's good to see you. Please, have a seat."

"Ma'am, good to see you, too."

Karen settled into the chair opposite her boss, a flutter of nerves stirred in her stomach—reminiscent of those first uneasy days after transferring from London to York.

Kelly sat up, her gaze fixed on Karen.

"So," Kelly began, her tone neutral, "are you ready to be back?"

Karen nodded. "Yes, ma'am. I'm ready. More than ready, in fact."

Kelly's eyes narrowed, studying Karen's face with the scrutiny of a senior officer. "And how's Zac coping? It can't be easy with what you've both been through. I can't even imagine..."

Karen hesitated, choosing her words, aware of the

*The Bones of Deceit*

weight each one carried. "It's... a process. He's making progress, but it's slow. The nightmares are still pretty bad, and he's struggling with anxiety. There are good days and bad days. But he's tough, tougher than anyone I know. He'll get there. We both will."

Kelly nodded, her expression softening, a rare show of emotion from the stoic superintendent. "And you? How are you holding up? I need to know you're fit for duty."

"I'm okay," Karen said, surprised to find she meant it, the truth of the words resonating within her. "Being here, getting back to work—I think it'll help. Give me some purpose, you know? Something to focus on beyond... everything else."

"Well, we're glad to have you back," Kelly stood and extended her hand. "Your team's been awaiting your return. They've done well, but they need their guv."

Karen thanked Kelly for her time and left the office, her steps lighter on her way towards the Serious Crime Unit. Applause erupted as she pushed open the door. Her team stood there, grins plastered across their faces, clapping and cheering as if she were a returning hero.

Belinda was the first to reach her, enveloping Karen in a tight hug which spoke volumes about the worry and care she'd felt during Karen's absence. "Welcome back, boss!" she exclaimed, her voice thick with emotion. "So bloody glad you're back. I can sleep at night again." Bel laughed and blew out her cheeks.

Ty and Ed were next, followed by Claire, Dan, and the others, each offering their own words of welcome and support. Karen felt overwhelmed by the warmth of their reception, blinking back unexpected tears which blurred her vision.

"Alright, alright," she laughed, trying to lighten the

moment. "You'd think I'd been gone for years! It's only been a few months, for goodness' sake."

After the excitement settled, Karen saw the questions in their eyes, the unspoken concerns, and curiosities. "I know you're all wondering about Zac and Jade. They're... they're getting there. It's not easy, but they're both fighters. Zac's still struggling with PTSD, but he's in therapy, working through it day by day. Jade's doing better—I'm hopeful she'll be back with us soon. Maybe even sooner than we think."

The team nodded, understanding and empathy clear in their eyes. Belinda stepped forward, a proud smile on her face, though Karen could see the toll of responsibility in the slight shadows under her eyes.

"I've been holding the fort while you were away. It's been a challenge, but a good one. Taught me a lot about leadership and how none of these shitbags listen to me!"

A chorus of laughter filled the room.

Karen puffed out her chest with pride, both in Belinda and in her decision to entrust her with the responsibility. "I knew you were the right choice, Bel. You've done brilliant from what I've heard. I couldn't have asked for better."

Bel shrugged with a bashful grin, but Karen caught the glimmer of gratitude in her eyes.

"So," Karen clapped her hands together, eager to dive back into the familiar rhythm of work, "catch me up. What's been happening while I've been away? Any cases I should know about?"

Belinda nodded. "The update might have to wait. We've taken a call—a body. Well, skeletal remains. York Minster."

Karen's skin prickled. A rush of adrenaline mixed with a twinge of something else—excitement, perhaps? She'd missed this. The buzz of a fresh case, the challenge of unravelling a mystery, the satisfaction of bringing justice to those who could no longer speak for themselves. It had been a few years since she'd had a 'bones' case.

"Right then," she said, straightening her jacket and squaring her shoulders. "Looks like I'm jumping back in at the deep end. Just the way I like it. Let's go, team. Time to get to work."

# 4

Karen and Bel pulled up behind a long line of police and forensic services vehicles parked outside York Minster. Stepping from the car, Karen took a moment to admire the magnificent building towering before her. She'd passed it countless times since moving to York but had only ventured inside once. Never had she imagined she'd be paying another visit on police business, let alone for such a grim reason.

Officers first on scene had sealed off the Minster behind police tape, with a growing crowd of onlookers gathering at the perimeter. Curious faces peered over shoulders and hushed tones rippled through the throng while Karen and Bel made their way to the scene guard. They signed into the scene log before a uniformed officer guided them towards the Undercroft.

Descending into the subterranean world beneath the Minster, Karen marvelled at the fascinating blend of ancient Roman remains, Norman foundations, and interactive displays which brought the Minster's rich history to life in its museum. The air grew cooler, and the sounds from above faded, replaced by the echo of their footsteps on stone.

"Bloody hell, Bel." Taking in her surroundings, Karen's eyes widened. "It's like walking through time here. Makes you wonder what other secrets this place might be hiding." Her voice carried a hint of awe.

Bel nodded, impressed. "It's incredible, isn't it? To think, all this history right beneath our feet." She ran her hand along a nearby wall, feeling the centuries-old stone beneath her fingertips.

They reached the work site where forensics officers in white Tyvek suits were on their knees. Camera flashes bounced off the walls. The click of shutters and the soft murmur of technicians at work filled the air. Karen stepped forward to view the remains, which were still partially buried, her eye taking in every detail.

Bart Lynch, the Crime Scene Manager, hovered behind his team, overseeing their work as he added notes to his book. His brow furrowed in concentration whilst he directed one of his team members. He gave a nod as he saw Karen coming closer.

Izzy Armitage, the pathologist, was already there, conducting her assessment of the skeletal remains. Her flame-red hair was tucked under a protective cap, her gregarious demeanour replaced by intense focus. Karen stepped back, allowing the experts to do their job while she walked round the scene, making her own silent observations. She scanned every nook and cranny, her mind piecing together potential scenarios.

A short while later, Karen and Bel met up with Izzy and Bart for their first thoughts. The four of them huddled together, their voices low, conscious of the echoing chamber round them.

Bart raised a brow, his pen poised over his notebook.

"Right. Here's what we've got so far. Workers discovered the remains while renovating this section of the Undercroft. We're dealing with buried skeletal remains. We can't determine much beyond the fact it's an adult human skull."

Izzy nodded in agreement, her face serious. "I'll need a forensic anthropologist to examine the bones once they're excavated. There's only so much I can tell you at this stage. The positioning and condition of the remains will be crucial in determining more."

Karen frowned, processing the information. Her mind raced ahead, considering the implications and the resources needed. "How long do you reckon it'll take to excavate the remains?"

Bart pursed his lips. "To preserve the remains as best we can, we'll need the rest of the day, at least. This isn't any regular crime scene—it's a historical site. We can't afford to make any mistakes."

"Alright," Karen replied. "Keep me updated on any developments. I want to know the moment you find anything significant. There's nothing we can do here for now, but we can get the ball rolling on the investigation." She was already drafting a list of tasks and assignments for her team.

Blinking against the sudden brightness as they emerged, Karen noticed Ty and Ed standing by the police tape, watching the crowd grow. Camera phones were out in force, and a few enterprising individuals were live streaming the scene. Probably on TikTok. Karen called her detectives over.

"Right, you two," she said. "I need you to interview the site manager. Find out who has access to the site and get details on any other works done here in the past. Also, speak to the head of maintenance for the Minster.

We need to build a timeline of activity in the Undercroft."

Ty and Ed nodded, already pulling out their notebooks.

"On it," Ty said, his usual easy grin replaced by a look of determination. "How far back are we going?"

"As far back as we need to. Ten, fifteen, twenty, or even fifty years. See what you can find."

Karen spoke to Bel as the two detectives set off to conduct their interviews. "Fancy a coffee? I've got a feeling it's going to be a long day."

They found a nearby coffee shop and ordered their drinks, the rich aroma of fresh ground beans a welcome distraction from the scene playing out a few yards from them. While waiting, Karen noticed Crumbs Cupcakery across the street. A flood of wistful memories washed over her—Jade, oversized cupcakes, and giddy plans for another girls' night out. The memory felt both vivid and distant, a bittersweet reminder of what she'd lost.

Bel followed Karen's gaze, noting the sudden shift in her superior's demeanour. "You alright?"

Karen shook herself out of the memory, forcing a small smile. "Yeah, fine. Just... remembering something." She left it at that, not ready to delve into the emotions stirred up by the sight of the cupcake shop.

Their coffees arrived, and Karen took a long sip, letting the warmth and caffeine work its magic. She pushed the bittersweet memories aside, focusing instead on the case at hand. There would be time for reminiscing later. Right now, they had more pressing issues like who did those bones belong to? And how long had they been lying there, a silent witness to centuries of history, waiting to be discovered? Sipping her coffee, Karen started to formulate a plan for what promised to be a complex yet fascinating investigation.

# 5

Karen left a few of her officers to oversee the scene and returned to the station, her mind whirring with the details of the case. As soon as she came through the doors of the Serious Crime Unit, she called out, "Can I get you all together for a quick catch-up, please?"

Her officers and support staff gathered round, a mix of curiosity and anticipation on their faces. Karen stood before the blank board, marker in hand, ready to piece together what little they knew.

"Right, let's go over what we've got," she began, adding 'York Minster Remains' to the top of the board. "Workers discovered skeletal remains during renovations in the Undercroft. We're dealing with at least one adult skull."

She turned to face her team. "We're calling in specialist officers for the search and recovery. Izzy's arranging for bone specialists and a forensic anthropologist to examine and date the remains."

"Do we know if it's just one body?" Dan asked, leaning against a nearby desk.

Karen shook her head. "Not yet. Could be one, could be more. We won't know until the recovery process is complete."

She paused and surveyed the faces of her team. "This will be a full murder investigation. But not like anything we've dealt with before. The historical nature of the site means we can't rely on our usual methods—no CCTV, and no recent witnesses."

Karen turned back to the board, jotting tasks. "I want a review of all misper reports for the last decade. But be prepared—it could go back much further. And we don't have confirmation on gender, race, or age yet, so cast a wide net."

The enormity of the task settled over the room. Karen felt it, too. But there was also a spark of excitement. This was what she needed. Normality and a sense of purpose. Looking at the sea of faces, she sensed they wanted it, too, with her back at the helm.

"We need to figure out how and why these remains ended up there," Karen continued. "At some point, there must have been earlier building works or excavations. Is that when it happened, or are we looking at something even older?"

She turned to Claire. "Can you deal? We need to research the Minster's history and focus on any construction or renovation work in the Undercroft. Liaise with Ed when he gets back from interviewing the site manager."

Claire nodded, already spinning on her chair to face her PC screen, ready to start her research.

"Any questions before I talk to the super?" Karen asked.

The team shook their heads, each already preparing for the tasks ahead.

"Alright, let's get to work. I'll arrange for some extra

bodies to help us out," Karen said, dismissing them with a nod.

While the team filtered back to their desks, Karen headed for Detective Superintendent Laura Kelly's office.

---

SHE KNOCKED on the open door.

"Come in, Karen," Kelly called, looking up from her computer. "How's it going with the Minster case?"

Karen settled into a chair opposite Kelly's desk. "It's... complex." She ran a hand through her hair. "We're dealing with skeletal remains in a historical site. It's going to be a challenge."

She outlined the preliminary findings and the steps she'd set in motion. Kelly listened, her brow furrowing as she considered the implications.

"Izzy's organising a forensic anthropologist," Karen concluded. "We're going to need all the expert help we can get on this one."

Kelly nodded. "Agreed. This isn't going to be a quick or easy investigation. Keep me updated on any significant developments. And Karen," she added as Karen stood to leave, "it's good to have you back."

Karen managed a small smile. "Thanks. I'm glad to be back."

She left Kelly's office and made her way to her own, closing the door behind her. For a moment, she stood there, letting out a long breath. The familiar surroundings of her office grounded her, reminding her of countless cases solved and mysteries unravelled.

But this case was different. Seated at her desk, Karen considered the possibilities and motives swirling in her mind. Did the person who'd buried the body think the remains would never be found? Did they believe they'd got away with it?

First, she jotted down ideas, questions, and potential leads in her notepad before reviewing the online case file. She needed to set up timelines and review dates.

# 6

Karen stretched in her chair before rising from her desk. She paused by her window and stared at the ground behind her building. When she was on leave, she'd missed the view. She recalled walking barefoot beneath the trees, experiencing the sensation of the grass beneath her feet in the warmer months. It wouldn't be long before she could do it again.

The past hour had flown by, and she needed to top up her water bottle. Nothing had changed in her time away. Used mugs sat in the sink; tea stains and coffee sludge lined the bottom of a few. Sugar crystals sprinkled the worktops, and open cartons of out-of-date milk filled the fridge. Her anger, a typical response, was curiously muted, replaced by an odd sense of familiarity.

She smirked. Yes, it was good to be back.

Back at her desk, a strange feeling came over her. It had been weeks since she'd sat here in charge of an investigation, and yet it seemed like the first day at a new job where everything appeared new and odd.

Yet, as she shuffled paperwork, a twinge of guilt

knotted in her stomach—how could she immerse herself in work when Zac was still battling the traumatic nightmares that plagued him every night?

For a moment, her thumbs hovered over her phone before she shot off a quick text to Zac.

*Hope you're doing okay. Love you x*

She paused, then sent a similar message to Jade. Her thoughts lingered on them both, hoping Zac was managing on his own. It pained her to be away from him, but she knew it was necessary. His recovery depended on breaking the cycle of dependency formed between them.

Turning to her computer, Karen logged in and watched as her inbox populated with an endless stream of emails which kept coming. She stared in surprise as the number appeared. "Over seven hundred emails," she groaned, rubbing her temples.

A knock at the door interrupted her dismay. DI Anita Mani stood in the doorway, a grin on her face. "Is it safe to enter, or are you still adjusting to being back in the hot seat?"

Karen's face broke into a genuine smile. "Anita!" She stood, circling her desk to embrace her colleague. "Come in, come in. Oh my God, so good to see you."

"Heard you were back." Anita settled into a chair. "How's it feel?"

Karen sank back into her own seat. "Strange. Good, but strange. It's been... a lot."

"And how are things at home? How's Zac coping?" Anita asked, her voice tinged with genuine concern.

Karen's expression softened. "It's been tough, really tough," she admitted, tracing her fingers in patterns on the desk. "He's making progress, but it's slow. Some days are better than others. The flip in personality and behaviour without warning is what I'm finding hard to deal with. One moment he's my Zac, and the next..." She shook her head.

Anita nodded, her dark eyes filled with understanding. "And Jade? How's she holding up?"

"She's improving," Karen replied, a hint of relief in her voice. "Not ready to come back yet, but she's getting there. The counselling seems to help, and her family's been a rock for her."

"Well, I'm glad you're back," Anita said with a smile. "We've missed you. The place hasn't been the same without you barking orders and keeping us all in line."

Karen appreciated the sentiment from her friend and colleague. "Thanks, Anita. It means a lot. More than you know."

"So, tell me about this new place you've moved to." Anita leaned back in her chair with interest. "I heard you'd found somewhere new."

Karen sighed, brushing her fingers through her dark hair. "It was a hard decision, but the right one. We couldn't go back to Zac's, not after... everything. Too many memories, too much pain associated with it. The new place is nice, though. Quiet neighbourhood, good security. It feels like a fresh start, which is what we need right now."

She described their new home, a property in a gated development north of the city. "There's a twenty-four-hour manned guard at the entrance, regular foot patrols. The force has been amazing—they've fitted panic buttons in every room, linked straight to the control room. We've got a state-of-the-art alarm system and trackers on our phones and cars."

Anita let out a low whistle. "Sounds like Fort Knox."

"It's helped Zac to become less anxious," Karen admitted. "And to be honest, it's helped me, too. I don't have to worry when I'm at work."

Anita reached out, squeezing Karen's hand. "I can't imagine what you've all been going through. But you know we're here for you, right? Anything you need."

Karen nodded, a lump formed in her throat.

"I should get going." Anita rose. "But call if you need anything, okay? And I'll visit Zac soon, I promise."

"He'd like that," Karen said, managing a smile. "Thanks, Anita."

Karen straightened up as Anita was leaving. There was work to be done, and she was ready to face it.

# 7

Karen pulled into the driveway of their new home, the security gate closing behind her with a reassuring clang. She sat in her car for a moment. The day had been long and challenging, but there was a surge of renewed energy running through her veins. It felt good to be back at work, to be making a difference again, *and to be out of here*, she thought, looking at the house.

A flash of guilt rushed through her. She felt bad. Was it selfish of her to even think that?

She grabbed her bag and made her way to the front door, fumbling with her keys. The house was quiet as she stepped inside, the only sound the low murmur of the television from the lounge. Karen hung up her coat and kicked off her shoes, padding towards the source of the noise.

Zac lay sprawled on the sofa, his eyes glued to a nature documentary. Looking up as she came in, a small smile played on his lips.

He sat up, stifled a yawn, rubbed his eyes, and mumbled a "Hey." "How was work?"

Karen sank next to him. She let out a contented sigh and nestled into the cushions. "Long," she admitted. "But really good. How about you? How was your day?"

Zac shrugged, his eyes darting away for a moment before meeting hers again. "Quiet. But I got dressed, tidied up, and took a walk round the garden."

Karen's heart swelled with pride and relief. It might have seemed like a small thing to others, but she knew how much of a struggle even these simple tasks had been for Zac lately. "That's fantastic," she said, squeezing his hand. "I'm so proud of you."

A faint blush coloured Zac's cheeks. "It's not much," he mumbled.

"It's progress," Karen insisted. "And that's what matters."

They sat in a comfortable silence for a few moments, the TV droning on in the background.

Then Zac turned to her, curiosity in his eyes. "So, tell me about your day. Anything interesting happen?"

Karen chuckled. "You could say that. We got called to York Minster. Some workers doing renovations in the Undercroft found skeletal remains."

Zac's eyebrows shot up. "Seriously? In the Minster?"

Karen nodded, launching into a detailed account of the discovery and the challenges they were facing with the investigation. Zac listened with interest, asking questions and offering insights. For a moment, it felt like old times, before the kidnapping, before the trauma. Just the two of them, discussing a case, bouncing ideas off each other.

"Sounds like you've got your work cut out for you," Zac said when she'd finished. "Historical cases are always tricky."

"Tell me about it," Karen agreed. "But it's a fascinating

one. And it feels good to be back in the thick of things, you know?"

Zac nodded, a shadow passing over his face. "Yeah, I know."

Karen pursed here lips. She knew Zac missed work, missed feeling useful and productive. But he wasn't ready yet, and pushing too hard could set back his recovery.

"Hey." Karen cupped his face in her hands. "You'll be back at work before you know it. You're making progress every day. And I'm so proud of you for that."

Zac leaned into her touch, his eyes closing. When he opened them again, there was a determination there that Karen hadn't seen in weeks.

"Thanks," he said. "I'm trying."

"I know you are," Karen replied. She stood, stretching. "Right, I'm starving. How about I put some dinner on?"

Zac nodded. "Sounds good. Need any help?"

Karen hesitated. Part of her wanted to say yes, to encourage Zac to be more active. But she could see the fatigue in his eyes and knew even the small steps he'd taken today had likely drained him. "No, I've got it, and I'm looking after my man," she said. "You relax. I'll call you when it's ready."

Karen blew out her cheeks and made her way to the kitchen. It had been a good day. She was back at work, feeling useful and engaged. And Zac had managed a day on his own, had even ventured outside. It wasn't much, but it was progress.

She began picking ingredients from the fridge, already planning out the meal. Moving round the kitchen, she felt optimistic. Perhaps things were improving.

## 8

Karen slipped out of the house, leaving Zac and Summer still asleep. The early morning air was crisp as she climbed into her car and set off for York Hospital for a provisional post-mortem on the remains recovered so far. Her mind raced with thoughts of the case, her family, and her team. Though it was late by the time she'd returned from work, it was a relief to step through the door and know Zac had survived. The night had passed without drama. No panic attacks. No nightmares. No sweat-sodden bedsheets.

Last night's text from Jade had been a welcome distraction, a moment of normalcy in the chaos that had become their lives. Though Karen had longed to call her friend and colleague, to hear her voice and reassure herself Jade was on the mend, she knew Jade's mum was still staying with her and didn't want to intrude on their precious family time. She made a mental note to visit in the next day or so, perhaps bringing along some of Jade's favourite biscuits and a decent bottle of wine.

Working the case felt good, a return to routine Karen

needed, but Jade's absence left a noticeable void in the office. The banter, the shared looks of exasperation during tedious meetings, and the unspoken understanding between them were all missing, leaving Karen feeling off-kilter as she navigated the investigation without her trusted right hand.

At least there had been progress overnight. An email update had appeared in her inbox, and she'd scanned the points first thing. Teams had recovered some remains, and they were in the lab, waiting to be examined. It wasn't much, but it was a start.

The cream Mini Paceman, oddly cheerful, contrasted sharply with the hospital's stark surroundings as Karen parked. She passed through the main entrance, her footsteps echoing in the cavernous space. The foyer was almost empty at that early hour. A few bleary-eyed staff members shuffled about, either starting their shifts or thankfully ending them.

She stopped at the coffee shop, its warm lights a beacon in the clinical surroundings. Ordering a much-needed caffeine boost, Karen savoured the rich aroma that wafted up from the cup, hoping it would shake off the last vestiges of fatigue clinging to her. With a grateful nod to the barista, she set off towards the mortuary, her mind already buoyed by the caffeine rush on an empty stomach.

A mortuary assistant showed Karen in, leading her through the corridors to the main examination suite. As the doors swung open, the unexpected atmosphere struck Karen. Instead of Izzy's usual energetic, upbeat tunes, a haunting melody filled the air. It wasn't a tune she was familiar with, but then again, Izzy's eclectic taste always kept her guessing.

Izzy Armitage stood by an examination table, her focus intent on the partial skeletal remains laid out before her. The skull, bones from the right arm and hand, part of the rib cage, and a section of the upper left arm were arranged with care.

"Morning, Karen," Izzy greeted her, looking up from her work. "The forensic anthropologist has been on site all night as they removed the bones. The specialist team is still at the Undercroft, continuing the excavation. It's a painstaking process, given the compression of both the earth and hardcore matter surrounding the victim."

Karen nodded, her eyes drawn to the fragmented remains. Part of her had hoped to see the entire skeleton, eager to push the investigation forward. But she knew the importance of careful, methodical work in cases like this. To avoid delays in the investigation, she'd opted for a provisional PM to gather early insights and clues, with a further detailed PM upon retrieval of all the remains.

"What can you tell me so far?" Karen asked, stepping closer to the table and folding her arms across her chest.

Izzy's gloved hands hovered over the bones as she spoke. "According to the forensic anthropologist, our victim is a Caucasian female, likely in her early twenties. There's evidence of a historic healed fracture on the right radius. More concerning are the fractures to the rear of the skull. Blunt force trauma is the likely cause of death, but given the condition of the remains, we can't be conclusive yet."

Karen absorbed the information, her mind already working to narrow their search parameters. "Anything else?"

Izzy's eyes lit up. "Yes. We recovered a necklace close to the remains." She moved to a nearby workbench, retrieving a small clear evidence bag.

Inside, Karen saw a delicate chain with a pendant.

"There's a name on the back. Sarah."

With widened eyes, Karen shot Izzy a look.

"See for yourself."

Karen took the bag and flipped it over to study the engraving.

"That's good news." Karen studied the necklace. "Between this and the healed fracture, we might narrow our search better than I'd hoped for."

"As long as the necklace belonged to the victim. It wasn't on her remains, only close by."

Karen nodded. A thought occurred to her. "Izzy, are the bones too old to extract DNA?"

The pathologist shook her head. "It might still be possible. We'll start with surface decontamination, then pulverise the hard tissues. They'll be incubated in extraction buffer and proteinase K, which together will dissolve the organic and inorganic portions of the bone tissue."

Izzy warmed to her subject; her enthusiasm was evident. "Grinding the sample into a powder exposes a greater surface area to the various chemicals employed in the DNA extraction process, releasing a greater amount of DNA from the hydroxyapatite mineral matrix. We'll then purify the DNA from the other dissolved materials using a variety of techniques."

Karen burst out laughing, grateful for Izzy's expertise. "Thanks, Izzy. I understand that as much as I understand the origins of our solar system but keep me posted on any developments."

Leaving the mortuary, Karen walked back to the car with purpose in her stride. They had a long way to go, but every piece of information brought them closer to identifying their victim and solving this decades-old mystery.

# 9

Karen strode into the SCU, her mind buzzing with the new information from Izzy. She called for a quick team update, and within moments, her officers gathered round her. Some found empty chairs, others perched on desk edges, while a few stood close by, eager to hear the latest developments.

"Right, listen up," Karen began, her voice carrying across the room. "I've been to the mortuary. Izzy's given us crucial information about our victim."

She held up the clear evidence bag and its contents, ensuring everyone could see it. "We've recovered this necklace from near the remains. It has the name 'Sarah' engraved on the back. Though we can't be certain it belonged to the victim, we'll assume it does for the moment as it could be key to identifying her."

A murmur of interest rippled through the team as Karen continued.

"The victim is a Caucasian female, in her early twenties. Evidence points to a healed fracture in her right radius. We need to search hospital records because this injury may have been treated at some point. I appreciate the further back we look, the more likely we will deal with paper records."

"That's assuming she received treatment in the UK," someone commented.

Karen nodded. "True, but we'll start with Yorkshire and widen the search."

Dan, resting on a nearby desk, raised his hand. "Karen, any idea of the time frame we're looking at?"

Karen shook her head. "Not yet, but we're working on it. Izzy's team is attempting to extract DNA, which might give us more to go on, but from the description she gave me on the process, it sounded time-consuming, so don't expect a result in a matter of a few hours."

A junior officer piped up from the back. "Have we considered how she ended up there? Any theories on motive?"

"At this stage, it's all speculation," Karen replied. "However, that's the area we need to concentrate on, though."

The team fell into a discussion, throwing out ideas and possibilities. Karen listened, noting the more plausible suggestions.

After a few minutes, she held up her hand for silence. "Ty, what did you get from the site manager?"

Ty straightened up from where he'd been leaning against the wall. "Not much. The current renovation only started a few weeks ago. They were just as surprised as anyone else to find the remains. They are a new firm of contractors for the Minster, so they don't have any prior knowledge of what preceded them."

Karen nodded, then turned to Ed. "What about the person in charge of maintenance? Any insights there?"

Ed pushed his glasses up his nose before speaking. "Yes. There was an archaeological dig at York Minster in the late seventies. According to the maintenance manager, the last significant Undercroft work was also done around the same time. He didn't have precise dates but said he would dig out the records and get back to me."

Karen nodded. "Brilliant. That gives us a potential time frame to work with. Ed, I want you to dig deeper into this. Pardon the pun. Speak to the head of maintenance again. Get all the details you can about the dig—the dates it took place, those involved, how long it lasted, what its purpose was. We want those details as a matter of urgency."

She turned to address the team. "This is a significant breakthrough. While we chase the Minster I want everything we can find on that dig. Check newspaper archives, university records, and local historical societies, anything that might give us more information."

Karen paused and cast her eye round her team. Despite the challenges ahead, a surge of optimism raced through her. They had several promising leads to follow, which was more than she'd dared hope for at this stage.

"Alright, let's get to work," she said, dismissing the team with a decisive nod.

With the team scattering to their respective tasks, Karen pondered her last unsolved case with the skeletal remains. In London, early in her career as a detective, Karen had been called to the discovery of a set of bones during the demolition of an old commercial building in Liverpool Street. The century-old foundations had made identifying the victim impossible, and the case had haunted her for months afterwards. She remembered the frustration of piecing together fragments of a life long forgotten, the endless hours poring over dusty archives and faded photographs.

This fresh case might prove as challenging, but at least they had a potential name, a time frame, a necklace, and a unique location.

It was a good start.

## 10

LATE IN THE DAY, another breakthrough excited the team. The office buzzed with renewed energy as Dan burst into Karen's office, his eyes alight with excitement.

"We've got good news," he announced, out of breath.

Karen sprang from her chair, following Dan back to the main floor. The atmosphere crackled with anticipation as they joined the rest of the team.

"What have we got?" Karen asked. Her gaze swept across her team as she parked one arse cheek on the nearest free desk and rested her hands on her thigh.

Belinda stepped forward, a stack of papers in her hand. "We have the victim's identity," she said, her voice steady but tinged with excitement.

Karen's eyebrows shot up. "Already? How?"

"We cross-referenced the name in archived Missing Persons reports from 1980 to 1990," Dan explained. "Focused on females in their twenties living in the York area. Then we narrowed it based on distinguishing features, injuries, or operations."

"And the necklace," Ty added from his desk. "That was a result."

Belinda weaved through the desks to the incident board. With practiced efficiency, she pinned up several glossy photographs of a young woman with long, dark hair cascading past her shoulders and a radiant smile that seemed to light up the room. The images captured unique moments in the woman's life, from casual snapshots to more formal portraits.

"This is Sarah Lockwood," Belinda announced to the team. "She was twenty-three years old, a former archaeology student at the University of York who vanished without a trace in the summer of 1987. Her disappearance has remained one of York's most perplexing cold cases for over four decades."

Karen studied the photos. "How certain are we?"

Belinda pinned up another image—a black-and-white X-ray. "We found a hospital record for her. She broke her right radius and received treatment here in York. This X-ray matches the healed fracture Izzy found on the remains. I checked with the orthopaedic consultant in the fracture clinic to be sure the fracture matched the healed fracture, and she was as certain as could be it was a match."

"Brilliant, Bel, well done," Karen chimed.

Ty stood, holding the evidence bag containing the necklace. "And this matches the description given by her parents when she disappeared. It's not a mass-produced item. It's a unique piece—handmade silver with a small amber pendant."

Karen nodded, impressed by her team's swift work. "Excellent job, everyone. Bloody brilliant to be honest. But we can't get ahead of ourselves. We need to be certain before we take this any further."

She turned to address the room. "I want background checks on Sarah Lockwood. Everything you can find—her family, friends, university records, any part-time jobs she might have had. We need a profile of Sarah and to find out who was in her life at the time she disappeared."

The team nodded, already reaching for phones and tapping at keyboards.

Karen turned to inspect Sarah's pictures. "Are her parents still alive?"

"Yes, both parents are in their eighties now. I feel sorry for them to be honest. More than forty years of carrying grief and not knowing what happened to their daughter."

Karen didn't reply. She couldn't imagine how that felt, the prolonged uncertainty and grief. Her mind wandered to her own family, to her sister, Jane, and felt a sharp pang of empathy. The feeling among the team hung heavy with the unspoken sorrow of Sarah's parents and countless others who had endured similar agonies. Karen lingered on the photographs, searching for clues in Sarah's frozen smile, wondering what secrets lay hidden behind those youthful eyes.

"Bel," Karen continued, "first thing tomorrow morning, we'll inform Sarah's family about the discovery. I'll pick you up at eight-thirty."

Belinda nodded, her expression sombre. "Sure, no problem,"

As the team filtered off, Karen stood before the incident board, studying Sarah Lockwood's smiling face. If it was indeed her remains, she'd had her whole life ahead of her and was reduced to bones hidden away for decades. Karen felt sadness settle over her at the tragedy. They had a responsibility to uncover the truth, regardless of how long it had been buried.

## 11

Karen returned home late, exhaustion robbing her body of energy. Her legs seemed as heavy as lead weights as she trudged up the drive and unlocked the front door. The house was quiet, save for the low murmur of the television in the bedroom upstairs. She slipped off her shoes and coat and walked through the hallway to the kitchen. Hunger clawed at her stomach, but at this time of night she didn't fancy making anything, so settled for a bowl of cornflakes with a generous sprinkling of sugar.

Placing the bowl in the dishwasher, she checked all the doors and windows before switching off the lights, activating the alarm, and heading upstairs.

Zac lay sprawled across the bed, fast asleep. The flickering light from the TV cast dancing shadows across his face. Karen reached for the remote and switched it off, plunging the room into darkness.

The sudden silence roused Zac. He jerked awake, eyes wide and unfocused. "Karen?" His voice was thick with sleep and tinged with anxiety.

"It's only me," she comforted, settling on the bed. "Sorry I'm so late."

Zac pushed himself up, rubbing his eyes. "What time is it?"

"Nearly midnight," Karen admitted, ready for his reaction.

His brow furrowed. "Midnight? Christ, Karen. You said you'd be home hours ago."

"I know, I'm sorry. The case—"

"The case," Zac echoed, his voice flat.

Karen sighed. "Zac, we've talked about this. My job—"

"Your job almost had us both killed," he snapped, then at once looked contrite. "I'm sorry. Fuck. I didn't mean... I worry, that's all."

Karen reached out, taking his hand in hers. She observed the subtle trembling in his fingers, a constant reminder of the trauma he had experienced. "I understand, babes. I do. But we can't live in fear and dwell on what happened forever. We have to look forward and get you better and back to work."

Zac's gaze dropped to their intertwined hands. "Can't..." He murmured.

She played with the engagement ring on her finger, remembering the day the jeweller had come to their house. It should have been a joyous occasion, choosing a symbol of their love and commitment. Instead, it had felt almost clandestine, another concession to the fear ruling their lives.

They hadn't even discussed wedding plans. The thought of a celebration seemed almost obscene in the face of everything they'd been through. Karen wanted their lives to return to normal, but what did normal even mean anymore? The Zac she'd fallen in love with seemed buried beneath layers of anxiety and trauma.

Emotions had never been her strong suit—she was a DCI, not a therapist—but this was different. This was Zac. The man who once made her laugh so hard she cried, now barely smiled. Every time she tried to reach him, her words felt clumsy, her reassurances hollow. She was supposed to be his rock, the one who held it together, but all she could feel was the weight of her own inadequacy. How could she face down murderers and worse with unflinching resolve, yet feel powerless in the face of his pain? The worst part was the growing fear he might never be the same—and it would be her fault for not knowing how to fix it.

"I'm going to check on Summer," Karen said, needing a moment to collect herself.

She padded along the hallway to Summer's room, easing the door open. The girl lay curled on her side, one arm wrapped round a stuffed rabbit. Karen stood in the doorway, watching the steady rise and fall of Summer's chest.

Love swelled in Karen's heart as she gazed at her step-daughter-to-be. She couldn't imagine her life without Summer in it now. The girl had wormed her way into Karen's heart, filling a space she hadn't even known was empty.

After a few minutes, Karen left Summer's room and headed for a quick shower. The hot water eased away some of the day's tension but did little to quiet the whirlwind of thoughts in her mind.

When she slipped into bed beside Zac, he was already fast asleep again. Karen stared at the dark ceiling, her mind racing. Things were difficult now, yes, but she was determined to make them better. They'd been through a shitstorm; surely they could find their way back? With that thought, she drifted off.

Karen wasn't sure how long she'd been asleep when a blood-curdling scream jolted her awake. She bolted upright, eyes wide, gasping for air, heart pounding, to find Zac thrashing beside her.

"No! Please, don't—" he cried out, still caught in the grip of his nightmare.

"Zac! Zac, wake up," Karen shouted as she shook his shoulder. "It's okay. You're safe. It's only a dream."

Zac's eyes flew open, wild with terror. For a moment, he didn't seem to recognise her. Then awareness flooded back, and he collapsed against her, trembling.

"Fuck, it was so real," he gasped, his voice muffled against her naked chest. "I could feel the cable ties cutting into my wrists, smell the damp walls..."

Karen held him close, running her fingers through his sweat-dampened hair. "Shh, it's okay. You're home. You're safe. I've got you."

She continued to murmur soothing words as Zac's breathing evened out. The tremors racking his body subsided, but he clung to her as if she were a lifeline.

Karen's heart ached for him. These nightmares were a frequent occurrence, each one leaving Zac more drained and fragile. She wished she could take away his pain and erase the memories haunting him.

Karen gently pushed Zac back onto the pillows as his hold on her relaxed. His eyes were already heavy-lidded, exhaustion pulling him back towards sleep.

"Stay?" he mumbled.

"Always," Karen promised, settling in beside him.

She watched Zac's face soften as he fell asleep. Karen knew she wouldn't get much more rest tonight. She'd lie awake, guarding Zac's sleep, ready to chase away the nightmares if they returned. Though it didn't feel right to bring it up now, Karen felt it would be good for Zac to talk to Doctor Morales about adjusting his therapy sessions. She would suggest it in the morning.

Karen listened to Zac's steady breathing, her resolve strengthened. She would fight for their happiness. For the life they deserved.

## 12

Karen arrived at Belinda's and sent a quick text to say she was waiting outside. Belinda emerged a few minutes later. Karen noted the dark circles under Bel's eyes and the determined set of her jaw. Though clearly tired, Belinda rushed toward the car.

"Morning." Belinda slid into the passenger seat.

Karen nodded in response, putting the car in drive. "Ready?"

"As I'll ever be," Belinda replied wrestling with the seat belt.

During the drive to Long Marston, Karen and Belinda discussed their approach to breaking the news to Sarah's family. The sadness surrounding their visit lingered between them.

"We need to be direct but compassionate," Karen said, her gaze on the road ahead. "They've been waiting a long time for answers."

"The shock might give them a heart attack," Bel joked.

Karen smiled at Bel's dark humour. "Even more reason to tread with care."

Belinda nodded. "Agreed. it could go tits up. Shock, grief, anger, disbelief, you name it."

The rest of the journey passed in contemplative silence, both women preparing themselves for the task ahead.

Driving into Long Marston, Karen was charmed by the mix of quaint thatched cottages and modern houses, all with lovely gardens. The Lockwood family home stood out—an aging but dignified structure that spoke of decades of care and memories.

Karen parked the car and sighed as she stepped out. She and Belinda exchanged a look of silent understanding upon approaching the front door. The well-maintained garden caught Karen's eye, and she wondered about the lives lived within these walls over the years since Sarah's disappearance.

Karen's finger lingered over the doorbell for a beat before she pressed it, her heart heavy with the news they were about to deliver. Shortly after, the door opened to reveal a frail elderly woman. Her eyes widened at the sight of the two officers. Concern flashed across her face.

"Mrs Olivia Lockwood?" Karen asked.

At the woman's nod, she continued, Karen held up her warrant card, as did Belinda.

"I'm Detective Chief Inspector Karen Heath from York Police, and this is Detective Constable Belinda Webb. May we come in? We need to speak with you."

Mrs Lockwood's hand trembled as she stepped back to allow them entry. "Of course, please, come through to the living room." Olivia led them through to where her husband, George, sat in an armchair. She introduced the officers to George before taking a seat.

Karen and Belinda sat across from Mr and Mrs Lockwood. Karen cast her eye round the room. A dark beamed

*The Bones of Deceit* 55

ceiling made the space feel cramped. The sofas were old and lumpy, the carpet thin and worn, but a wood-burning stove sat nestled inside an enormous brick fireplace. Karen imagined how cosy it would feel to sit in front of it in the depths of winter.

"Mr and Mrs Lockwood, I'm afraid we have some difficult news. During a recent excavation at York Minster, we discovered remains we believe may belong to your daughter, Sarah."

Mrs Lockwood let out a gasp followed by a choked sob, her husband's arm at once going round her shoulders. Mr Lockwood's face crumpled, but he remained silent, his focus on comforting his wife.

Karen and Belinda sat in silence, allowing the couple a moment to process the information. The room filled with the sound of Mrs Lockwood's muffled cries and Mr Lockwood's whispered words of comfort.

After a few minutes, the front door opened and closed. Footsteps approached the living room, and a middle-aged man appeared in the doorway, carrying two bags of shopping in Tesco carrier bags. His eyes darted from the elderly couple to the two officers.

"Mum, Dad, is everything okay?"

Karen rose and introduced herself.

The man nodded and introducing himself as Alistair Lockwood, the son.

"What's going on?" he asked, worry creasing his brow. "I do Mum's weekly shop for her and stop in for a cuppa and a catch-up."

Karen thought that was nice of him. "We have found human remains, and there's evidence to suggest that they may belong to Sarah," she said returning to her seat.

Alistair faltered for a moment, his eyes wide with shock. He moved to sit beside his parents. Karen saw a flicker in his eyes. It was gone in an instant, replaced by a mask of grief.

"How do you know it's her?" Olivia asked. She wiped away a tear with a tissue.

"We found this," Karen said, pulling a photo from her handbag of the necklace and engraving. Karen pointed out a forensic examination of the remains suggested they belong to a female in her twenties.

George Lockwood closed his eyes for a few seconds. "We gave that to her on her eighteenth birthday."

Karen also explained the evidence of a historic fracture.

Mr and Mrs Lockwood stared at one another, silent words passing between them.

After the initial shock subsided, the Lockwoods shared memories of Sarah. Mrs Lockwood retrieved a photo album, her hands shaking as she opened it.

"Sarah was so bright, so full of life," Olivia said, her voice wavering. "She loved archaeology. It was her passion from a young age."

George nodded, a sad smile on his face. "She was always digging up the garden, looking for ancient artefacts. We used to joke she'd excavate the entire village if we let her."

Flipping through the album, Karen and Belinda saw Sarah's life unfold before them. A gap-toothed child grinning at the camera, a teenager holding up a science fair trophy, a young woman in a graduation gown, her eyes shining with excitement for the future.

"This picture of Sarah was taken before her work on the York Minster dig," Olivia commented, gesturing to the photo of Sarah smiling radiantly and giving a thumbs-up outside the Minster.

At the mention of the dig, Karen noticed a subtle shift

in the room's atmosphere. Alastair's posture stiffened. George's eyes darted towards his son before turning away. Karen filed away these observations for later consideration.

"Sarah was so eager about that dig," Alastair said. "It was a tremendous opportunity for her career."

"She grabbed the chance. They both did," Mrs Lockwood added, glancing at her son.

Karen nodded, her mind working to piece together the dynamics at play. "Alistair, you worked on the dig with your sister?"

"Different roles, but yes, I did."

"As you're someone close to her, we'd be grateful for any insights you might have about the dig or Sarah's work. I'll take a statement from you."

Alastair's expression appeared earnest. "Of course, I'd be happy to assist in any way I can. Anything to find out what happened to my sister. It was a shock for all of us when she disappeared. It's been hard for us ever since." He placed an arm round his mum for comfort.

Karen thanked him but remained noncommittal, sensing there might be more to his offer than simple cooperation. "We'll be in touch, but in the meantime we'll leave you to come to terms with the news. Here's my card," Karen said, handing over her business card. "Call me if there's anything you need."

Mrs Lockwood got to her feet as Karen and Belinda prepared to leave. She walked over to the mantelpiece and picked up a framed photograph, her fingers tracing the image within.

"Please," she said, pressing the photo into Karen's hands. "Find out what happened to our Sarah. She deserves justice after all these years. We may not be here for much longer, and we'd like to have peace."

Karen looked at the smiling face of Sarah Lockwood, her heart heavy considering the grieving mother's plea. "We'll do everything in our power to uncover the truth, Mrs Lockwood. You have my word."

"That was hard. Bless them," Bel said as she stopped by the passenger door of Karen's car.

Karen sighed and nodded. "Awful to carry such pain for so many years. We've made that wound a lot more painful. I only hope we can find out what happened to Sarah in the last moments of her life. Her parents deserve closure. Let the dust settle, then I'll speak to Alistair in the morning. Square it up with him, will you?"

"Sure."

Karen unlocked the car and started it before making their way back to the station.

## 13

Detective Superintendent Laura Kelly sat in her office reviewing budget projections ahead of a senior management meeting next week. The loud, jarring ring of her phone interrupted the gentle hum of the air conditioning. She glanced at the caller ID and rolled her eyes in frustration recognising the number for Kim Foster, the Police and Crime Commissioner.

"Detective Superintendent Kelly speaking," she answered, her voice calm despite feeling annoyed at the interruption.

The commissioner spoke with a clipped and stern tone. "Detective Superintendent Kelly, I have been briefed on the situation involving York Minster. I need to talk to you about this. This is a sensitive matter."

Kelly straightened in her chair. "Yes, sir. We're making progress—"

"Progress isn't the issue," he cut in. "It's the attention this case is attracting. We need discretion, and we need it resolved fast. There are... pressures from above."

Kelly frowned. "I assure you, sir, my team is handling

the investigation with utmost professionalism. DCI Heath is leading the case, and she's one of our best—"

"Heath?" the commissioner interrupted again. "She's only back from leave, isn't she? After that nasty business with her partner?"

"Yes, but she's more than capable—"

The commissioner's voice lowered. "Listen, Kelly," he continued, "this goes beyond solving a decades-old murder. There's more at stake here than you realise. From what I can gather, there were several influential families involved in sponsoring the dig. I'm sure they don't want their names being dragged through the mud."

Kelly's mind raced, processing the hidden layers of complexity beneath what had seemed a straightforward cold case. "I understand, sir. You can trust in our discretion, but I'm not sure what families you're referring to?"

"Never mind that at the moment. Let me handle it. I need to make sure we finish this investigation with the least amount of fuss."

After a few more terse exchanges, Kelly ended the call. She leaned back in her chair, her brow furrowed as she contemplated the extra pressures that information would place on the investigation. The political implications added a whole extra dimension to an already challenging case.

She turned to her computer, pulling up the case file and reviewing the progress and evidence gathered so far.

After a moment's hesitation, Kelly decided transparency was best. She hated the whole politics bullshit which made her job of being independent much harder. She picked up her phone and dialled Karen's extension. "Karen? Could you come to my office, please? There's something we need to discuss."

Kelly continued her budget analysis as she waited for

Karen to arrive. Time wasn't on her side, and she needed it clear in her own mind before presenting her case.

The knock on her door came sooner than expected. "Come in," Kelly called out.

Karen entered, her face a mix of curiosity and concern. "You wanted to see me, ma'am? I've only been back a short while after visiting Sarah Lockwood's parents."

Kelly gestured to the chair across from her desk. "Have a seat. Perfect timing. We need to talk about the York Minster case."

Karen took a seat, while Kelly rested her elbows on the desk. "I've had a call from the commissioner. It seems our case has attracted high-level attention."

Karen's eyebrows rose. "Is it good or bad?"

"Both," Kelly replied. She paused, choosing her words. "The commissioner stressed the need for discretion and a swift resolution. There are... political considerations at play."

Karen's expression hardened. "Political considerations shouldn't interfere with a murder investigation."

"In an ideal world, no," Kelly agreed. "But we don't live in an ideal world. The commissioner hinted at influential families being involved, and there's concern about their names being dragged through the mud by our investigation."

"Any names mentioned for these sponsoring families?"

Kelly shook her head.

Karen leaned back in her chair, processing this information. "So, what are we dealing with here? Are we being asked to back off?"

Kelly shrugged. "No, not explicitly. But we need to tread with care. The implications of this case could be far-reaching, beyond solving a decades-old murder."

"With all due respect, ma'am," Karen said, her voice strained, "our primary concern should be justice for Sarah Lockwood. For over four decades, her family has sought answers."

"I agree," Kelly said. "And it's what I told the commissioner. But we can't ignore the wider context. We need to be prepared for potential obstacles and interference."

Karen nodded. "Do you think there's a connection between these 'influential families' and Sarah's disappearance?"

"It's too early to say, probably not, but they were sponsors," Kelly replied. "But it's a possibility we need to consider. The commissioner's interest suggests there's more to this than meets the eye."

"So, what's our next move?" Karen asked.

Kelly met her gaze. "This is between you and me for now. We continue the investigation as planned, but with an extra layer of caution. I want you to keep me informed of every development, no matter how small. Expect increased scrutiny."

"Understood, ma'am. I'll continue as planned."

"Good," Kelly said with a small smile. "That's why you're leading this case. But remember, discretion is key. We need to be smart about how we proceed."

Before Karen left, Kelly added, "And Karen? Be careful. If there are powerful people involved in this, they might not appreciate us digging into the past."

Karen paused at the door. "I'll be careful, ma'am. But we owe it to Sarah and her family to uncover the truth, no matter where it leads us."

## 14

KAREN AND BELINDA settled into the video room as they delved into the details of the 1987 archaeological dig at York Minster. Surrounded by stacks of files and the soft hum of computers, they both recognised the magnitude.

"Right," Karen said, spreading out a collection of old documents on the table. "Let's see what we can find about this dig."

Belinda nodded, her fingers flying over her keyboard as she accessed the digital archives. "I'm looking into the university records first. If Sarah was involved, there should be some mention of it."

A comfortable silence settled over the room as they worked, punctuated only by the occasional rustle of papers or tapping of keys. Karen found herself immersed in the yellowed pages of old reports, her mind piecing together the events of over four decades ago.

After an hour of intense research, Belinda's voice cut through the quiet. "Still can't find much on Sarah, other than she's listed as a volunteer in the university's archaeology department records."

"Anything about her specific role?"

Belinda shook her head.

Karen frowned as she tapped her pen against the desk. "We need more. What about news articles from the time? A dig at York Minster would have attracted a fair bit of attention."

"On it," Belinda replied, already typing away.

While Belinda searched, Karen went back to her documents, her head throbbing from too much information. The connection between Sarah and the dig site where they found her remains wasn't coincidental.

"Here's more!" Belinda exclaimed a few minutes later. "Several articles from the local paper about the dig. They were excited about it."

Karen moved to Belinda's side, peering at the scanned newspaper clippings on the screen. Her eyes widened at the headlines.

"'Treasures Unearthed at York Minster'," Karen read aloud. "Look at this, Bel. They found valuable artefacts during the dig. This discovery excited the archaeological world, as nothing similar had previously been unearthed in the UK."

Belinda nodded and scrolled through the articles. "Roman coins, medieval relics, even mentions of possible Saxon artefacts. Sounds like it was quite the haul."

Karen tapped her chin with her pen while in deep thought. "Valuable artefacts, a young archaeology student who goes missing... Bel, are you thinking what I'm thinking?"

Belinda met Karen's gaze, her expression grim. "That Sarah might have stumbled on to something she shouldn't have?"

"Exactly." Karen paced the room. "We need to consider all motives. If Sarah discovered something valuable, or perhaps saw something she wasn't supposed to..."

"It could have made her a target," Belinda finished.

Karen nodded. "Who else was involved in the dig? Were there any disputes over the artefacts? And most importantly, what happened to all those treasures they found?"

Belinda was already typing away. "I'll start compiling a list of all known participants in the dig. We should be able to locate many of them, though I imagine a few might have passed away by now."

"Good," Karen said. "And let's get in touch with the Minster's administration again. I want to know everything about how they handled the discoveries back then and where those treasures ended up."

Karen's mind raced with possibilities as she worked. Could Sarah have discovered an artefact someone wanted to keep secret? Or had she witnessed theft or fraud related to the dig's findings? The more they uncovered, the more complex the case became.

After another hour of intense research, Karen stood and stretched her back. "Right, Bel. What do we have?"

Belinda raised her eyes from her computer. "I've got a few names for the dig list team, including Sarah. A mix of students, professors, and professional archaeologists. However, I don't think record keeping was high on their agenda. It's all scribbles on paper, and it appears as if it's incomplete. My guess is as the years passed, more of the documentation ended up wasting away on dusty shelves or in boxes, their whereabouts unknown now."

"I feared that. You only have to review old, archived police files to see how much information is missing or makes little sense."

"Yep. I've got a bunch of other names. David, Melvin,

Angela, Stan, Keith, Maureen, Carole, and Ian. No bloody surnames. Who were they? Part of the dig team? Onlookers? Press? Other interested parties? I've not got a Scooby Doo, and there's no way of tracing them or determining if they are persons of interest." Belinda let out a long sigh.

"Any names stand out from what you have found?" Karen asked.

"A few," Belinda replied. "There's Professor Emmett Fairfax, who was leading the dig. He's still alive, retired now, but living in York. And there's a James Hargreaves, who was a grad student. He's a prominent archaeologist."

Karen nodded. "Good work. Anyone else of note?"

"Alastair Lockwood, as we know. He was involved in cataloguing the finds."

Karen frowned and recalled their earlier meeting with the Lockwood family.

She paced the room, her mind working through the information. "Alright, I'll come back to that soon."

Belinda nodded. "What about the artefacts? Should we search for where they ended up?"

Karen thought that was a good idea. "Get in touch with the Minster and any museums that might have received items from the dig. We need to account for everything found."

As Belinda added to her growing to-do-list, Karen stared at the whiteboard she'd been scribbling on, now covered with new information about the 1987 dig. The case was growing more complex by the hour, but she felt they were on the right track.

"One more thing, Bel." Karen turned back to her. "Let's make sure the team keeps it under wraps at the moment. Until we know more, I don't want to tip our hand about the potential connection between the dig and Sarah's death."

Belinda nodded and then returned to her notepad.

Returning to their work, Karen felt a nagging suspicion that the 1987 dig site's secrets weren't just hidden; they'd been deliberately concealed. Powerful people had kept it hidden for decades, and now, unearthing it might come with consequences none of them were prepared to face.

Two hours later, Karen and Belinda stood before the large whiteboard, markers in hand, as they constructed a timeline of events surrounding Sarah Lockwood's disappearance. They worked back and forth, noting known dates and events, starting from Sarah's enrolment in the archaeology programme and ending with the recent discovery of her remains.

Filling in the timeline highlighted its missing parts. There were weeks, sometimes months, where they had no information about Sarah's activities or whereabouts.

"Look at this." Karen tapped her marker against a large blank space. "What happened during this period? We need to find out."

Belinda made a note. "I'll see if other dig members remember anything that didn't make it into the official reports."

With the timeline complete, they stepped back to survey their work. The visual representation of events made the complexity even more apparent.

"Now for the interviews." Karen turned to Belinda. "Let's compile a list of the dig participants we need to speak to."

They moved to a different desk, where Belinda pulled up the list she had created earlier. Together, they began the painstaking process of locating each person.

"Professor Fairfax," Karen read aloud. "You said he's still in York?"

Belinda nodded. "Yes, I have an address for him. Semi-retired now but still active in the local historical society and a part-time lecturer."

"Good, he's top of our list, after Alistair," Karen said. "What about James Hargreaves?"

"He's a professor at Cambridge," Belinda replied. "I have his contact details for his office there."

"Good. Next?"

Belinda studied a list of Minster staff present during the dig. "We have Father Robert O'Brien. He was a young priest back then, involved in cataloguing the finds with Alastair. Might be worth talking to him. He's still part of the clergy at the Minster."

Karen nodded.

They continued through the list, noting those they could locate and marking others as deceased or whereabouts unknown. It was a sobering reminder of how much time had passed since Sarah's disappearance.

A text message interrupted Karen's work. She glanced at it, Zac's name flashing across the screen. For a moment, she hesitated, her fingers hovering over the phone. The case demanded her full attention, but she couldn't ignore the pang of worry she felt for Zac and Summer.

"Everything alright?" Belinda noticed Karen's distraction.

Karen sighed as she typed out a reply to Zac. "Yes, just Zac checking in. It's... it's been a bit of a change, being back at work."

Belinda gave her a sympathetic smile. "I can only imagine. But you're doing great. We've made more progress in a day than I thought possible."

Karen appreciated Belinda's words. "Thanks, Bel. Now, where were we?"

They continued working late into the evening, the

room transforming round them. Whiteboards filled with notes and theories, stacks of files grew on desks, and a web of connections formed on one wall, linking people, places, and events.

As the day ended, Karen and Belinda stood in the middle of the room, appraising their handiwork. The sheer volume of information they had gathered was impressive, but Karen knew they had only scratched the surface.

"It's a start," she said, her voice tinged with both satisfaction and determination. "But we've got a long way to go."

Belinda nodded in agreement. "At least we've got a clearer picture of what we're dealing with. And a plan for moving forward."

Karen looked at the timeline once more, her eyes drawn to the gaps they still needed to fill. "First thing tomorrow, we schedule these interviews. I want to speak to Fairfax as soon as possible, tomorrow ideally, and then Sarah's brother at the most convenient time."

"I'll get on it first thing," Belinda assured her.

Exhausted, Karen gathered her things to leave, her shoulders aching. The case was complex, but she enjoyed that part the most, the ones which tested her.

## 15

Karen showered to wash away the last remnants of sleep and padded into the kitchen, the aroma of freshly brewed coffee and toast filling the air. Zac stood at the cooker, spatula in hand, tending to a pan of scrambled eggs. Summer sat at the table, her attention fixed on her phone, thumb scrolling.

"Morning." Karen reached for a mug.

Zac glanced over his shoulder. "There's coffee in the pot."

Karen poured herself a cup, savouring the rich scent. She leaned against the counter, watching Zac plate up the eggs. The domesticity of the scene felt surreal, a stark contrast to the grim reality of her current case.

Summer looked up from her phone. "How's the skeleton case going?"

Karen hesitated, surprised by the direct question. She took a sip of coffee, buying herself a moment to consider her response. "It's... progressing. We've identified the victim."

Summer's eyes widened with interest. "Really? Who was it?"

Karen moved to the table and sat across from Summer. "A young woman. She was a former archaeology student who disappeared in 1987."

"Wow," Summer breathed. "That's so long ago. How did you figure out who she was?"

Karen glanced at Zac, who had turned from the cooker to listen. His face was impassive, but she sensed the tension in his posture.

"We used old missing persons reports and medical records." Karen kept her tone neutral. "Sarah had suffered a unique fracture in her arm which helped us identify her."

"That's so cool." Summer leaned forward. "What about DNA? I read they can extract DNA from old bones now."

Karen nodded, impressed by Summer's knowledge. "That's right. We're working on that, too, but it's a complex process."

"What about the dig site?" Summer asked. "Was there anything else found with her?"

Karen hesitated again, aware of Zac's gaze. "There was a necklace. It helped with the identification."

Summer's eyes widened. "That's amazing. It's like a real-life mystery novel. How do you even start investigating something that happened so long ago?"

Before Karen could respond, Zac cleared his throat. "Summer, don't you have a history project to finish?"

Summer rolled her eyes. "Dad, this is way more interesting than my project on the Industrial Revolution."

"Your project's due tomorrow," Zac reminded her, his tone firm. "You need to focus on that."

Karen watched the exchange, noting the underlying

tension in Zac's voice. She understood his concern, his desire to shield Summer from the darker aspects of police work.

"Your dad's right, luv," Karen said. "Your schoolwork comes first."

Summer sighed. "Fine. But can you tell me more about the case later?"

The ring of her mobile cut Karen off as she opened her mouth to respond. She glanced at the screen and frowned. "It's your mum," she said to Summer as she stood. "I'd better take this."

She stepped out of the kitchen to answer the call. "Michelle, hi."

"Karen." Michelle's voice was taut with tension. "I've seen the news about your case. A body found in York Minster?"

Karen pinched the bridge of her nose. "Yes, that's right."

"And you're leading the investigation?"

"I am," Karen confirmed.

"I'm concerned," Michelle replied bluntly. "Is Summer safe without you keeping a close eye on her?"

Karen leaned against the wall and closed her eyes. "Of course she is, Michelle. We've taken every precaution—"

"But you can't guarantee it, can you?" Michelle interrupted. "Your work is dangerous, Karen. I don't want Summer exposed to that."

"Michelle, I promise you, Summer's safety is our top priority," Karen tried to keep her frustration in check. "We have security measures in place—"

"Did that help when Zac was kidnapped?" Michelle hissed.

Karen flinched at the reminder. "That was a unique

situation," she said, her voice strained. "We've increased our security since then."

"I want to speak with Zac and discuss changing our custody arrangement," Michelle snapped. "I don't think it's safe for Summer to be with you and Zac right now."

Karen's heart sank. "Michelle, please. Let's not be hasty. This is ridiculous, and I don't think it's right for you to be making rash and impulsive decisions like this. Zac and I agreed during his recovery I would be your contact. Zac doesn't need you bending his ear at every opportunity. So, I suggest you back off. We've got it under control. We can talk about this—"

"I'll have my solicitor contact you," Michelle said and hung up.

"Wow." Karen lowered the phone and stared at the blank screen.

Michelle had always been a bit of a thorn in her side, but today she felt less like a concerned mother and more like a wrecking ball, smashing through the fragile progress Karen and Zac had made. She understood the woman's fear—honestly, she shared it—but Michelle's sharp words and overreaching demands stung. Karen was trying, desperate to hold everything together: to help Zac heal, to protect Summer, and to keep their lives from unravelling under the weight of their shared trauma. But every time Michelle started throwing round accusations and ultimatums, Karen felt like she was failing everyone. She leaned her head against the wall, her eyes burning with unshed tears, and let the ache of being stuck in the middle wash over her.

After a few deep breaths, she clenched her jaw and composed herself before returning to the kitchen. Zac and Summer were in the midst of a heated discussion when Karen walked in.

"But, Dad, why can't I learn more about police work?" Summer questioned, her voice rising in frustration. "It's interesting!"

Zac's face flushed; his jaw clenched. "It's dangerous work, Summer. You don't need to know about it."

"But Karen does it," Summer argued. "And she's fine."

Zac's eyes flicked to Karen, then back to Summer. "It's different for Karen. She's trained for it."

"So I could train for it, too," Summer insisted.

"Absolutely not," Zac said firmly. "I don't want you anywhere near any kind of danger."

Karen stepped forward, placing a hand on Summer's shoulder. "Luv, your dad's just worried about you. The work we do can be dangerous, and it's natural for him to want to protect you."

Summer looked at her, eyes pleading. "But you're careful, right? You stay safe?"

Karen's heart clenched at the innocent question. She knelt beside Summer's chair, meeting her eyes. "I am very careful. And I have an entire team of people working with me to make safety a top priority. But your dad's right—it can be hairy. That's why we don't want you to worry about it."

Summer nodded, her enthusiasm dampened. Karen pulled her into a tight hug, breathing in to smell her shampoo. Over Summer's shoulder, she met Zac's eyes, seeing the conflict there—his love for her warring with his fear for their safety.

"I've got to head to work," Karen said, as she loosened Summer from her grip. She kissed the top of her head. "Have a good day at school, Trouble. I want to hear all about your history project later."

Summer offered a small smile. "Okay. Be safe, Karen."

Karen's throat tightened at the words. "Always," she promised.

She grabbed her bag and coat, and gave Zac a quick kiss. "I'll call you later. It was Michelle on the phone."

Zac rolled his eyes and nodded. "Take care, and thanks for keeping her off my back, I don't want to deal with her tantrums right now."

Karen left the house, burdened by the responsibility—to her family, to her job, to the victim whose story she was trying to uncover.

## 16

Karen sat in her car outside Jade's new apartment, annoyed she hadn't come sooner. The Lockwood case had kept her busy, but it was no excuse for neglecting her friend. She checked her phone for any important messages as she stepped from the car, the cool air a sharp contrast to the warmth of her Mini.

Karen pressed the buzzer and waited.

A long pause followed before the sound of movement inside. The door opened, revealing Jade. Karen's heart clenched at the sight of her friend. Jade looked pale and drawn, dark circles under her eyes hinting at sleepless nights. Her hair, often neatly styled, hung limp round her face. She was wearing an oversized sweater which swallowed her frame, making her appear smaller and more vulnerable than Karen had ever seen her.

"Karen," Jade said, her voice a mix of surprise and relief. "I wasn't expecting you."

Stepping inside as Jade moved back to let her in, Karen replied, "I should have come sooner. Sorry. I've been meaning to visit more often, but…"

"You were only here a few days ago. You don't have to check up on me. I still have a pulse," Jade rolled her eyes.

Karen bit back the guilt threatening to overwhelm her. "I've been busy with…"

"The case," Jade finished for her, a hint of understanding in her tired eyes. "It's okay. I've seen it on the news. I know how it is."

Karen leant in and gave Jade a hug, which lasted for ages, neither wanting to pull away. It felt so good to see her, Karen's eyes misted over.

Jade loosened her grip and led her back in to her apartment.

They settled in the living room. Karen noticed the less-than-tidy space and a crumpled blanket on the couch, suggesting Jade had been sleeping there. An empty mug and half-eaten plate of food cluttered the coffee table. Karen spotted a laptop hidden under some magazines, its screen showing a news website.

"Where's your mum?"

"She's doing a food shop and a few chores for herself. Not sure when she's back."

"How are you doing, really?" Karen asked, settling into an armchair across from Jade.

Jade attempted a smile. "I'm… managing. The nightmares are less frequent now." She fidgeted with the edge of her sleeve. "The psych says I'm making progress, but some days it doesn't feel like it. I'm seeing Doctor Morales later today, so that will be a barrel of laughs."

Karen nodded. "Recovery isn't linear. You're bound to have good and bad days. But you're strong, Jade. You'll get through this."

"How's the team?"

"They are good and miss you. I miss you. But you'll be back before you know it."

Jade's gaze dropped to her hands. "Sometimes I'm not so sure. I feel... different. Like I don't quite fit in my skin anymore." She looked up and changed the subject. "How's the Lockwood case going?"

Karen hesitated, surprised by the abrupt change. "It's progressing. We've made a few breakthroughs, but there's still a lot to uncover."

Jade nodded, a spark of interest in her tired eyes. "What breakthroughs? Have you interviewed the original dig participants? What about the treasures and artefacts, were they found?"

"Jade," Karen raised a brow, "you're supposed to be focusing on your recovery, not worrying about work."

"I know, I know," Jade replied, a hint of frustration in her voice. "But I need this. Thinking about cases, trying to solve puzzles... it helps. It gives me something to focus on besides..." She trailed off, her gaze distant, and Karen could almost see the memories of her ordeal flickering behind her eyes.

Karen reached out and placed a comforting hand on Jade's arm. "I understand. But I'm worried about you pushing yourself too hard. Your health comes first."

Jade's eyes met Karen's, a mix of determination and vulnerability in them. "Please, Karen. I'm not asking to come back to work. Just... keep me in the loop? It makes me feel less useless, less... trapped in my head. It would be a distraction."

Karen studied her friend, recognising the struggle behind her words. She saw the Jade she knew—the brilliant detective, the tenacious investigator—fighting to surface beneath the trauma. After a moment, she nodded. "Okay. I'll keep you informed about major developments. But you have to promise me you won't do anything else. Your recovery comes first, alright?"

Relief washed over Jade's face. "I promise. Thank you. You don't know how much this means to me."

They spent the next hour talking, Karen sharing select details about the case. She watched Jade come alive, asking insightful questions and making connections even Karen hadn't considered. It was like watching a withered plant unfurling its leaves in the sunlight.

Karen saw Jade stifling a yawn. "I should get going," she said, standing. "You need your rest."

Jade nodded, looking exhausted. "Thank you for coming, Karen. And for... well, for everything."

Karen pulled Jade into a tight hug. Jade stiffened for a moment before relaxing into the embrace. She wondered if Jade might not keep her promise about not investigating, but she understood her friend's need to feel connected to their work. It was part of who Jade was, and part of her healing process.

"Take care of yourself, and say hi to your mum from me," Karen said as she stepped out. "If you need anything —anything at all—you call me, okay? Day or night. And you could always pop in to say hi to everyone. I know they'd love to see you."

Jade nodded, a small but genuine smile on her face. "I will. Thanks."

Karen returned to her car. Concern for Jade's wellbeing warred with hope at seeing glimpses of her old self. She knew the road to recovery would be long and challenging for Jade, but perhaps this connection to their work would help her find her way back to herself.

## 17

KAREN ARRIVED at Alistair Lockwood's modest terraced home not long after. This visit differed from her previous encounter with Alistair. Today, she wasn't here to break any more bad news, but to understand—to see Sarah Lockwood through her brother's eyes and as a key witness in the last days of Sarah's life.

The overgrown flowerbeds clashed sharply with the house's neat appearance.

Alistair answered the door, his face a mixture of wariness and resignation. "DCI Heath, please, come in."

Bookshelves towards the end of the hallway were overflowing with academic texts and journals, making the interior of the house cluttered but clean. Alistair led Karen to a small sitting room, where framed photographs covered every surface. He noticed Karen's lingering gaze.

"Most of these are of Sarah and my parents," he said softly, picking up a frame from a nearby table. "This one was taken when she started university. She was so excited, so full of life."

Karen took a seat, accepting the photograph Alistair

handed her. It showed a young Sarah, her smile radiant, eyes sparkling with enthusiasm. Her parents either side of her. "She looks happy."

Alistair nodded, lowering himself into an armchair opposite Karen. "She was. Sarah had this... zest for life, for knowledge. Even as a child, she was always asking my parents questions, always wanting to know more."

He paused, a fond smile playing on his lips. "I remember when she was about nine, she dug up half of our mother's garden looking for 'ancient treasures'. Mum was furious, but Dad couldn't stop laughing. He said we had a budding archaeologist on our hands."

Alistair's eyes sparkled with the memory.

"When did she first become interested in archaeology?"

Alistair leaned back, his gaze distant. "It was a school trip to the British Museum when she was twelve. She came home buzzing, talking a mile a minute about mummies and hieroglyphics. From that day on, she was determined to become an archaeologist. When I followed that route and she gained an insight into my work, it only consolidated her interest in doing the same."

Alistair continued to share anecdotes about Sarah's childhood and teenage years. Karen detected a shift in his demeanour. The initial wariness had faded, replaced by a bittersweet nostalgia.

"Sarah was always the brave one," he said, a hint of admiration in his voice. "Where I was cautious, she was bold. She wasn't afraid to challenge authority or question the status quo. It's what made her such a promising archaeologist."

Karen nodded for him to continue. "And as a sister? What was she like?"

Alistair's expression clouded, a flicker of pain crossed

his face. "She was... incredible. Supportive, funny, always there when I needed her. But I..." his voice caught.

"But what?" Karen prompted.

Alistair shook his head. "I wasn't always there for her as we grew up. I was so caught up in my career, my own ambitions. Sometimes she reached out when she needed me, and I was too busy or too distracted to notice."

"What was your relationship like?" Karen asked. "Were you close?"

Alistair hesitated, guilt flashing across his face. "We were, once. But as we got older, we drifted apart. I regret not spending more time with her."

"In the time leading up to Sarah's disappearance, did you notice any changes in her behaviour? Was she worried about anything?"

Alistair's brow furrowed as he thought back. "She was excited about the dig for certain. But now you mention it, there was something... She seemed distracted, almost nervous at times."

"Did she confide in you about any concerns?"

Alistair shook his head. "Not directly, no. But I remember overhearing her on the phone once, arguing with someone. I couldn't make out what it was about, but she sounded upset."

Karen made a note of this. "Did you ask her about it?"

"I tried." Alistair sighed. "But she brushed it off, said it was nothing. I should have pushed harder, should have made her talk to me." His voice cracked slightly on the last words.

Karen gave him a moment to compose himself before continuing. "What about her work on the dig? Did she ever mention any issues or conflicts with her colleagues?"

Alistair's expression turned thoughtful. "She mentioned something about disagreements over how certain artefacts should be catalogued. But didn't go into details."

Karen continued to probe Alistair for more details, carefully noting his reactions. She noticed how he sometimes hesitated before answering, how his eyes would dart away when certain topics came up.

With the interview almost over, Karen posed one last question. "If Sarah were here today, what would you want to say to her?"

Alistair's composure broke at this question. Tears welled in his eyes as he struggled to speak. "I... I'd tell her I'm sorry. Sorry for not being there for her, for not listening when she needed me. And I'd tell her how much I've missed her, every single day since she's been gone."

He stood, moving to a bookshelf and pulling out a worn leather-bound journal. "This was Sarah's diary from her first year at university. She gave it to me when she graduated, said it would help me understand her journey." He handed it to Karen, his hands trembling. "I never read it. I always thought there would be time later."

Karen accepted the diary, understanding the significance of this gesture. "Alistair, I..."

"Please," he interrupted, "return it when you've read it."

"Alistair, thank you for sharing this with me."

Alistair sank back into his chair, looking older and more vulnerable. "You know, DCI Heath, the hardest part isn't the public scrutiny. It's the knowledge I failed her. Not just at the end, but throughout her life. I was her big brother. I should have protected her, supported her dreams. But she was too headstrong, and I sometimes found it hard getting through to her."

"From everything you've told me, it's clear Sarah

adored you. She looked up to you, followed in your footsteps."

"But I let her down," he cried, his eyes glistening with raw emotion.

"We all make mistakes," Karen said. "What matters is how we choose to move forward. By sharing these memories, by helping us understand who Sarah really was, you're honouring her memory."

Alistair wiped his eyes. "She deserved so much better. She had such potential, such passion. The world is poorer for having lost her."

Karen listened and built a more complete picture of the young woman whose life had been cut tragically short as Alistair continued to share stories about Sarah—her triumphs, her struggles, her dreams for the future.

When Karen finally stood to leave, Alistair walked her to the door.

"Thank you. For listening, and for caring about who Sarah really was."

Karen smiled. "Thank you for sharing her with me. It helps, you know. Understanding the person behind the case makes our work more meaningful."

With a quick look at Sarah's diary beside her, Karen started her drive.

The visit had lasted over two hours, but Karen felt she had gained invaluable insights into Sarah Lockwood's life and character.

## 18

BACK AT THE STATION, Karen entered the incident room and glanced over her assembled team. The air crackled with a mixture of excitement and tension as they prepared to discuss the progress of the case. She took a moment to observe each team member, noting the determination etched on their faces.

"Right, let's get started," Karen said, moving to the front of the room. "We've made progress in the Lockwood case, but a great deal remains to be done."

She outlined the current state of the investigation, highlighting the connections they'd uncovered between the 1987 dig, the valuable artefacts, and Sarah's disappearance. The team listened, interjecting with questions or observations.

Ty added, "The conversation with the Minster and their beliefs about what was discovered contradict the records. It seems like most artefacts were catalogued, but the Minster thinks more items were unearthed but not recorded."

"Clerical error or oversight?" an officer suggested.

"Perhaps either. It was all paperwork back then, not electronic records like these days," Karen continued. "Maybe they catalogued everything, but some of the paper trail got lost over the years?"

A few in her team nodded, while others scrunched their faces as they considered it.

Ed nodded in agreement. "I've looked into the legal aspects. There are interesting loopholes in artefact ownership laws from that period."

"Is it possible someone took artefacts?" Dan asked.

Karen shrugged. "It's possible. Either that, or it was a ham-fisted dig, where the left hand didn't know what the right hand was doing, and things disappeared down a black hole in the middle?"

"But how would it link into Sarah's disappearance?" Dan pushed. "Whatever went on during the dig led to her losing her life and being stuffed into a brick-and-rubble coffin. That's the only time anyone excavated or examined that part of the Undercroft. Nobody beyond the excavation would have been aware of the happenings below."

Karen had to agree. "We already know there are gaps in the records round Sarah's work on the dig. I'm not sure why. Once more, there is a possibility of careless paperwork. Only those present or aware of it could have hidden her body there before sealing it up again. We have to start with the dig team."

"The secrecy surrounding Sarah's disappearance concerns me," Belinda noted. "It's as if someone went to great lengths to keep her hidden. Did they consider her insignificant?"

Karen didn't have an answer. "Whatever she was aware of or witnessed contributed to her death. And if someone stole pieces and didn't record them, then where are they now?"

The discussion continued. Preet, often quiet in meetings, cleared her throat. "I have an idea," she said, her voice hesitant at first but growing stronger. "What if we considered an undercover operation? To infiltrate the world of artefact collectors and dealers? We may hear about missing pieces exchanging hands on the black market?"

The room fell silent while everyone considered this proposal. Karen raised a brow, intrigued by the suggestion.

"Go on, Preet," she encouraged.

"There's a prolific black market for stolen and rare artwork and historic pieces. I had an insight into it while I was in the robbery squad. We recovered items stolen from exhibitions, historical sites, and all sorts. Many end up in the hands of wealthy foreign buyers and collectors, never to be seen again." Preet let her insights sink in before continuing. "The items might change hands many times, and at eye-watering sums. If artefacts vanished from the dig, they likely would have been traded this way, and I wouldn't be surprised if some are still being offered for sale."

Preet's suggestion sparked a heated debate.

"That could give us access to information we'd never get otherwise," Ty commented.

"But the risks," Claire countered, her brow furrowed with concern. "We'd be dealing with potentially dangerous individuals."

Karen listened to all sides, her mind working through the implications. She spotted Kelly hovering near the door, listening. Their eyes met, and Kelly gave a slight nod, showing her interest in the undercover proposal.

Karen knew what her boss was thinking. Kelly's slight nod carried the weight of careful calculation. Yes, she'd pushed to keep this investigation quiet, but an undercover operation offered something traditional police work couldn't—plausible deniability. If done right, they could gather intelligence without alerting York's key players they were under investigation. The rich and powerful would be more likely to let their guard down round someone they thought was one of their own rather than uniformed officers asking uncomfortable questions.

"The fewer official inquiries, the better," she said carefully. "An undercover presence, properly managed, actually gives us more control over how this plays out in the public eye. And if things go south, we can pull our officer without drawing attention to the wider investigation."

Belinda raised her hand, to cut through the chatter. "We need to consider the practical aspects. Are resources and manpower available for this operation?"

Ed chimed in, his legal mind already at work. "There are significant legal considerations, too. We'd need to be careful about entrapment issues and ensure all evidence gathered would be admissible in court."

The discussion intensified, with team members arguing for and against the idea. Karen called for order, raising her voice to be heard over the debate.

"Preet." She turned to the young officer. "Can you elaborate on your idea? What did you have in mind?"

Preet straightened in her chair, gaining confidence as all eyes turned to her. "I was thinking we could create a persona as a wealthy collector interested in Viking artefacts. Using this cover, we make connections within the antiquities market, leading us to information about any missing artefacts from the '87 dig."

Preet outlined her plan. Karen nodded, impressed by the consideration given to the proposal.

"It's a solid idea," Karen said. "But we'd need to create a very convincing cover identity. The risks would be significant."

The team discussed the logistics, debating the best approach to ensure the safety of whoever went undercover while maximising the chance of gathering useful intelligence.

Karen signaled for quiet as the meeting ended. "I appreciate everyone's input on this. It's an interesting proposal. I'll consider the undercover operation and consult with Detective Superintendent Kelly. In the meantime, I want everyone to continue with their current lines of inquiry. I'm going to see Professor Fairfax."

She assigned tasks to each team member, ensuring all aspects were being pursued. As the team dispersed, Karen caught Kelly's eye and nodded towards the hallway.

Once outside, Karen and Kelly engaged in a hushed conversation about the undercover proposal.

"It's risky," Kelly admitted. "But it could help, and I'll take the flack if it goes tits up."

Karen nodded. "I agree. The potential benefits are significant, but so are the dangers."

Kelly considered for a moment. "I'll give conditional approval, pending a more detailed operational plan. But, Karen, tread with care. This case is already attracting attention from high places."

"Understood."

## 19

Karen stopped outside the modest bungalow on the outskirts of York. The garden was well-tended, with trimmed hedges and a riot of colourful flowers. As she glanced at the neighbouring properties, they too looked as neat and well looked after. She was more interested in the house of Professor Emmett Fairfax, a key witness, holding crucial information about the 1987 dig and Sarah Lockwood's disappearance.

She rang the doorbell, the muffled chimes echoing inside the house. After a moment, the door creaked open, revealing a man in his early seventies. His white hair was neatly combed, and he peered at Karen through thick-rimmed glasses.

"Professor Fairfax?" Karen presented her warrant card. "I'm DCI Karen Heath. Thank you for agreeing to speak with me."

Fairfax nodded, his expression a mixture of wariness and curiosity. "Yes, of course. Please, come in."

He led her into a cluttered living room, every surface covered with books, papers, and archaeological artefacts.

Karen took a moment to take in the room, noting the organised chaos of a lifetime's academic pursuit.

"Please take a seat, tea?" Fairfax gestured to an armchair.

"No, thank you." Karen pulled out her notebook from her handbag. "Professor, I'd like to ask you about the archaeological dig you led at York Minster in 1987."

Fairfax settled into his chair, his fingers drumming on the armrest. "Ah yes, the '87 dig. It was quite an extensive project. We were there for six months, you know."

Karen nodded. "Could you tell me more about the specifics of the dig? What were you hoping to find?"

"Well," Fairfax began, his eyes lighting up with academic enthusiasm, "our primary goal was to investigate the Norman foundations of the Minster. We were interested in any evidence of earlier Saxon structures on the site."

While Fairfax spoke, Karen noted a slight tremor in his hands. His gaze switched to a framed photograph on a nearby shelf.

"And did you find what you were looking for?" Karen prompted.

Fairfax hesitated, his enthusiasm dimming. "We... we made several interesting discoveries, yes. Remnants of Saxon stonework, remarkable and precious Roman and Viking artefacts. It was all very exciting."

Karen rested her elbows on her thighs. "I understand there were undergraduates and former students involved in the dig as well. Do you remember a young woman named Sarah Lockwood?"

At the mention of Sarah's name, Fairfax's nervousness became more pronounced. He reached for a glass of water on the side table, his hand shaking as he took a sip.

"Sarah? Yes, I remember her. Bright young woman, very enthusiastic about archaeology. It was such a tragedy when she went missing. It took us all by surprise, and for many, it was hard to concentrate on the dig after she disappeared."

Karen kept her eyes on Fairfax, marking the beads of sweat forming on his brow. "Professor, were there any... unusual occurrences during the dig? Anything that might shed light on what happened to Sarah?"

Fairfax's eyes darted round the room, as if searching for an escape. "Unusual? No, no, I don't think so. It was all routine and very academic."

Karen pushed a little harder. "We've uncovered information suggesting there were influential families either involved or connected to the dig. Perhaps a vested interest? Can you tell me anything about that?"

Fairfax's posture stiffened. "Influential families? Well, yes, I suppose you could say that. The Minster has always attracted interest from certain circles. We had... benefactors who took a keen interest in our work and offered us financial support."

"Who were these families?"

"The Pearsons were one such family. I remember seeing Mr Pearson arrive at the Undercroft as we were leaving for the night."

"Do you know why he was there?"

Fairfax shrugged. "No idea. He never spoke to us. I only saw him the once."

"He arrived alone?"

Fairfax nodded.

It made little sense to Karen and concerned her more than anything else.

"These benefactors," Karen pressed, "did they have any particular areas of interest? Any specific artefacts they were hoping you'd find?"

Fairfax's nervousness was clear now. He stood, moving

to the bookshelf and fiddling with artefacts there. "I gather they were interested in the history of York, naturally. The Viking period was of fascination to many."

Karen followed him with her eyes, noting his evasive body language. "Professor Fairfax, I get the sense there's something you're not telling me. Were there any discoveries not reported officially?"

Fairfax froze, his back to Karen. For a long moment, the only sound in the room was the ticking of an old grandfather clock in the corner. When he turned back to face her, his expression was a mix of fear and resignation.

"DCI Heath," he said, his voice soft, "you have to understand the position we were in. The things we found… they were important to the right people and valuable. But there were… pressures. Expectations. Money."

"What pressures, Professor? What did you find?"

Fairfax sank back into his chair, looking every one of his seventy-plus years. "There were artefacts, you see. Not just Viking, but older. Much older. And far more valuable than anyone imagined."

"And these artefacts," Karen prompted, "what happened to them?"

Fairfax shook his head, a haunted stare in his eyes. "I can't… I shouldn't say more. There are people involved, powerful people. It's not safe."

Though Karen felt a breakthrough was near, Fairfax seemed paralysed by fear. She changed tack.

"Professor, I understand your concerns. But a young woman lost her life. Her family has been waiting for answers for over forty years. Anything you can tell us, no matter how small, could help bring them closure. I'm not here to get you into trouble. That's not my intention."

Fairfax glanced at her, clear in his expression. He

*The Bones of Deceit*

opened his mouth to speak, then closed it again, shaking his head.

"I'm sorry," he said. "I wish I could help, but I can't remember much more. My recollection of the past isn't as clear these days. Please, I think you should go now."

Karen knew she had pushed as far as she could for now. She stood, handing Fairfax her card. "If you think of anything else, anything at all, please contact me. Day or night. Perhaps we can talk again?"

Fairfax rose and followed Karen to the door. Karen turned in the open doorway and looked at Fairfax. In the space of her visit, it looked as if he'd aged another few years. He looked weary and lost as he offered her a weak smile.

On her way back to her car, Karen thought about their conversation again. Fairfax's hints about unreported discoveries and the powerful people involved had opened a whole new avenue of investigation.

## 20

Karen's phone buzzed as she sat at her desk poring over the case files after her visit to Fairfax. She glanced at the screen, frowning at the unfamiliar number. "DCI Heath," she answered, her voice crisp and professional.

"I have information about the 1987 dig that might interest you," a distorted voice crackled through the speaker. "Meet me at the Railway Museum in an hour. Come alone."

Before Karen could respond, the line went dead. She stared at her phone for a moment, her mind racing. Anonymous tips were always a gamble, but in a case this cold, she couldn't afford to ignore any leads.

Karen strode into the incident room, scanning for Belinda. "Bel, can I borrow you in my office?" she called.

Once inside, Karen closed the door and filled Belinda in on the anonymous call. "It might be nothing, but..."

"But it might be everything," Belinda finished. "What's the plan?"

Karen leaned against her desk, arms folded. "I'll go to the meeting. You'll be my backup, out of sight, but close enough to intervene if needed. We'll record everything, of course. The meeting is in an hour, so I'll grab you on the way out."

"Sure, I'll finish what I'm doing," Bel replied, opening the door and heading back to her desk.

---

An hour later, Karen wandered through the Railway Museum, her senses on high alert. She paused by a display of old steam engine parts, pretending to read the plaque while scanning the area.

"DCI Heath," a voice behind her made her turn. A man in his sixties, wearing a tweed jacket and flat cap, stood there, his hands tucked deep inside his jacket pockets, looking round the hall. "Let's walk and talk, shall we?"

They walked through the museum taking in the exhibits like any ordinary visitors. The man introduced himself in hushed tones only as "John".

Karen racked her brain to recall a "John" on the dig list, but she couldn't remember Bel mentioning the name. Someone had missed him from the list, or more likely, he'd used a fake name for the meeting.

John continued. "I saw you're investigating the discovery of remains from the Undercroft. I was part of the dig team in '87, but only for a few weeks."

"How is this connected to my investigation of the remains?"

"Because I think it's all connected."

"Go on."

John nodded. "A woman on the dig went missing. Are they her remains?"

"I can't say anything as the family has just been informed, and the name hasn't been made public yet."

"Okay, well, I guess it must be Sarah, because as far as I'm aware, she's the only person who went missing. That's why I needed to speak with you."

Listening carefully, Karen sought to connect the new information to what she already knew. "Why come forward now?"

John's face darkened. "Sarah was going to blow the whistle on the whole thing. It's why I think she disappeared."

Karen's pulse quickened at John's revelation. She kept her face neutral, maintaining a calm exterior despite the surge of adrenaline coursing through her veins.

"What are you referring to, John?" she asked. "What was Sarah planning to reveal?"

John's stare darted round the museum, as if checking for eavesdroppers. He led Karen towards a quieter corner, near a display of vintage railway signage.

"It wasn't only about the artefacts," he announced. "There was an entire network involved. Influential families, politicians, even the church officials. They were using the dig to line their pockets, and there was big money at stake."

"What do you mean?" she pressed.

John hesitated, his weathered hands fidgeting with the hem of his jacket. "Smuggling. The Viking artefacts were only the tip of the iceberg. They recorded most of the finds, but they didn't catalogue certain items of immense value and shifted them before most of the dig team even saw them."

Karen gestured for him to continue. She knew the recording device hidden in her jacket would capture every word.

"Sarah stumbled onto it by accident when she witnessed people loading boxes into the back of a van before they assessed and recorded them," John added, his voice tinged with regret. "She was brilliant, you know. Noticed discrepancies in the paper cataloguing, items going missing. She started asking questions, digging deeper."

"And that's why you think she disappeared?" Karen concluded, her voice grim.

John shrugged, his eyes haunted. "I would say yes. I should've done something back then. But I was afraid. These people had power. Genuine power."

"John, I need names. Who was involved?" Karen held back from mentioning anyone as she wanted to see if John volunteered names.

The old man shook his head, fear etched across his face. "I can't... I don't know for certain. Just rumours."

"We can protect you," Karen assured him.

John was already backing away. "I've told you enough," he said, his voice shaky. "If I were to look for a place to start, I would start with the Pearson and Fairfax families. The Pearsons were in the middle of it all and had money. They funded a lot of the dig."

Before Karen pressed further, John turned and hurried away, blending into the crowd of museum visitors.

Karen stood for a moment, processing the flood of new information. After a few moments, she headed for the exit where she met with Belinda. On their return trip to the car, Karen filled Bel in on her conversation with "John".

"This is big, Karen. Huge."

The drive back to the station was a blur of traffic lights and pedestrian crossings. The name Pearson echoed in her thoughts, a potential key to unlocking the mystery surrounding Sarah Lockwood's disappearance.

The possibilities swirled in Karen's mind as she found a parking spot near her building. Belinda had already called ahead requesting preliminary background checks on the Pearson and Fairfax families.

"Bel, I'll catch up with you in the unit, I need to update DS Kelly first."

"No probs," Bel replied as she stepped from the car.

## 21

ALL EYES WERE on Karen as she stepped to the front of the busy incident room, having just left Kelly's office. Kelly had expressed both concern and interest as she'd listened to Karen's account of her meeting with "John". With the addition of new names in the pot, Kelly reinforced the need for caution and reassessment at every stage. Her primary concern was to ensure they didn't ruffle feathers with potential suspects or cross paths with the top brass.

Karen hushed her team and recounted her meeting, watching as expressions of surprise and intrigue spread across her colleagues' faces.

"Right," Karen said, clapping her hands together. "We're dealing with something much bigger than we thought. Claire, what have you got on the families?"

Claire stepped forward, tablet in hand. "The Fairfax family has deep roots in York. They've been involved in local politics for generations. Richard Fairfax sat on the city council. His son, Emmett Fairfax, as we know was a prominent archaeologist who led several high-profile digs in the area, including the 1987 York Minster excavation. Emmett has no other immediate family."

Karen's eyes narrowed.

Claire continued. "As for the Pearsons, they're old money. Banking. They've got connections all over the country, but their primary seat of power has always been here in Yorkshire. David Pearson senior passed away fifteen years ago. Boating accident. Well, fell overboard after an afternoon of drinking. Drowned."

"There you go. I've been saying for years that drinking is bad for your health!" Dan laughed.

"Grim," Karen said. "Living relatives?"

"Yes. He left behind a son, David Junior, and a daughter, Andrea. She now lives in the US with her husband and three children. Her husband is in the oil business, a senior executive."

"And David Junior?" Ty Ed asked.

Claire pulled a face. "He didn't do so well. Not sure his dad would have been proud of him."

"Why not?" Karen chipped in.

"Junior went into property. A private landlord with a portfolio of over seventy-five properties. But he's being investigated by the HRMC for tax evasion. Apparently, they think he owes over five hundred grand in unpaid taxes. But Junior claims he spends over six months a year abroad at his secluded luxury villa, so his tax liability should be lower." Claire shrugged. "I'm not a tax expert, so I do not know what's what."

Karen stared at the photos pinned to the board of the Fairfaxes and Pearsons.

"Where is Junior now?" Karen asked.

"Not sure. No fixed address for him in the UK. Stays in hotels or with friends. He's here, though. We checked with

Border Control. He came through Manchester airport five weeks ago."

"Any direct links between the families and Sarah Lockwood?" Karen asked.

"Nothing concrete yet," Belinda admitted. "But I'm still digging. There's a lot of history to sift through."

Karen turned to the rest of the team. "Alright, here's what we're going to do. Ty, I want you and Ed to focus on the Fairfax family. Start with Emmett and work your way back. Look for any other connections to the 1987 dig and any suspicious activities in the years since."

Ty nodded, already making notes.

"Preet," Karen continued, "you and Claire take the Pearsons. Same drill. I want to know everything about them—business dealings, political connections, the works. Pay special attention to anything round the time of Sarah's disappearance."

"On it," Preet replied.

Karen paused, her gaze sweeping across the room. "Remember, we're dealing with powerful people here. Be discreet in your inquiries. We don't want to rouse suspicion, especially Junior. I don't want him doing a runner because I'd like a word with him about his father."

"If we can find him," Preet said.

"True."

Returning to her office after the team dispersed, her phone buzzed—a text from Zac.

*Everything okay? You seemed distracted this morning.*

Karen sighed, guilt tugging at her conscience. With everything happening on the case, she'd not thought about home. She typed out a reply, promising to fill him in later.

Placing her phone on the table, Karen's eyes were drawn to a photo of Sarah Lockwood.

"We're getting closer, Sarah," Karen murmured. "We're going to find out what happened to you."

A few moments later, Bel appeared in Karen's doorway and came round to Karen's side of the desk.

Bel fiddled with the recorder before replaying the recording of the conversation. They cross-referenced John's claims with the official dig records, searching for any discrepancies.

"Check this." Belinda pointed to a section of the report on Karen's screen. "The inventory lists 'miscellaneous metalwork' but doesn't give any specifics. That's unusual for an archaeological report."

Karen nodded, her suspicions growing. "And here. There's a gap in the dating sequence. It's as if they've omitted an entire section of findings."

"And they've got records stating minerals. Gems?"

Karen shrugged.

The deeper they investigated, the more discrepancies surfaced. The team listed funding sources vaguely, glossed over certain areas of the dig site, and left unexplained gaps in the daily logs.

"This reeks of a coverup." Karen leaned back in her chair with a sigh. "But why? What could be so important about these artefacts that it would lead to murder?"

Belinda chewed her lip. "Maybe it's not about the artefacts themselves, but what they represent. If they're as old as John claims, they could rewrite history."

Karen nodded, her mind working through the implications. "It's a good thing. It's progress and a reshaping of history. But could upset a lot of powerful people. A lot of people and institutions have a vested interest in maintaining the current historical narrative."

"So, what's our next move?" Belinda asked.

Karen tapped her fingers on the table. "We need to

talk to Fairfax again. He knows more than he's letting on, and now we have some leverage to make him talk. And if he doesn't, then I'll threaten him with withholding information."

"I'll set it up. We can visit him first thing tomorrow."

"Sounds good, Bel. I need to update the super about our undercover op and will head home after that."

"No problem. Enjoy your evening."

"You, too." Karen scooped up her folder detailing the undercover op Preet had fleshed out and headed off to find Kelly.

## 22

Karen strode through the quiet corridors of the building. Tiredness crept into her bones, and her mind felt exhausted. The last few days had taken its toll on her. After nine weeks at home, being back at work was a shock to the system. Long, unsociable hours, forgetting to eat, and *thinking hard*, were things she'd fallen out of the habit of doing.

She paused outside the open door to Kelly's office and knocked once.

Kelly looked up from her desk, a towering stack of files pushed to one side. "Karen, come in and take a seat. I thought you would be home by now?"

"I'm heading off but wanted to go over the final details of the undercover operation plan again." She placed a thick folder on the desk with a soft thud.

Kelly closed notebook and scanned the contents of the folder as Karen began her comprehensive briefing.

"We've found a chance to go to important auctions where we think certain people could be," Karen explained. "Preet's made excellent progress in establishing her cover as a wealthy collector with a penchant for rare and valuable items. She's heard of a chap called Marcus Brennan, in his sixties, and a wealthy antiquities collector with a shady reputation. Belinda found his name mentioned twice in online articles about historical artefacts and his opinion on items found in the '87 dig and other digs around the world. We think he'll be a good place to start."

While Karen described the plan, Kelly listened and asked questions where needed.

"Brennan is known for planning private viewings, and word is he'll be organising one next week for some 'special items'." Karen emphasised her point with air quotes. "We might find items related to our case there, but we can't be sure. This is more about an opportunity to brush shoulders with Brennan, gain his trust, and see if he throws up anything of interest. He's well connected and known for handling items with a shady past."

Kelly raised a brow, a flicker of intrigue crossed her face. "And you're confident Preet can handle this level of pressure?" she probed, her tone both curious and cautious.

"Absolutely. She's proven herself more than capable in far trickier situations while in the robbery squad. Her knowledge of antiquities has been invaluable in maintaining her cover and building credibility within the circles Brennan is in. She has undertaken undercover roles while in robbery, so I'm confident she has what it takes."

They delved into a detailed discussion of the potential risks and contingencies, with Karen outlining the safety measures in place to protect Preet. As the thorough briefing concluded, Kelly leaned back in her chair satisfied.

"This is good work, Karen," she said, her tone warm with approval. "I'm impressed with the level of detail and forethought you've put into this operation. It's clear you've considered every angle."

Karen let out a long breath as her anxiety lessened. Kelly's approval meant everything, especially given the high stakes of the case and the potential dangers involved.

"Thank you," Karen replied, allowing a small smile to soften her expression. "We've all been working hard to make sure this goes as smoothly as possible."

Kelly nodded, her expression turning serious once more. "I agree this operation should go ahead." She reached for her phone. "I'll contact the covert ops team at once. We need to get the ball rolling straight away. I'll update you later."

"Great. I'll give Preet the green light."

Karen thanked Kelly before heading off.

---

Karen parked outside Jade's apartment, the streetlights casting a soft glow on the quiet neighbourhood. She hesitated for a moment, wondering if she should have called ahead, but decided the impromptu visit felt right. With her bag and a file of case notes in hand, she went to Jade's door.

The doorbell chimed, and after a few moments, Jade appeared. Her face lit up. "Karen! I wasn't expecting you... again so soon. You were only here this morning."

"I know. Can't keep me away, right? I was on my way home. I know it's late, but thought I'd drop by." Karen offered a warm smile. "I hope I'm not disturbing you?"

Jade shook her head and rolled her eyes, stepping aside to let Karen in. "Well, I'm so busy. Life is just one tornado of activity now. It's hard to catch my breath!"

Karen smiled. Her heart swelled as she saw a fleeting moment of the old Jade shine through.

"Come in, I'll put the kettle on. We'll have to keep the noise down as Mum has gone to sleep."

While Jade busied herself in the kitchen, Karen glanced round the living room. It was tidier than this morning, a sign Jade was keeping herself occupied during her recovery or her mum had tidied. A half-finished jigsaw puzzle sat on the coffee table, and a stack of books on forensic psychology caught Karen's eye.

Jade returned with two steaming mugs of tea. "Good day?" she asked, making herself comfortable in an armchair across from Karen.

Karen took a sip of her tea before answering. "It's been busy. A lot going on. How did your appointment go?"

Jade's smile faltered. "It was fine. Usual stuff. She talks. I talk. She talks a bit more. I talk a bit less!" Her smile returned. "I'm... okay. Definitely felt better today. I've not had a nightmare in two days. I consider that progress, however, certain moments bring back a rush of memories."

"That's understandable. And what happens now with Doctor Morales?"

"We've decided to stick with the twice-a-week schedule for another two weeks and then review it," Jade confirmed. "She's been helpful. We've been working on grounding techniques for when the anxiety hits."

They chatted for a while about Jade's recovery progress, with Karen offering words of encouragement and support. With the conversation slowing, Jade glanced at the file Karen had brought.

"Is it... about the case?" she asked.

Karen nodded and grabbed the file. "I promised to keep you in the loop. We've made progress on the Lockwood investigation."

She filled Jade in on the latest developments, careful not to overwhelm her with too many details. Jade listened with interest and folded her arms across her chest.

"We've uncovered a potential link between a historic artefact smuggling operation and high-profile figures in York's history." Karen highlighted the key figures. "We believe Sarah may have discovered certain individuals who were forging documentation on the discoveries and then stealing them before they were recorded."

"And you think the Pearson and Fairfax families were involved?"

Karen shrugged. "Maybe. Nothing concrete but worth pursuing as a line of enquiry. I'm going to talk to Sarah's brother tomorrow. Now the family has had time to process it, I'd like to know more about her."

Jade leaned in. "Have you looked into offshore financial records of those families? You might find payments hitting their accounts from their deals. I doubt they'd keep too much money here in the UK?"

Karen smiled, recognising Jade's eye for detail. "That's a fair point. I'll have Ed investigate it tomorrow."

Jade's spirits lifted as the evening went on, and she seemed more like her old self to Karen. Another hour passed before Karen realised the time and gasped.

"Shit, I better be off before Zac sends out a search party."

Jade rose and walked her to the door.

"Thanks for stopping by. And for keeping me updated. It means a lot."

Karen squeezed her friend's shoulder and then

hugged her. "Anytime. You're still part of the team, don't forget that. You'll be back with us in no time."

While Karen drove home, she was hopeful. Jade still had a long way to go, but tonight had shown the determined, brilliant detective she knew was still there, ready to fit back in when the time was right.

## 23

THE FOLLOWING MORNING, Karen and Belinda were once again at Professor Fairfax's home. The elderly academic looked even more haggard than before, his eyes shifting between the two detectives after they entered.

"Professor Fairfax," Karen began, her tone firm but not unkind, "we need another conversation about the 1987 dig."

Fairfax slumped in his armchair, defeat written across his features. "I suppose you've uncovered something?"

Karen pulled out a file from her bag. "We've found discrepancies in the official reports, Professor. Omissions, vague descriptions, unexplained gaps. Care to explain?"

Fairfax's eyes widened, a flicker of fear crossed his face. "I... I don't know what you mean."

"You do," Karen insisted. "We believe items discovered went missing, Professor. Someone left them out of the reports."

Fairfax's composure crumbled. He buried his face in his hands, his shoulders shaking slightly. When he raised his eyes, they were red-rimmed. "Understand," he began, his voice trembling, "the pressure we were under. We needed to toe the line or lose our funding."

Sensing Fairfax was on the verge of opening up, Karen softened her approach. "Tell us what happened, Professor. Help us understand."

Fairfax took a deep breath and stared ahead. "The artefacts we found… they were incredible and far more valuable than previously thought. It wasn't just a few isolated pieces—we uncovered a treasure trove."

Belinda leaned in, her curiosity piqued. "But wouldn't that be an incredible discovery? Why keep it quiet?"

Fairfax laughed. "One would assume so, wouldn't one? But there were… interested parties. People who felt this discovery could destabilise the accepted historical narrative. But that was their story when self-gain was their only concern."

"And Sarah Lockwood? Where does she fit into all this?"

Fairfax's face fell, guilt etching deep lines round his eyes. "Sarah… she was brilliant, idealistic. She couldn't understand why items were being taken away and not being recorded. She threatened to go public."

"And then she disappeared," Karen finished.

Fairfax sighed, a single tear rolled down his cheek. "I've lived with the guilt for over forty years, but I had no proof of what happened to her and why. It was my duty to defend her, to be there for her. But I was a coward. We all were."

Karen leaned back, processing this new information. "Professor, I need you to tell me everything. Every detail you can remember about those artefacts, about the people who wanted them kept secret, about the night Sarah disappeared. Can you do that?"

Fairfax looked at her, a mix of fear and confusion in his eyes. "I'll try."

Fairfax's voice sounded frail and uncertain. His mind jumped from one thing to another, his statement coming out in a convoluted mess that made it hard for Karen to piece it together. She wondered what useful information would come from it, but both her and Bel listened for the next thirty minutes as the old man droned on.

---

"THAT WAS A WASTE OF TIME," Bel fumed, while they made their way back to the car.

With a shrug, Karen unlocked the doors and settled into her seat. "Not completely. Its once again confirmed the connection between Sarah's disappearance and her death, and the smuggling of artefacts. She was hushed and her body dumped. I want to know if the Minster authorities and clergy had an inkling about the smuggling, or were they kept in the dark, too?"

"True. I think he was horrified when you told him where Sarah's body was discovered."

"Yep. And it confirms her killer came back after the dig was finished to bury her body, suggesting she was stored somewhere. Which could have been anywhere."

"We need to focus on those who oversaw and sponsored the dig. The team hasn't identified any new information or leads on the members of the dig. So far, they all check out, but we're still working to locate a few who currently live or have lived abroad."

Karen agreed as she started the car and set off. "I'll drop you off at the station. I need to meet up with Preet. The undercover op is up and running, and today is day one, and after that, I'm going to see Dean Lyle at the

Minster. Ty called the dean for me yesterday, so he's expecting me. Call me if you need me."

## 24

Detective Superintendent Laura Kelly stood by her office window and looked out over the grounds. Early March heralded the end of winter and the prospect of spring round the corner. And yet, the slate-coloured sky offered little hope. The bare branches of the trees lining the walkways between the buildings swayed in the easterly wind, their dark limbs in stark contrast against the gloomy sky. She watched a few officers hurry between buildings, their breath forming small clouds in the damp air. Round the base of a few trees, determined daffodils poked their heads above ground, not ready to bloom but keen to be the first to announce spring was here.

She pursed her lips. The complexity of the investigation was growing by the day, and she found herself absorbed in the details Karen had provided. A soft knock at her door broke her concentration.

"Come in," she called, expecting one of her officers.

To her surprise, Councillor Victoria Hartley strode into the office, her tailored suit and perfectly coiffed hair a stark contrast to the functional police surroundings. Kelly turned, masking her bewilderment.

"Councillor Hartley, this is unexpected. How can I help you?"

Hartley's lips curved into a smile. "Laura, I hope you don't mind me dropping by unannounced. I thought it was time we had a chat about this... situation at York Minster."

Kelly gestured for Hartley to take a seat, her guard up. "Of course, Councillor. What aspects of the investigation concern you?"

Hartley settled into the chair, crossed her legs, and fixed Kelly with a penetrating stare. "Concerns, Laura? Oh, I have quite a few. This case is attracting a lot of attention, and not all of it is positive. There are whispers in certain circles about the... direction of your investigation."

Kelly took to her seat and leaned back, her face a mask of professional neutrality. "I assure you, Councillor, we're conducting a thorough and impartial investigation. The discovery of human remains, especially in such a historically significant location, demands nothing less."

"Oh, I don't doubt your dedication," Hartley said, her tone firm. "But you must appreciate the fragility of this situation. York Minster is not just a building; it's a symbol of our city's heritage. And now, with rumours of missing artefacts and potential cover-ups... Well, it's causing quite a stir."

Kelly had never liked the woman. Brash, loud, stuck-up, and about as attractive as a month-old sandwich found at the back of the fridge. "Councillor, with all due respect, our job is to uncover the truth, regardless of how uncomfortable it might be. A young woman lost her life, and her family has waited over forty years for answers. Surely you can appreciate the importance of that?"

Hartley's smile tightened. "Of course, the loss of life is tragic. But we must consider the broader implications. This investigation has the potential to affect many people who had nothing to do with the dig or a suspicious death. Are you prepared for the consequences of that?"

"Consequences? What are you implying, Councillor?" Kelly demanded, her tone sharpening. "And more importantly, where are you hearing these 'rumours' from? We haven't released a press statement, nor have we discussed this outside of my team."

Hartley uncrossed her legs and cleared her throat, her voice lowering. "I'm suggesting... political considerations are at play here. Powerful people with vested interests in maintaining the status quo. People who might not appreciate the upheaval your investigation could cause."

Kelly nodded and raised a brow as Hartley's words sank in. They were treading on the toes of well-known people, challenging narratives that had stood for many years.

"Are you asking me to compromise my investigation, Councillor?" Kelly asked, her voice steady despite the anger bubbling beneath the surface.

Hartley stood, smoothing her skirt. "Not at all, Laura. I'm simply advising caution. Tread carefully. You're navigating treacherous waters, and it would be a shame to see such a promising career capsized by... overzealousness."

As Hartley made her way to the door, Kelly called out, "Councillor, I appreciate your concern, but my team will continue to investigate the facts wherever it leads. It's our job, and we do it without fear or favour."

Hartley paused and turned back, her hand on the doorknob. She smirked, her eyes fixed on Kelly. "As you wish, Superintendent. I've said my piece. I hope, for your sake, you know what you're doing."

With those final words, she was gone, leaving Kelly alone with the effect of her words hanging in the air.

The door hadn't even clicked shut before she slumped back in her chair, jaw clenched so tight her teeth might crack. Bloody woman. Always had to have the last word, didn't she? She strutted through the station like she owned the place, no doubt carrying a designer handbag worth more than my monthly salary, her heels clicking on the corridor floor as if it were a catwalk.

Who did she think she was fooling with a fake posh accent anyway? Probably practiced it in front of her mirror every morning, right after spending an hour plastering on enough makeup to supply a Sephora counter. The kind of woman who'd take the last biscuit from the tin and then comment on everyone else's weight.

She reached for her lukewarm coffee, wishing it was something stronger. This day was going to be a long one, and that woman's perfume—expensive and overpowering enough to give anyone a headache—still lingered in the air like a bad memory.

Reaching for her phone, she needed to update Karen right away.

## 25

Preet stood in front of a full-length mirror in a hotel room preparing herself. She had replaced her usual practical work attire with an expensive designer dress, new hairstyle, and makeup. She practiced her new walk, the click of high heels unfamiliar and slightly unsteady.

Three undercover officers bustled round her, making final adjustments to her appearance and running through her cover story one last time. Preet listened, her nervousness masked by a cool confidence she wasn't yet used to.

The lead officer, Sergeant Craig Roberts, a veteran of many undercover operations in the force, handed Preet a burner phone and a designer handbag. "I've modified both with hidden tracking technology," he explained.

Preet nodded.

They moved to a table covered in documents—all created to support Preet's new identity as a wealthy art collector with a particular interest in Viking artefacts. Preet memorised key details, her brain working hard to absorb all the information.

The team ran Preet through a series of role-play

scenarios, testing her reactions to potential questions and situations she might encounter. She stumbled a few times but recovered, impressing the team with her quick thinking and adaptability.

With the preparation ended, Preet took a moment alone. She stared at her reflection, trying to see herself as others would—a confident, sophisticated collector. For a moment, doubt crept in, and she wondered if she was up to the task.

Karen entered the room, her presence at once putting Preet at ease.

"Look at you, all fancy and nowhere to go," Karen teased as she studied Preet up and down.

"Too late to back out?" Preet joked.

"Yep, so grow a pair of balls and get stuck in. This is an important operation for us, and I'm proud of you for volunteering."

"Thanks, Karen."

"Remember, Preet," Karen said, "you're not just playing a part. You're a key element to us in uncovering the truth about Sarah Lockwood and whatever happened during the dig. Trust your instincts, and remember we've got your back. Listen, observe, and report back."

"Got it."

Karen wished her luck before heading off again to her next meeting.

The undercover team gathered for a final briefing. They went over emergency protocols. Preet listened and remained silent.

"If anything feels off, anything at all, you use the code word," Craig stressed. "Your safety is paramount. We can always regroup and try again, but we can't replace you."

Excitement and apprehension warred within Preet as the briefing concluded; a final mental checklist confirmed her readiness. Craig handed her a set of car keys which suited her new persona.

"I'm ready," she muttered as she stepped out into the corridor and walked towards the lifts. The doors slid open with a chime, revealing a plush interior which matched the luxury of her attire. Preet stepped inside, her heels sounding loud in the enclosed space. On her way down to the lobby, she rehearsed her cover story, fixing the details firmly in her memory.

The lobby bustled with activity, well-heeled guests moving about with an air of casual affluence. Preet strode through, her posture perfect, exuding the confidence of someone accustomed to such surroundings. She nodded to the concierge as she passed, receiving a deferential smile in return.

Outside, Preet headed for the car park and searched out the C-Class silver Merc. She slid into the driver's seat, the leather cool and smooth against her skin. She started the car and approved of the dash which lit up like a Christmas tree. *Very fancy.*

Pulling away from the hotel, Preet glanced in the rearview mirror. The reflection showed not the police officer she knew herself to be but the sophisticated art collector she was pretending to be. With a smile, she merged into traffic, heading towards her first meeting in the world of high-stakes artefact collecting.

## 26

Karen stood before the imposing facade of York Minster, taking a moment to appreciate its grandeur before entering.

Inside, the hushed atmosphere enveloped her. Her footsteps echoed on the ancient stone floors as a junior member of staff led her through ornate corridors to the dean's office.

The dean, Richard Lyle, a dignified man in his sixties with silver hair and piercing blue eyes, greeted Karen with polite reserve. His handshake was firm but brief, and he gestured for her to take a seat in one of the high-backed chairs facing his desk.

"DCI Heath, welcome. I appreciate the visit. It's been a stressful few days for everyone here. The recent discovery both saddened and alarmed me. It's taken us all by surprise," he said, his voice carrying the cultured tones of a lifelong clergyman. "How may I help you today?"

Karen smiled and glanced round the room before returning her gaze to him. "Thank you for seeing me,

Dean Lyle. I'm here to discuss the ongoing investigation and our need for further cooperation from the Minster."

The dean's expression remained neutral on the whole, but Karen noticed a slight tightening round his eyes. He steepled his fingers under his chin, a gesture that seemed both thoughtful and defensive.

"Of course, we want to help in any way we can," he replied, his words measured. "However, I'm sure you understand the delicate nature of our position. The Minster is more than a historical site. It's a place of worship and spiritual significance."

Karen nodded, acknowledging his point. "I understand, Dean Lyle. We don't intend to disrupt the Minster's operations or services. However, the case requires us to delve deeper into the events surrounding the 1987 dig, and my officers are struggling to get the required information to conduct a thorough investigation."

The dean's fingers tapped together, a subtle sign of his discomfort. "The dig was quite some time ago, DCI Heath. I'm not sure what relevance it could have to your current investigation."

"We believe it's crucial to understanding the circumstances of Sarah Lockwood's disappearance," Karen explained, her tone firm but respectful. "We'd like access to any records from that period, as well as permission to examine certain areas of the Minster involved in the dig." She held off from referencing the smuggling operation for now.

Dean Lyle's brow furrowed, his discomfort now more visible. "Those events occurred before my time here, so I'm in the dark as much as you. I'm not sure it's possible, but I can see what we can do, DCI Heath. Many of those records are part of the Minster's private archives. And allowing access to restricted areas could damage delicate historical features."

Karen was about to press further when a knock at the door interrupted them. The door opened, revealing a younger clergyman with a warm smile and a stack of papers in his hands.

"Oh, I'm sorry," he said, his eyes widening at the sight of Karen. "I didn't realise you were in a meeting, Richard."

The dean's annoyance was evident, but he maintained his composure. "Canon Wheatley, this is DCI Heath. She's here about the ongoing police investigation and the need to access our archives round the time of the dig."

Canon Michael Wheatley pursed his lips. "Ah, yes. The discovery in the Undercroft, correct?"

Karen nodded, intrigued by the canon's apparent enthusiasm. "Yes. We're trying to gather more information about the 1987 dig."

Wheatley placed his papers on a side table and turned to the dean. "You know, Richard, we could offer access to the records. The ones in the public archive, at least. It wouldn't breach any confidentiality."

The dean's lips thinned as he glared at Wheatley, displeased with his intervention. "I'm not sure it's wise, Michael. We need to consider the implications."

Karen watched the interaction with keen interest, taking note of the subtle tension between the two clergymen. There was more to their relationship than met the eye.

"Perhaps we could start with the public records," Karen suggested, seizing the opportunity. "The information would give us a foundation to work from without compromising any sensitive information."

The dean hesitated, his gaze flicking between Karen and Wheatley. Finally, he sighed. "Very well. We can offer access to the public archives. But anything beyond that will need further discussion and approval."

Karen nodded, sensing this was the best she could hope for now. "Thank you, Dean Lyle."

Canon Wheatley stepped forward as she rose to go. "You know," he said, his voice lowered, "the church has a long history of protecting its own. Sometimes such protection extends to... well, let's just say, complicated situations. It was a dark period in our history, and it's something the clergy are keen to leave in the past."

The dean cleared his throat, cutting off any further comment from Wheatley. "Thank you for your time, DCI Heath. Canon Wheatley will show you to the archives."

Karen followed Wheatley out of the office. Her mind raced with the implications of his cryptic comment. There was more beneath the surface here, layers of history and secrecy she would need to unravel. Karen was so deep in thought, she collided with a tall, lean man in clerical attire.

"Pardon me," he murmured, his kind blue eyes clouded with worry.

Wheatley introduced him as Father Robert O'Brien, a long-standing member of the Minster's clergy and told the Father the reason for Karen's visit.

Karen raised a brow when she spotted a flicker of unease cross Father O'Brien's face at the mention of the investigation. Belinda had identified his name as a member of the '87 dig. "Ah, Father O'Brien, I'll need a word with you as I want to ask you a few questions about the dig."

Alarm flashed across the father's face as his head snapped back. To Karen, the elderly priest seemed nervous, his hands fidgeting as he claimed to remember little about the dig.

"It was so long ago, you see," he said, not quite meeting Karen's eyes. "I don't think I'll be of much help." With that, he turned and scurried off.

"Is he always so nervous?"

Wheatley shrugged. "Not normally," he replied as he led her through a maze of corridors, their footsteps echoing off the stone walls. "I apologise for the dean's reticence," Wheatley said as they walked. "He's very protective of the Minster's reputation."

Karen studied the canon's profile and noted the sincerity in his expression. "And you, Canon Wheatley? What's your stance on this investigation?"

He paused, turning to face her. "I believe in truth, DCI Heath. Even when it's uncomfortable. The church has made mistakes in the past. Most faiths have. It's led to wars and division through the centuries. Hiding them has only ever led to more pain."

They reached a heavy wooden door, which Wheatley unlocked with an ancient-looking key.

"These are the public archives." He pushed the door open to reveal rows of shelves filled with books and documents. "I'll leave you to your research, but please, if you need any help, ask."

Wheatley turned to leave and called out to Karen, "Canon Wheatley, were you here during the 1987 dig?"

He paused, a shadow passing over his face. "No, I wasn't. But I've heard stories. Some of them... well, they're not the tales the dean would want circulating."

With his cryptic remark, he left Karen alone in the archive room before she could say more. She stood for a moment, taking in the musty smell of old paper and the history surrounding her. There were secrets here, buried in these documents and in the memories of those who had lived through that time.

Karen fired off a text to Bel to inform her she'd bumped into a rather cagey Father O'Brien, who seemed reluctant to talk.

Scanning the shelves, Karen's mind was already working, piecing together the subtle clues and tensions so far. The dean's reluctance, Wheatley's hints at past mistakes and cover-ups—it all pointed to something beyond a simple archaeological dig.

She pulled out a folder labelled "1987 Excavations" and opened it, scanning the yellowed pages.

Bel's reply interrupted her reading.

*Father O'Brien's name keeps coming up. He seems to have been present at key moments during the dig.*

Karen frowned and replied, remembering the priest's off behaviour.

*I think it's time we had a more in-depth conversation with Father O'Brien.*

Bel replied with a thumbs-up emoji.

## 27

KAREN EMERGED from the York Minster archives, her eyes strained and her nose itching from the dust. She sneezed, rubbing her nose as she made her way to her car, her mind whirling with the information she'd gleaned from the old records.

In need of a pick-me-up, she took a detour on foot and headed across the pedestrian walkway in front of the Minster and dipped into Minster Gates, a narrow road filled with unique little shops that excited visitors to the city. It was nice to feel normal and blend in with the crowds of shoppers who milled about, peering into shops selling fudge, antiques, and jewellery. It reminded her of The Lanes in Brighton. The last few days had blurred into an endless round of meetings and conversations, all merging into a large melting pot of words in her mind.

A trendy coffee shop took her fancy. She popped in to grab a cappuccino to go.

Caffeined up, Karen returned to her car and headed off.

On the drive back to the station, a call came through

on her phone. Karen activated the hands-free system, recognising Belinda's number.

"Hi, Bel," she answered, her voice still nasal from the dust.

"Karen, we've been called to a suspicious death. They found a body near the river," Belinda's tense voice came through the speakers. "A journalist according to a wallet found in his jacket. We've found a rucksack close by. I believe it belongs to him. We found a voice recorder in the rucksack, but it's empty, and there are printed articles that interest us."

Karen's heart rate spiked. "Details?"

"Male, mid-thirties. Found submerged, facedown. Based on what he had with him, we think this might be related to our case."

"I'm on my way," Karen said, already changing course. "Have you called in Izzy?"

"She's en route," Belinda confirmed.

Karen ended the call, her curiosity piqued. A murdered journalist? Coincidental?

The crime scene was a flurry of activity when Karen arrived. She parked behind a line of police vehicles and made her way along the muddy bank towards the river. SOCOs in white suits surrounded the body which lay close to the path running alongside.

Izzy Armitage glanced across as Karen approached, her expression grim. "White male, mid-thirties," she reported, echoing Belinda's earlier assessment. "Cause of death appears to be blunt force trauma to the head. But someone could have hit him and held his face under water until he drowned. I won't know for certain until the PM."

Karen noticed the man's right hand clenched round a piece of paper.

Karen knelt, pulling on a pair of latex gloves. With gentle movements, she extracted the sodden paper from the victim's grip. The ink had run, but Karen could make out a partial rubbing of something resembling an artefact. The style looked Viking.

"Bag this," she instructed a nearby SOCO.

Belinda appeared at her side, notepad in hand. "Victim is Andrew Wheatley, investigative journalist. He was working on a story about artefact smuggling through the generations. I found a stack of photocopied articles in his rucksack, as well as a few recent ones relating to the remains at the Minster."

Karen's eyes widened. "Artefact smuggling? Any connection to Viking artefacts?"

Belinda shook her head. "Not sure yet, but we're looking into it."

Karen stood, surveying the scene again with fresh eyes. "Alright, I want this area locked down tight. Full search of the riverbank in both directions. And, Bel, keep this under wraps for now until we know more and have briefed the super. If there's a connection to our case, we don't want to tip anyone off."

With her team beginning their search, Karen spotted Hyde arriving. She waved him over.

"Ed, glad you're here. We have a journalist. Can you check into recent stories he was working on, especially anything related to artefact smuggling or the antiquities market. Can you organise a search of his address?"

Ed nodded. "I'll get on it. Any concerns about confidential sources?"

"That's what I'm worried about," Karen admitted. "If he was on to something big, it could explain..." she gestured to the grim scene round them.

Karen's unease grew with each step of the initial investigation. The location, the method of killing, even the position of the body—it all felt familiar. She thought of Sarah Lockwood, wondering if, after all these years, they were dealing with the same group of people.

The sun had set by the time Karen stepped away to call Kelly. Floodlights illuminated the crime scene, casting harsh shadows across the muddy bank. Karen shivered as the chill crept into her bones. She stamped her feet to ease the stiffness in her toes.

"Ma'am, it's Karen," she said when the call connected. "We've got a situation."

Karen updated her on the murdered journalist and the potential connection to their ongoing investigation.

"This is worrying, Karen, especially after my call to you about Councillor Hartley's visit." Kelly paused. "If word gets out a journalist was killed while investigating artefact smuggling, and it might be connected to a decades-old cold case, the press will have a field day. And I don't need the crime commissioner or councillor on my case any more than they are already."

"I know," Karen agreed. "We're keeping it quiet for now."

"Yes," Kelly said. "Keep me posted, but for now we're needed at HQ. The CC has called a meeting to discuss the case."

"What? Seriously?"

"Yes. They've not given me any details, so meet me there and let's see what it's about."

Hanging up, Karen's head spun with thoughts of how to juggle all these elements of the investigation while keeping a lid on it.

## 28

Karen and Detective Superintendent Kelly sat in a large, imposing conference room at police headquarters. The air crackled with tension as they awaited the CC's arrival.

"You okay?" Kelly asked.

"No. you?"

"No."

The door opened, and a group of senior officers filed in, their faces grave. Karen recognised the Chief Constable and several other high-ranking officials. They took their seats without small talk, a clear sign of the seriousness of the situation.

"I called this meeting to discuss the York Minster investigation," the Chief Constable began, his expression thoughtful. "The discovery of remains in such a historically significant location has put us in a complex position. We need to ensure justice is served while handling this with appropriate sensitivity."

He leaned forward, his tone balanced. "I support your team's thorough approach, but I need to understand your strategy. We've received calls from several parties expressing concerns about the scope of your inquiries, particularly regarding historical and current figures. This isn't about stopping the investigation—it's about ensuring we can defend our methods if questioned."

The CC paused as he looked at his notes.

"The eyes of the city are on us," he continued, glancing between Karen and Kelly. "We have a responsibility to solve this case but also to protect the integrity of all involved until we have concrete evidence. I want regular updates on your progress and early warning of any significant developments. If we need to allocate additional resources or provide support, I need to know."

Having laid out his thoughts, he turned to an officer in the next chair.

Karen listened, her jaw clenched, as the officer outlined a list of individuals concerned about the case. The names included local businesspeople, Councillor Hartley, and even the Dean of the Minster. Her stomach tightened as she recognised some names, especially David Pearson Jnr, whom the team had been unable to locate, but yet could still find time to lodge his concerns.

When given the opportunity to speak, Karen defended her investigation. "With all due respect, sir," she said, her voice unwavering despite the anger simmering below, "you are right, we have a duty to follow the evidence and serve justice, regardless of where it leads. This case has already cost one young woman her life, and a journalist as well. We can't ignore it. And since we've started our investigation, I don't think it would put us in a good light if we slowed or focussed on one little aspect of it. There are too many armchair sleuths, true crime bloggers, and freelancers who'd search for answers for months and years to come. I don't think we need an extra spotlight on us?"

The CC nodded, appearing to agree with Karen's assessment.

She noticed a few officers shifting in their seats, torn between their duty and political pressures.

"DCI Heath," one of the senior officers said, his voice cold, "you need to understand the delicate nature of this situation. Are we making good inroads?"

Karen glanced at Kelly, who gave her a subtle nod of support.

"Yes, sir, we are."

Before tensions could rise, Kelly intervened. "Gentlemen," she said, her voice calm but authoritative, "I think we're losing sight of the bigger picture here. Solving a case this old would be a massive win for the force. It would show the public we never give up, and justice can prevail even after decades. We have a cold case, a grieving family, and the distinct possibility of smuggling of priceless artefacts. Can you imagine the public's perspective? Nothing but favourable in my eyes."

During Kelly's speech, Karen felt the atmosphere change. While not convinced, a few officers seemed more supportive of the investigation. Others remained displeased.

The Chief Constable leaned back in his chair. "I appreciate your passion, DCI Heath, and your perspective, DS Kelly. Proceed with caution and keep me informed of every development. I don't want it getting out of hand. Am I clear?"

Both Karen and Kelly nodded their agreement.

As the meeting drew to a close, Karen felt drained but relieved she wasn't alone. She exchanged a brief glance with Kelly as they gathered their things, acknowledging the annoyance they both felt.

In the hallway outside the conference room, Karen

turned to Kelly. "Thank you," she said, "for backing me up in there."

Kelly nodded, her expression serious. "It was the right thing to do. But, Karen, they'll be monitoring our every movement. I admit, I play the political game, but these guys take it to a whole new level."

Karen sighed, running a hand through her hair. "I know. But we can't back down now. Not when we're so close to uncovering the truth."

Kelly leaned closer as they headed toward the car park, lowering her voice. "I'll do what I can to control interference from the brass. You focus on the investigation. But... be discreet. And watch your back."

"I will do, ma'am."

"What's the latest on Preet? Any updates?"

"Not yet. She's attending a high-end auction this evening. The covert ops team are keeping tabs on her. I'll catch up with her tomorrow."

"Good, let's hope we make progress," Kelly replied, fishing her car keys out of her bag before heading for her car.

## 29

Preet stood in the opulent lobby of a high-end auction house. Despite her outward composure, her heart pounded. Wealthy collectors surrounded her, each eyeing the catalogue of Viking artefacts up for bidding.

Moving through the crowd, Preet eyed the other attendees. She noted their interactions, picking up snippets of conversation about provenances and private collections.

A tall, distinguished man approached Preet. She recognised him from the briefing photos as Marcus Brennan, a key figure in the artefact trading world, and someone known for handling artefacts from dubious sources.

"Good evening," Brennan said, his voice smooth as silk. "I don't believe we've met. Marcus Brennan."

"No, we haven't. Amira Daman," Preet replied, using her cover name. "It's a pleasure, Mr Brennan."

Brennan inched closer to Preet, his tone soft and slow, his manner charming but with an undercurrent of suspicion.

"The surname sounds familiar. Any connection to the prominent Daman family in India?"

Preet afforded herself a small coy smile and shrugged. He'd fallen for it, as expected, as soon as she'd introduced herself. The Daman family was in the top ten wealthiest families in India and worth over twenty billion dollars. With significant interests round the globe, the temptation was too strong for Brennan not to be interested in connecting with her family.

"Perhaps," Preet replied.

Brennan's eyes widened as he tested her knowledge of Viking artefacts.

Preet in return recited information she'd taken from the briefing notes Sergeant Craig Roberts had put together.

"So, Ms Daman, what brings you to our little gathering? Any particular pieces catching your eye?"

"I'm interested in the ninth-century hammer pendant. The craftsmanship is exquisite, and its provenance is fascinating."

During their conversation, Preet noticed Brennan subtly scanning the room, seemingly searching for someone. She filed this observation away, wondering about his clear nervousness.

Preet kept her face neutral. "I'm curious about the authentication process of these artefacts. It must be quite rigorous."

Brennan's eyes narrowed, but his smile remained fixed. "Oh, absolutely. We take great care to ensure the authenticity of every piece. In fact..." He paused, seeming to decide. "I have a few special items not in the main auction. Perhaps you'd be interested in a private viewing?"

Preet accepted, recognising this as a potential breakthrough, but also aware of the increased risk. "I'm interested, Mr Brennan. We'll talk later."

With the first lot presented, the air crackled with anticipation, and Preet could feel Brennan's scrutiny from across the aisle, making her acutely aware of his presence. The strategy indicated she would take part in the bidding, so she would need to be careful to keep her cover as a serious collector while gathering as much information as possible about the other buyers.

The auctioneer's voice filled the room. "Lot twenty-three, a silver hammer pendant, circa 850 AD. We'll start the bidding at fifty thousand pounds."

An online bid set the tone. Preet raised her paddle, noting who else showed interest. A woman two rows ahead, a man near the back, and Brennan himself all joined the bidding war before the online bidder secured the item.

During a break in the auction, Preet darted through the crowd and headed for the ladies. Once alone in a cubicle, she sent a message to her team, updating them on the invitation from Brennan and seeking guidance.

*Made contact with Brennan. Invited to private viewing. Requesting next steps.*

When Preet went back to the auction room, she found Brennan engaged in a heated argument with another man. She couldn't hear the words, but the body language suggested a serious disagreement. The other man, grey-haired and wearing a tailored suit, jabbed a finger at Brennan's chest before storming off.

Brennan caught her gaze. His face settled into a pleasant facade, leaving Preet to ponder what she'd unexpectedly witnessed. He approached her, his composure restored.

"Ah, Ms Daman. I hope you're enjoying the auction. Still interested in a private viewing?"

"I am, Mr Brennan. I'm looking forward to it. Here's

my card," she said, handing Brennan her business card. "Call me with the details. Please don't waste my time. I'm a very busy woman and will leave for the US in a few days on business. We're acquiring a piece my father has purchased for two million dollars. So, I'm not looking for the normal pieces, only rare items beyond the reach of most collectors."

Brennan raised a brow and smiled as he slipped the card inside his jacket.

As the auction resumed, Preet found herself more alert than ever. The tension in the room seemed to have escalated as more lots were sold. All the while, she kept her eye on Brennan, waiting to see what he did next.

## 30

Kelly sat at her desk, the glow of her computer screen illuminating her tired face. It was late, but she was reviewing reports from Karen's team, trying to stay ahead of the complex investigation. Her phone buzzed, the caller ID showing the Police and Crime Commissioner's number, Kim Foster.

Kelly tutted and answered the call.

"Detective Superintendent Kelly, I need an update on the Lockwood investigation. Now." The commissioner's voice was terse as he made his demands.

Kelly picked up on the strain in his voice, sensing the pressure he was under from above.

"Your progress email to me confirmed the decision to mount an undercover operation. How certain are you it will yield anything of substance?"

"Commissioner, I assure you DCI Heath and her team are making significant headway. We've identified the victim and are pursuing several promising leads—" Kelly worded her response, highlighting the progress made while downplaying the more controversial aspects of the investigation.

Foster interrupted, his tone sharpening. "That's not good enough, Kelly. We need results, not promises. If we don't resolve this case quickly there is talk of budget cuts. You're throwing a lot of resources on a cold case."

Kelly felt a tightening in her chest, recognising the veiled threat to her department's resources. She gripped the phone tight, forcing her voice to stay calm. Despite Foster's constant interruptions, Kelly pushed on and explained the reasons for the covert operation. "I understand the pressure, Commissioner, but rushing a complex investigation leads to mistakes. We're being thorough to ensure—"

"Thorough?" Foster scoffed. "What we need is closure, not a media circus. There are people interested in seeing this wrapped up, Kelly. People with influence."

*So I hear.*

She sensed Foster's increasing frustration, his breath becoming sharp on the other end of the line.

"Your job, Detective Superintendent, is to solve crimes with minimal disruption. Don't forget."

After ending the call, Kelly sat there staring at her phone. She reviewed the conversation, picking apart Foster's words and trying to discern the true motivations behind the pressure. The mention of "people with influence" nagged at her, hinting at a web of connections Karen had already mentioned.

Kelly retrieved Karen's case file on her computer, along with reports from the investigation. She spent time considering the best way to navigate the political minefield while supporting her team and maintaining the integrity of the case. The complexities of the Lockwood investigation, with its ties to historical artefacts and powerful families, seemed even more treacherous.

The conversation with Foster had clarified there were forces at play, eager to see the Lockwood case closed. But Kelly knew rushing the investigation or bowing to political pressure would compromise everything she and her team stood for.

"Sod this, I'm done for today," she hissed as she pushed back in her chair, gathered her things, and switched off her PC.

## 31

WITH A CUP of coffee in one hand and her notebook in the other, Karen scanned the incident board for any further information added overnight. Other than a few extra lines of enquiry, the board remained unchanged. One person she still needed a word with was Father O'Brien, who was part of the dig team and involved with cataloguing alongside Alistair Lockwood. At some point today, she would pay him a visit. O'Brien had appeared jittery when she'd visited the dean, which bothered her.

It had been a busy start to the morning already. Karen, Bel, and Preet had convened for an early morning debrief with Kelly, all of them eager to discover what Preet had discovered at the auction the previous evening. Kelly appeared happy, and Karen was relieved Preet had handled the pressure. They agreed to continue with the covert op for another few days to see where Brennan led things, especially because Brennan had called Preet last night inviting her to a discreet get-together he was organising for the following night.

The news sounded promising with the opportunity for Preet to discover who Brennan was mixed with and whether they were persons of interest to the investigation.

Karen stepped away and headed for Bel's desk.

"Bel. We need to examine how the original investigation was carried out by York police. I know it's a pain in the arse, but let's crack on with going through the paper-based reports in the police archives."

---

KAREN AND BELINDA sat in a small, cluttered office at the police archive, surrounded by boxes of old case files. The musty smell of aged paper filled the air as they sifted through decades-old reports.

It took a while, but as they worked, Karen picked up on a pattern of inconsistencies in the police reports surrounding the time of Sarah's disappearance. She leaned across the table, tapping a finger on a particular document.

"Bel, look at this," Karen said. "The dates on these reports don't match with the timeline we've established. It makes me think the investigating team was not in receipt of all the facts and details."

Belinda shifted from her own stack of papers, pushing her glasses up her nose. She took the report from Karen, and scanned the page.

"You're right," she said, reaching for a marker. She stood and moved to the large whiteboard they'd brought in, noting the discrepancies.

Belinda continued to make notes before she returned to her chair. "Karen, I've found something else, too." She turned to old financial records spread out before her which formed part of the investigation in the late eighties. "There's a series of unusual transactions linked to several prominent local families in the weeks following Sarah's disappearance. Namely, the Pearsons and Marshalls."

Karen stood, moving to peek over Belinda's shoulder.

"These families... they're still influential in York today?"

"We know about the Pearsons," Bel said. "The Marshalls are new to this investigation, but not new to the police. The Marshalls have been in and out of the nick more than I've had hot dinners. Shaun Marshall died a few years back. Ross, his son, took over the *family* business. Fraud, laundering, theft of high-value paintings and antiques destined for the overseas market. What do you think it means?"

"I'm not sure yet," Karen replied. "But it's worth investigating further. Where's Ross now?"

"Last time I knew, no fixed address. Spends more time on the Costa Del Crime than the UK. Known contacts include David Pearson Jnr."

"Why am I not surprised?"

Belinda nodded. "There's more. Current officials. Look at this one—Councillor Victoria Hartley. She was just a junior clerk back then, but her name keeps appearing in these files because her father, Matthew Hartley, was a York councillor back in the eighties."

"Fuck."

Delving deeper into the archives, Karen uncovered a report which made her pause. "Belinda, you need to see this!" she called out. "Officers received a tip-off about a possible sealed vault beneath York Minster, which allegedly contained artefacts from the dig. But I don't see it mentioned anywhere else in later reports."

"Shouldn't someone have mentioned something so significant several times unless the source was wrong, or it was never discovered?" Belinda frowned.

The shrill ring of Karen's phone interrupted their discussion. She glanced at the screen, seeing Ed's name appear.

"It's Ed." She answered the call and put it on speakerphone. "Ed, you're on speaker with Belinda and me. What have you got?"

Ed's voice crackled through the speaker. "I've been digging into the backgrounds of the Pearson and Fairfax families as you asked. I've traced a bank account in Morocco linked to the Pearsons. A healthy current balance of over three hundred and fifty thousand in it. First set up in 1982, and since then has seen deposits every few months. Plenty of cash going in and out over the years."

"From who?"

"Still working on that. A company called Cantor International. That's all I have, but it's a UK company, so Companies House and HMRC are my next port of call."

"And Fairfax?"

"One sec," Ed replied. "Right, I've got it now. Emmett Fairfax has a little over one hundred and twenty thousand in Lloyds TSB. There's also a closed account in the name of his late father, Stuart Fairfax. The closing balance was sixty-four thousand."

"Closed? What happened to the sixty-four grand?" Karen asked.

"Transferred into Emmett's account when his father died."

Karen and Belinda exchanged a glance of curiosity.

"Thanks, Ed," Karen said when he finished. "This is

excellent work. Keep digging but be careful. We don't want to tip anyone off."

After ending the call, Karen turned to Belinda. "We need to see Fairfax now."

Belinda nodded gathering her phone, coffee mug, and notes.

## 32

"Who else is on our list to talk to?" Karen asked, steering her car through slow-moving traffic.

She stopped at a zebra crossing and watched as a mother pushed her buggy across the road in a hurry. A contrast to the elderly man who stepped off the pavement and hobbled across, a walking stick in one hand and a Sainsbury's bag in the other. Karen wondered why he had his head bowed and was staring at the ground, but she didn't notice the curvature of his upper spine until he passed. *Poor bloke,* she thought. Despite his health challenges, he still had to grab his groceries and other essentials. *Are there no neighbours to help?*

"Father O'Brien," Bel replied.

"Right, I'll see him after Fairfax."

Karen squeezed into a parking bay further along the road and walked the remaining distance to the address.

Emmett Fairfax answered the door. His chest sagged upon seeing his visitors. Fairfax's eyes darted between them. "Please leave me alone," he pleaded.

"Professor Fairfax," Karen began, her voice firm but not unkind, "we need to talk to you again. We've uncovered discrepancies in the official records and hoped you'd be able to shed light on them."

Fairfax's face paled, but he maintained his composure. "I've already told you everything I know, Detective Chief Inspector."

"Sorry, but this needs to be done. We can do it here or at the station. Your choice."

Fairfax sighed and nodded before letting the officers in and leading them through to his lounge.

Once he was settled in his armchair, Karen spread out some documents they had brought from the archives. "These tell a different story to what we first believed. We've found altered witness statements, omissions in official reports, and a pattern of misinformation."

Fairfax stared at the documents, his eyes widening in surprise. His hands trembled as he reached for one document.

"We need the truth," Karen pressed. "What items were taken and not recorded during the dig?"

Fairfax slumped in his chair, decades of secrecy crushing his chest. He was silent for a long moment, his internal struggle clear on his face.

Finally, he spoke. "It was never supposed to go this far."

Karen shifted forward and clasped her hands together. "What was it? What did you find?"

Fairfax took another deep breath and swallowed hard, his eyes rising to meet Karen's. "We found Viking artefacts, many of which were valuable and would fetch a fortune on the black market. But there were powerful people who wanted it kept secret. So, they told me they would lock away the evidence in a nearby vault until they decided about what to do with it. The team received a request to stop working when they discovered the pieces. When we were allowed back a few days later, someone had removed those artefacts and everything else associated with them. We never saw them again."

With Fairfax's confirmation and added details, filling the holes in their investigation, Karen and Belinda shared a knowing look.

"Who told you the pieces would be locked away?"

"Pearson. He was the mouthpiece for the group financing the dig."

"Pearson senior?"

Fairfax nodded as he stared at Karen.

"And did you ever witness boxes being loaded into a vehicle during the dig?"

Fairfax shook his head.

"Did you see any other individuals other than those on the dig team?"

"No."

"Are you sure?" Karen probed, doubting Fairfax's reply.

"I'm sure."

Karen glanced at Bel and nodded before they both stood.

"Thanks for your time. That will be all for now, but we may need to speak with you again. We'll see ourselves out."

---

"Do you believe him?" Bel asked as they walked back to the car.

"Nope. There's more to it. He knows the names. I'd love to pull him in along with anyone else connected to the dig and the smuggling operation. But, with Preet undercover, if anyone is still smuggling or selling stolen artefacts, I'd rather catch them in the act than scare them off."

## 33

Karen stood outside St Mary's Church. She was here to speak with Father O'Brien. Back in 1987, he had been a young priest at York Minster during the dig. The church was quiet, as the last parishioners had left only moments before.

Upon entering the church, the stillness struck Karen. Father O'Brien was at the altar, his back to her while he arranged flowers. She cleared her throat, and he turned, his face a mask of polite enquiry that didn't quite hide his nervousness.

"Evening, Father, moonlighting?" Karen said, her voice echoing in the empty church. "In case you've forgotten, I'm DCI Karen Heath. I was hoping we could talk about your time here."

O'Brien's smile was tight. "Of course, Detective. This isn't moonlighting. I conduct drop-in sessions at various churches. It's a way for us to reach deeper into the community to offer help and spiritual guidance. What would you like to know?"

Karen began the conversation, asking about his early

days as a priest. O'Brien guarded his responses, which she noticed, including how he rung his hands.

"And the 1987 dig," Karen said. "That must have been an exciting time at the Minster."

O'Brien's demeanour changed. He became defensive, his hands fidgeting with the sleeve of his cassock. "I'm afraid I'm not well-versed in that. It was all handled by the archaeologists, you see."

Beads of sweat formed on the priest's forehead. She changed tack. Reaching into her bag, she pulled out a file and spread papers across a nearby pew. They talked about a sealed vault beneath York Minster and documents suggesting the hiding of artefacts.

O'Brien's face paled as he looked at the evidence. "Where... where did you get these?" he stammered.

"That's not important right now, Father," Karen said. "What's important is what they show. Evidence of a cover-up. Hidden artefacts. Incorrect inventories. And I suspect you understand this better than you're suggesting."

O'Brien's composure cracked. He struggled to find the right words, his feeble attempts to explain the evidence only undermining his credibility. "These could be from anywhere," he said, his voice shaking. "You can't possibly think the church would be involved in something so nefarious."

Karen pressed harder, her voice firm as she demanded the truth. "Father O'Brien, we have evidence linking the church and others to the disappearance of Sarah Lockwood and the concealment of artefacts from the dig. I need you to tell me what you know."

O'Brien stood his ground.

"Now!" Karen demanded.

Still nothing.

Karen shrugged. "Fine, we can do this the hard way. I need to take you in for questioning."

Without warning, O'Brien broke down. Tears streamed down his face. He collapsed on to a pew. "I never wanted to be part of it," he sobbed. "I was only a young priest. They told me it was for the good of the church, we were protecting something important. They told me what to do."

Karen sat beside him, her voice softening. "Who were you protecting, Father? What happened?"

Between sobs, O'Brien confessed. He spoke of artefacts discovered during the dig, items which could "change history" as he'd been told. He mentioned names of those who were involved in the decision to hide the findings. Karen recognised a few. Stuart Fairfax, David Pearson, and Shaun Marshall. The intention wasn't for the items to be put on public display but to be sold on the black market for sizeable sums, where they would disappear into the private collections of billionaires round the world.

"And Sarah?" Karen asked, already knowing the answer having heard it from "John" at the Railway Museum. "What happened to her?"

O'Brien's face crumpled. "She... she found out. She was going to expose everything. I had no idea about their plans, I promise. When I heard she'd disappeared, I... I knew. But I was too afraid to speak and I had no proof."

Karen listened, storing every detail, her mind reeling at the implications.

"I've lived with this guilt for decades," O'Brien said, his voice breaking. "I should have said something sooner. I'm so sorry."

Karen placed a comforting hand on his shoulder. "It's

not too late to do the right thing, Father. We'll need you to make a formal statement. Will you do that?"

O'Brien nodded, relief mixing with fear on his face. "Yes, it's time the truth came out."

Leaving the church, with Karen supporting the shaken priest, she spotted a figure lurking from the shadows of a nearby building. Before she could get a clear look, they disappeared. Karen hurried O'Brien to her car, her senses on high alert, realising she wasn't the only one who wanted to speak with the father.

## 34

Preet checked her handbag one last time and glanced at Marcus Brennan's opulent mansion. He'd done well for himself, and no doubt funded by less than legitimate means. She was here for an exclusive event for high-end artefact collectors.

"I can do this," she announced as she reapplied her lipstick, giving herself one last check in the rearview mirror of her car before stepping out and heading towards the front door.

A man stood at the entrance and ticked her name off on a guest list pinned to a clipboard in his hand. He gave Preet a cursory nod and stepped to one side to let her pass. Preet joined the gathering, scanning the room, and noting the guests—a mix of wealthy collectors, academics, and what she suspected were black market dealers. The air was thick with the smell of expensive perfumes and the low hum of hushed conversations. Crystal chandeliers cast a warm glow over the proceedings, their light glinting off jewellery and polished silverware.

She made her way to Brennan, who greeted her with a

pasted-on fake smile. "Ah, Miss Daman," he said, his voice smooth as silk. "I'm glad you came this evening."

"I wouldn't miss it," Preet replied, matching his tone. "You have quite the collection of guests."

Brennan's lips curled into a smile. "Only the best for our little soirée. But come, there's something I'd like to show you."

He placed a hand on the small of her back and led Preet away from the main party, guiding her along a hallway lined with priceless artworks. They stopped before a heavy oak door, which Brennan unlocked with a key from his pocket.

Inside, displayed on velvet-lined trays, were artefacts which took Preet's breath away. She recognised several pieces matching descriptions from the 1987 York Minster dig. There were intricately carved bone combs, delicate silver brooches, and fragments of illuminated manuscripts. But they were minor items. He led her on to a larger display.

Preet gasped. "Oh my lord."

Brennan nodded and smiled.

Preet spotted another few items believed to have gone missing from the dig. A Viking helmet forged around 970 CE which had belonged to a minor Viking king. The only complete example in existence. She moved along the displays and stopped at the next one. Trays of coins, dated between 539 and 870 CE, along with a chest discovered which had been carbon dated to 675 CE according to the small plaque in front of it.

"Extraordinary," Preet murmured, her eyes wide with genuine awe.

While Preet examined the artifacts, Brennan remained watchful. His eyes narrowed, studying her reactions. "You have quite an eye, Miss Daman. From what sources do you acquire your pieces?"

Preet pulse throbbed in her temples as she navigated his interrogation. "Oh, here and there. Auctions or private sales with wealthy sellers who enjoy the Viking era. As you know, judging from your collection, it's a profitable era. And you know how it is in our world—discretion is key. I would never reveal my sources."

Brennan nodded, but his gaze remained sharp. "And your interest in Viking artefacts? That's quite a specific niche."

"A passion that started at university," Preet replied. "I find their craftsmanship unparalleled."

Another guest—a woman Preet recognised as Councillor Hartley—interrupted their conversation. She entered the room with the confidence of someone accustomed to power.

*Shit*, Preet thought. The last person she expected to see was a York councillor. Preet turned and moved away as if captivated by an exhibit she'd seen in another glass case. Thankfully, Preet had never met Councillor Hartley and hoped the woman had never seen pictures of her since joining Karen's team. Her racing heart and cotton-dry mouth betrayed her rising panic.

"Marcus," the councillor boomed. "Quite the gathering you've put together."

Brennan clasped the woman's hand and kissed both cheeks. "Councillor Hartley, always a pleasure. Have you met Miss Daman? She's quite the Viking enthusiast."

Preet waved from a distance and noted the familiarity between the two, filing away this information for later before stepping behind a glass display stand.

Brennan excused himself to talk to Hartley outside, leaving Preet alone with the artefacts. She took photos of each piece. Her heart raced, knowing that being discovered would be disastrous. She moved round the displays, ensuring clear shots of each item while appearing to show casual interest.

When Brennan returned, an older man Preet didn't recognise accompanied him. The newcomer had a weathered face and piercing blue eyes which appeared to look right through her.

"Ms Daman," Brennan said, "allow me to introduce Professor Messaoudi from Morocco. He's one of the foremost experts on Viking archaeology."

The professor eyed her, engaging in a discussion about Viking history. "So, Ms Daman, what's your take on the debate surrounding the extent of Viking presence in York during the tenth century?"

Preet drew on her extensive preparation, matching the man's knowledge and even correcting him on a few points. "While the traditional view has been of a limited occupation, recent archaeological evidence suggests a much more significant Viking settlement. The finds at Coppergate, for instance, show a thriving urban centre with diverse craft production."

Professor Messaoudi raised an eyebrow, impressed. "Well-informed, I see. And what of the runic inscriptions found on the Minster excavations?"

"Fascinating pieces. They've provided valuable insights into the linguistic and cultural melding of the period. The mix of Old Norse and Anglo-Saxon elements in those inscriptions paints a picture of a truly multicultural York."

"Very good," Messaoudi replied. "Shall we join the main party? I'm a little thirsty," he added, holding his empty flute.

Preet nodded and slipped in line between the two men.

Later in the evening, Preet detected a slight shift in Brennan's behaviour. He became more open, sharing details about upcoming auctions and hinting at the provenance of some artefacts.

"You know, Ms Daman," Brennan said, "not all of these pieces come through... conventional channels. But I assure you, their authenticity is beyond question."

Preet steered the conversation, gathering as much information as she could. "I'm sure your sources are impeccable, Mr Brennan. In our world, reputation and authenticity are everything."

Brennan rested his hand on Preet's arm. "I'm hosting a more intimate gathering tomorrow evening. I'd be delighted if you would join us."

"I would be honoured. You have my number. Text me the time and location."

Preparing to leave, she spotted Brennan in an intense, hushed conversation with Councillor Hartley. Their faces were close, their expressions serious. At one point, Hartley stroked Brennan's cheek and he leaned his head into her touch. Were they more than acquaintances? It appeared so. Preet strained to hear, but the general noise of departing guests drowned out their words.

Preet left the mansion, keen to get away. The cool night air was a relief after the stuffy atmosphere inside. Settling into her car, she noticed someone in a nearby vehicle. For a moment, she feared someone had discovered her secret, but the car drove away, disappearing into the night.

Before setting off, she fired off a text to Sergeant Craig Roberts about the evening.

## 35

Following a hurried call from Sergeant Craig Roberts, Kelly spent the next hour digging into Councillor Victoria Hartley's background. The feedback from Preet had been a revelation to Kelly, and since getting off the call, she had been searching for any connection to the mysterious events of 1987.

The late hour was clear in the eerie silence of the empty corridors outside her office, and an untouched cold cup of coffee sat forgotten on her cluttered desk.

Though she couldn't prove it yet, it had become clearer why Hartley had paid her a visit and attempted to steer her away from continuing the investigation.

*Convenient*, she thought.

She knew Karen was downstairs in an interview room taking a statement from Father O'Brien. Karen had been keen to update her the moment she'd arrived back at the station. Stuart Fairfax, Shaun Marshall, and David Pearson had not only bankrolled the dig, but they were also more than likely connected to Sarah's death when she'd uncovered the discrepancies and missing artefacts.

The only disappointment was all three were deceased and couldn't face justice.

But it was Councillor Victoria Hartley who Kelly had in her crosshairs.

As Kelly read document after document, her eyes growing weary from the strain, she uncovered another surprising and significant link. Kelly discovered the woman's father had not only served as a councillor in the '80s but had also served on the committee for council funding allocations. She also discovered Victoria Hartley and her then-fiancé, Ross Marshall (Shaun Marshall's son), had controlled a dubious trust receiving city funds for the dig.

The revelation sent a jolt of adrenaline through her tired body. She leaned back in her creaking chair, her mind contemplating the far-reaching implications of this unexpected discovery. Could this be the breakthrough she'd been searching for, or another thread in a complex web of connections?

Kelly's computer emitted a soft ping, signalling an incoming email. Her heart quickened as she recognised the sender—a former colleague now working at Scotland Yard in London. She had reached out to him days ago, hoping his connections might shed light on Hartley's past. Reading the message, she felt a rush of both excitement and anxiety.

The email was a goldmine of information, detailing Hartley's activities in the years following 1987. It painted a picture of a woman on the rise but with questionable methods. However, most intriguing were the records of several suspicious financial transactions, large sums of money in her father's name moving to offshore accounts with no clear source or purpose, and upon his death, his accounts were closed and the monies transferred to a

Spanish bank account in Victoria Hartley's name. Kelly leaned in closer to the screen, her brow furrowed in concentration as she absorbed every detail. The transactions could be the key to unravelling the mystery playing on her mind. Councillor Matthew Hartley had been on the take. For what? To turn a blind eye from something?

She opened an attachment to the email. A grainy photo took her breath away. Matthew Hartley stood among a group of suited men dressed in blue aprons and collars. Masonic attire. She stared at the names beneath the image, her eyes widening in surprise. Stuart Fairfax, Matthew Hartley, David Pearson, and Shaun Marshall.

"Bastard," Kelly hissed.

Energised by this new lead, Kelly decided to confront Hartley. She called Hartley to say an important development needed to be discussed tonight as a matter of urgency.

Though not happy at the late-night intrusion, Hartley agreed to the meeting. Kelly wasted no time as she switched off her PC, grabbed her coat and bag, and dashed from her office.

---

KELLY ARRIVED about twenty minutes later and pressed the doorbell. Hartley, dressed in jeans and a jumper, answered and greeted her with forced politeness, the tension clear in her tight smile.

"This better be important," the woman grumbled as they moved to Hartley's private office off the main hallway.

Kelly started the conversation but steered it towards the Lockwood case. She watched Hartley, noting the flicker of unease in the councillor's eyes at the mention of Sarah's name.

"Councillor Hartley," Kelly said, "I've come across information I believe you might shed light on."

Hartley's smile didn't waver, but her fingers tightened round her pen. "Of course, Superintendent. What is it?"

The councillor's composure began to unravel as Kelly presented her findings, particularly the information concerning Hartley's father. Hartley's denials became less convincing, her hands shaking as she reached for a glass of water.

"I'm not sure what you're implying," Hartley said, her voice tight. "My father's position on the council isn't relevant to your current investigation."

Kelly raised a brow, her gaze steady. "It becomes relevant, Councillor, when we consider the dubious financial transactions which followed. They seemed to coincide with key moments in the cover-up of Sarah Lockwood's disappearance."

"Absolute bloody nonsense. What are you implying?" Hartley protested.

"I'm suggesting someone paid hush money to your father to keep quiet about the discoveries and later illegal thefts and sales of precious artefacts on the black market. If he looked the other way, he would be taken care of... get my drift?" Kelly smiled, enjoying the moment. "My question is, are you complicit, too? Did you know anything about it? Because as far as I can see, when his offshore accounts were closed, the balances moved to a Spanish bank account in your name." She waited for a second before adding, "And you were engaged to Ross Marshall at the time, who as we both know has a lengthy criminal record now."

The confrontation reached a climax as Kelly laid out her suspicions about the cover-up.

Hartley, her political mask slipping, resorted to threats. "You're treading on dangerous ground, Superintendent," she hissed. "Do you have any idea who you're dealing with? The connections I have?"

Kelly stood firm, making it clear she wouldn't be intimidated. "I'm dealing with someone who seems to be obstructing a murder investigation, Councillor. Your connections don't change the fact."

"Watch what you say, Superintendent."

Kelly continued to smile, enjoying the woman's discomfort, never taking her eyes off Hartley. "From where I stand, you're complicit and corrupt, and I'm going to make sure my case is watertight. I'm giving you the opportunity to do the right thing now!"

Before Kelly left, Hartley made one last, desperate attempt to bribe her into silence. "Think about your career, Superintendent," she said, her voice softening. "I could make things very comfortable for you. A promotion, political support... all you have to do is let this go."

Kelly stood and glared at the woman. "I'm not for sale, Councillor. And neither is justice for Sarah Lockwood."

After leaving, her chest swelled in triumph. She was sure they were on the right track and had poked a hornet's nest.

## 36

Karen yawned as she pulled into the Tesco car park, her mind still racing from the day's events. After taking Father O'Brien's statement, she braced herself for the whirlwind of drama and chaos the coming days promised. Kelly's text update only added fuel to her emotions. Her only regret was not being there to see the smugness wiped from Councillor Hartley's face. Still, she'd get a full update from Kelly in the morning before taking any further steps.

The fluorescent lights cast an eerie glow over the empty car park as she made her way into the store. She hurried through the aisles, grabbing essentials and ignoring the sense of tension in her stomach.

Twenty minutes later, she emerged from the store, her arms laden with bags. Approaching the car, something caught her eye. A white envelope tucked under her windscreen wiper, fluttering in the cool night breeze. Setting down her bags, she reached for the envelope.

She checked her surroundings before opening it. Inside was a crudely typed note with a chilling message: "*Drop the case or you'll be next.*" Reading the words sent a shiver down her spine; the threat was clear. Karen scanned the car park, her eyes straining in the darkness, but she couldn't see anyone lurking nearby.

Shit. Someone had followed her.

Calming herself, Karen clenched her jaw in defiance and tucked the note into her pocket. She loaded her shopping into the boot and took one last look at her surroundings. Once in the driver's seat, she started the car and left.

The drive home was tense with Karen checking her rearview mirror for any signs of being followed. Her mind raced, debating whether to report it. She knew if she reported the threat, Kelly might take her off the case. With a heavy heart, she decided to keep it to herself for now.

Karen took a moment to gather her thoughts as she arrived home. She couldn't let Zac or Summer see how shaken she was. She plastered on a neutral expression and headed inside.

The moment she stepped through the door, Karen sensed the tension in the air. Zac was waiting for her in the living room, his face a mixture of relief and worry. She set her bags at the bottom of the stairs, bracing herself for the difficult conversation she knew was coming.

"You're late," Zac said, his voice tight with anxiety.

Karen sighed. "I know. I'm sorry. I had to stop for a few bits on the way home." She fished round in one of her shopping bags and pulled out a two-pack of custard tarts, waving them in front of Zac. "Your favourite."

Zac stood and paced the room. "Do you have any idea what it's like, waiting here, not knowing if you're okay? Every time you're late, I imagine the worst."

"Zac, I—"

"No, Karen. These long hours... it's too much. You're putting the job before your family. I can't handle the worry."

Karen's frustration grew. She knew it wasn't Zac saying this, it was the PTSD, past trauma, and anxiety talking. "That's not fair. You know how important this case is. We're making progress, and—"

Their voices rose, the argument escalating. Neither spotted the figure at the bottom of the stairs until Summer's quiet voice cut through their heated exchange.

"Karen? Dad? What's going on?"

Karen and Zac fell silent, exchanging guilty expressions upon seeing the worry on Summer's face. Karen moved to the stairs, her voice softening.

"It's nothing, sweetheart. A misunderstanding. Grown-up stuff and nothing to worry about. Go back to bed, okay?" She leaned in and kissed Summer on the forehead, before running her hand through Summer's hair.

After reassuring Summer and sending her back to her room, Karen and Zac continued their discussion to the kitchen. The change of scenery seemed to calm them both, and they talked more rationally about their fears and concerns.

Zac leaned against the counter, his shoulders slumped. "I have nightmares, Karen. Every night. I see you being taken, like I was. And I can't do anything to stop it. I walk round the house with a ball of fear churning my insides the minute you leave the house."

Karen's heart ached at the pain in his voice. She reached out and took his hand. "I'm so sorry, Zac. I didn't appreciate it was still so bad."

For a moment, Karen considered telling Zac about the threatening note, but she held back. He was already struggling so much; she didn't want to add to his worries.

"I take precautions, Zac. I'm careful. And I have an entire team watching my back, our backs," she reassured him.

Zac looked at her, his eyes filled with a mixture of love and fear. "What if it's not enough? Karen, I've been thinking... maybe we should leave the force. We could move somewhere quieter, safer."

Karen stared at him, stunned by the suggestion. The thought of leaving her job, her purpose, was unthinkable. But as she looked at Zac, she understood the impact the kidnapping had on him.

"Zac, I... I don't know if I can. My job, it's part of me. We're both coppers, it's who we are."

"And it comes with huge risks," he countered.

"Zac..."

He raised a hand to cut her off. "But things have changed."

"Yes, but it's only temporary. We'll get through this. And before you know it, you'll be itching to get back to work. It's going to take time."

Zac fell silent. He shrugged.

Karen's stomach twisted. Every time they had this conversation, the guilt crept in, sharp and unforgiving. Her job was part of who she was, but at what cost? Zac was still haunted by what had happened, and every reminder of the risks she took felt like another blow to his already fragile sense of safety.

"I promise it will get better. We've got so much to look forward to. It's a shitty rough patch we're going through, but I'm not about to give up on us."

They talked late into the night, neither willing to concede their position but both recognising the need for compromise. Finally, they reached an uneasy truce.

"I'll try to be home more," Karen promised. "And I'll keep you better informed about my whereabouts. And as soon as this case is over, how about if you and I book a weekend away in the country? Somewhere quiet, with lots of wooded trails for us to walk?"

Zac nodded, taking her hand. "Sounds good. And I'll work on managing my anxiety. I know your job is important to you, and I'll try to be more supportive."

Though still unresolved, their argument ended with a fragile truce as they lay in bed. Karen lay awake, listening to Zac's restless turning beside her. She stared at the ceiling, the threatening note from earlier playing on her mind.

## 37

Karen stood at the kitchen counter, stirring a pot of porridge as she watched Summer enter the room and grab her own breakfast. The young girl slid into her usual seat at the table, her movements lacking their typical energy. Karen frowned, as Summer poked at her cereal without enthusiasm.

"Everything alright, love?" Karen placed a glass of orange juice on the table in front of Summer.

Summer shrugged. "I guess."

Karen sat across from her, sensing there was more to Summer's mood than simple morning grumpiness. "You know you can talk to me about anything, right?"

After a moment's hesitation, Summer spoke. "Karen, what's it like being in the police?"

The question caught Karen off guard. She'd always been open about her work. "Well, it's challenging but rewarding. Why do you ask?"

Summer's words tumbled out in a rush. "I've been reading about the police cadets. They learn lots of things, like first aid and crime prevention. Do you think I could join?"

Karen blinked, surprised by the level of thought Summer had put into this. "That's quite a big decision, Summer. It's not something to take lightly."

Karen explained the realities of police work, balancing the positives with the challenges, but before she could finish, the doorbell rang. She glanced at the clock, realising it must be Michelle, Zac's ex-wife, here to collect Summer.

Karen rose to answer the door. "That must be your mum. We'll finish this chat later, okay?"

Seconds later, Michelle appeared in the kitchen doorway, her expression tightening as she took in the scene. "Summer, are you ready to go?"

"Almost, Mum," Summer spooned cereal into her mouth with newfound enthusiasm. "Karen and I were talking about the police cadets. I'm thinking of joining."

Karen grimaced at the tightness in her chest. *Thanks, Summer.*

The atmosphere in the kitchen changed. Michelle's eyes narrowed as she glared at Karen. "Police cadets? What's this about?"

Karen tried to keep her voice calm. "Summer was asking about my work, that's all."

"And you thought it was right to encourage her?" Michelle's voice was sharp. "After everything that's happened. Have you forgotten what Zac endured?"

Karen sensed her temper rising. "Of course I haven't forgotten. But that doesn't mean—"

"Doesn't mean what?" Michelle interrupted. "That you should put ideas in her head about joining such a dangerous profession?"

"I'm not putting ideas in anyone's head," Karen retorted. "Summer asked, and I was giving her honest answers."

Their voices rose as they argued back and forth about the merits and risks of a police career. Summer shrank in her chair, her stare switching between the two women.

The sound of footsteps on the stairs announced Zac's arrival. He entered the kitchen, his face creased with concern. "What's going on?"

Michelle spun round to him. "Did you know about this? Karen's been talking to Summer about joining the police cadets."

Zac's eyes widened. He looked from Michelle to Karen, clearly unsure how to respond. "I'm sure Karen was answering Summer's questions. Right, Karen?"

Karen nodded, grateful for Zac's effort at mediation. But Michelle wasn't satisfied.

"And you're okay with that?" she demanded. "After what you went through? Do you want Summer exposed to those kinds of risks?"

Karen saw Michelle's frustration building even as Zac tried to calm her. She opened her mouth to argue further, but before she could speak, a shout cut through the tension.

"Stop it!" Summer cried, her voice cracking. "Just stop!"

The room fell silent, all eyes turning to the distressed girl.

Summer's face flushed, and tears brimmed in her eyes. "I hate it when you all fight. All I asked was about Karen's job. I didn't mean to cause trouble. I asked Karen. It was me who started this. So stop twisting things."

Karen felt a tightness in her chest when she saw the

conflict on Summer's face. Torn between her curiosity about Karen's work and her mother's fears.

Michelle's face softened as she looked at her daughter. "I'm sorry, sweetheart. We shouldn't have argued in front of you."

She turned to Karen; her voice was still tight but less hostile. "We can discuss this another time, when we're all calmer. But I need to be clear—I don't approve of encouraging Summer towards such a dangerous career."

Karen nodded, not trusting herself to speak without reigniting the argument. She watched as Michelle gathered Summer's things, ushering the girl towards the door.

Karen saw Zac's worried expression as he went to hug Summer goodbye. She felt a heaviness in her chest. Was she asking too much of her family? After everything they'd been through, was it fair to expose them to the constant stress and danger of her job? After Zac had suggested leaving the force, was this the further evidence he needed to solidify that opinion?

"I'm sorry," Karen said after Summer and Michelle had left.

Zac blew out his cheeks and ran a hand through his messy bed hair. He shrugged. "I wish I knew what to do." He slumped into a chair at the dining table and tipped his head back. Closing his eyes, he tutted.

"I know, babes." Karen stepped in behind his chair and draped her arms over his shoulders. Closing her eyes, she relished the feeling of Zac in her embrace. They'd not enjoyed much closeness in recent months, and she missed it so much.

"I'm sure Summer will forget about it and something else will grab her interest."

"Perhaps."

Even though she wanted to suggest the police cadets didn't mean she'd become a copper, and it could teach her valuable skills like first aid, public service, right from wrong, and responsibility, she kept it to herself for the time being.

## 38

It was nice to have calm restored to the house after Michelle left. It wasn't an ideal way to start the morning. Karen kissed Zac goodbye, her lips lingering on his for a moment longer than usual. The warmth of his breath mingled with hers, a comforting familiarity she needed. "Everything will be okay," she murmured, trying to convince herself as much as him. Her dark-brown eyes searched his face, seeking reassurance in his familiar features. With a last squeeze of his hand, her fingers intertwining with his, she pulled away. She straightened her back and headed out the door, unsure how today would pan out.

Throughout her drive to work, she was unnerved by a persistent feeling of being watched. Her eyes flicked to the rearview mirror, scanning the cars behind her. On impulse, she took a series of random turns, deviating from her usual route.

At a red light, her gaze locked on to a black car three cars back. She frowned, certain she'd seen the same vehicle several times during her drive. Though she couldn't make out the driver's face, something about the car made Karen feel uneasy. Her instincts kicked in, mind racing as she decided what to do. Race off? Call it in?

The light turned green, and Karen made an abrupt turn on to a quiet side street. She pulled over and stopped, her body tensing as she noted the car follow suit in her mirror. Not letting the moment pass, she stepped out of her car, hand gripped round her baton.

Karen approached the slowing vehicle, adrenaline surging through her veins. Before she could reach it, the engine roared to life. The car sped off past her, tyres screeching against the tarmac, leaving Karen standing alone on the street.

With a racing pulse, she memorised the car's registration as it rounded the corner and sped away. Shaken but determined, she returned to her car and continued her journey to the station.

Walking through the station car park, a sudden wave of dizziness washed over her. The world seemed to tilt, and she found herself back in the moment of her own abduction. The memory was so vivid—the rough hands grabbing her, the suffocating darkness of the hood they'd pulled over her head. Her breath hitched in ragged gasps as she leaned against the cold, damp stone wall, the rough texture grounding her slightly.

"It's not real," she responded, forcing herself to focus on the rough brick against her palms. "You're safe. You're at the station."

It took a few moments before the car park came back into focus. Karen took several deep breaths to slow her heart rate. When she felt steady enough, she pushed off the wall and made her way into the building.

Inside, she paused in the corridor, debating whether to tell her team about the incident with the car. She knew they would want to know—they were more than colleagues, they were friends who had been through hell together. But a part of her hesitated. Was it anything suspicious? An uncomfortable coincidence? Could she be certain there was a connection to her case? She didn't have the answers.

Karen ran a hand through her hair, torn between her instinct to confide in her team and her desire to protect the case—and her pride. For the moment, she'd tell Kelly and have the registration details checked.

## 39

With her mind buzzing this morning from her showdown with Councillor Hartley last night, Kelly busied herself at her desk. The soft hum of her computer and the muffled conversations of her colleagues further along the corridor created a familiar background noise.

The chime of her phone on the desk cut through her thoughts. Kelly answered, her brow furrowing as she listened to the curt message on the other end. A summons from her boss for an immediate meeting. The tone left her uneasy as she gathered her things and made her way to the lift. She tutted and shook her head, certain her summons was a result of last night.

The lift doors opened on the top floor. With a sharp intake of breath, Kelly straightened her jacket, the crisp fabric crackling softly, and jutted out her chin, her defiance evident in the set of her shoulders. She strode along the corridor, the sound of her heels muted on the carpeted floor. The conference room door loomed ahead. She paused before entering.

Inside, the Chief Constable sat at the head of the long

table, flanked by several high-ranking officials. Their serious expressions did nothing to ease Kelly's growing concern. She took her seat, aware of the thick tension in the room.

"Superintendent Kelly," the Chief Constable began, his voice grave. "We've called you here to discuss the progress of the Lockwood case."

Kelly nodded, her thoughts swirling as she prepared to defend her team's work. "Of course, sir. We've made significant strides in the investigation—"

"And yet," one official interrupted, "we seem no closer to an arrest. Can you explain why?"

Kelly pursed her lips before responding, choosing to hold back on revealing the evidence she'd uncovered on Councillor Hartley and the late-night visit. "The case is complex, with historical elements requiring careful investigation. I'm assisting DCI Heath and her team in pursuing several promising leads—"

The Chief Constable raised a hand, silencing her. "We're concerned about the high-profile nature of some suspects, Kelly. Do you have evidence against them?"

Kelly's jaw tightened. "With all due respect, sir, we can't allow external concerns to interfere with a murder investigation."

A murmur ran through the room. Kelly noticed glances exchanged between the officials, heightening her sense of unease.

"Perhaps," another official suggested, his tone deceptively casual, "it might be wise to assign a more... experienced detective to lead the case? We have one or two who would prove excellent at handling this and bringing a swift conclusion."

Kelly bristled at the implication. Would they be just as bent? "DCI Heath is more than capable—"

"Is she?" the official pressed. "Given her recent personal experiences, are we certain she's equipped to handle such a sensitive case?"

"Karen Heath is one of the most dedicated and skilled officers I've ever worked with," Kelly retorted, her voice firm. "Her recent experiences, if anything, have only sharpened her resolve to see justice done."

The debate intensified, voices rising as Kelly staunchly defended Karen and her team. The argument's intensity, a maelstrom of accusations and rising voices, finally broke through to a dawning realisation. This meeting wasn't just about the case. There was something else at play here—a power struggle, perhaps. Her colleagues seemed to see this as an opportunity to advance their own careers at Karen's expense. Or did they want to protect those involved?

The Chief Constable raised his hands, calling for quiet. When the room settled, he turned to Kelly, his expression unreadable. "Kelly, you've been with the force for a long time. Your dedication is commendable."

Kelly tensed, sensing a shift in the conversation.

"In fact," he continued, "your handling of this sensitive case could lead to... advancement. There's talk of an Assistant Deputy Chief Constable position becoming vacant soon in the Leicestershire Constabulary. You would be a strong candidate for such a role."

The implication hung in the air. Kelly felt like the air had been sucked out of the room. She stared at the Chief Constable, stunned by the implied bribe. The other officials watched her, waiting for her response.

Kelly's mind raced. She thought of Karen, of the victim whose killer still walked free, of the principles she'd upheld throughout her career. The silence stretched, taut as a wire.

Finally, Kelly spoke, her voice firm. "I appreciate the consideration, sir, but I stand behind DCI Heath and her team. They are the best people for this investigation, and I have full confidence in their abilities."

She saw disappointment and anger flash across a few faces, while others regarded her with newfound respect. The Chief Constable's expression hardened.

"I see," he said, his tone clipped. "Well, then. Superintendent, I hope your confidence isn't misplaced. You may go."

Kelly stood, her head held high despite the sinking sensation in her stomach. As she walked to the door, she knew she'd made powerful enemies.

## 40

With a deep set scowl, Kelly strode through the station, her walk morphing into a stomp as she made her way to Karen's office. Officers who caught sight of her expression stepped aside, obviously sensing the storm brewing beneath her calm exterior.

She reached Karen's door and knocked once before entering, not waiting for a response. Karen looked up from her desk, surprise flickering across her face at Kelly's abrupt entrance.

"We need to talk," Kelly said, her voice tight with suppressed anger. She closed the door behind her and took a seat across from Karen. She took a long, deep breath, closed her eyes, and clenched her fists, exhaling to calm herself.

Karen straightened, concern etching lines across her forehead. "What's happened?"

Kelly shook her head. "I've come from a meeting with the Chief Constable and others. They're not happy with the progress of the Lockwood case."

Karen raised a brow. "But we've made significant headway—"

"That's not the issue," Kelly interrupted. "They're worried about the high-profile nature of the suspects. And..." she paused with a tut, "they wanted to replace you with one of their own choices to lead the investigation."

Karen's face paled. "Replace me? But why?"

"They questioned your ability to handle the case, given your recent experiences," Kelly explained, her voice softening. "I defended you, of course. Told them you were the best person for the job."

Karen sat back, stunned. "I can't believe they'd try to take me off the case. After everything we've uncovered..."

"It gets worse. They tried to bribe me with a promotion to go along with it."

Karen's eyes widened. "They what?"

"Hinted at an Assistant Deputy Chief Constable position," Kelly said, her disgust obvious. "As if I'd sell out my principles for a promotion."

"Ma'am, I... I'm lost for words. Thank you for standing up for me."

Kelly waved off her thanks. "It's not about you, Karen. It's about the integrity of this investigation. Something bigger is at play here, and I think I know what it might be."

Kelly's tone took on a serious note. "I've been doing some digging into Councillor Victoria Hartley's background. As you know, her father was on the city council at the time of the York Minster dig and Sarah's disappearance."

Kelly continued outlining her findings from her contact, including the Masonic photo. "I uncovered suspicious financial transactions in her father's bank account in the years following 1987. After his death, Victoria became the principal beneficiary. I confronted Hartley about it last night."

"You did what?" Karen exclaimed.

Kelly grinned. "Probably not the best move, but I went to her house. You should have seen her face when I laid out the evidence. She tried to threaten me, hinted at her 'connections in high places'. Even tried to buy me off with promises of political support."

Ma'am, I... I'm blown away. That took serious balls."

Kelly shrugged, but there was a glint of pride in her eyes. "I don't like being pissed on or taken for a muppet," she growled. "It's our job to follow the evidence, no matter where it leads. I wasn't about to let her intimidate me, especially when I believe her father was on the take to turn a blind eye."

"Well, speaking of following the evidence, I've got news of my own. Father O'Brien came good and provided a statement late last night."

"What did he say?"

"He broke down and confessed to knowing about the hidden artefacts and the cover-up following Sarah's death," Karen explained. "He claims he was a young priest following orders, too afraid to speak up. But he gave us names. The father has confirmed all those we suspected. But the biggest revelation appeared to be the offspring of those first involved have carried on where their dads finished when they popped their clogs."

Kelly's eyes widened. "That's huge, Karen. No wonder they're trying to shut us down. We're getting too close to the truth."

"There's something else I need to tell you." Karen hesitated for a moment before continuing. "I think I'm being followed."

Kelly's face darkened with concern. "What do you mean?"

"Last night, on my way home, I found a threatening note on my windscreen. It said to drop the case or I'd be next. And this morning, on my way to work, I'm pretty sure someone was following me."

"Karen, why didn't you report this at once?"

Karen sighed. "I don't want to be taken off the case. And I don't want to worry Zac or Summer any more than they already are. Zac's anxiety has worsened since I returned to work."

Kelly sighed as she looked round Karen's office, deciding what to do next. "I understand, but you need to be careful. These people will go to great lengths to keep their secrets buried. Promise me you'll take extra precautions. I'll inform the control room to be vigilant and closely track all three of you."

"I will. And… thank you, ma'am. For everything you've done."

## 41

Karen was still processing everything when Belinda burst in minutes later, waving a file.

"Karen, you will not believe this," Belinda said, her voice breathless. "I've uncovered fresh evidence about Sarah's last known movements on the night she disappeared."

Karen looked at Bel, intrigued. She pushed aside the stack of papers in front of her and gave Belinda her full attention. "What have you found?"

Belinda laid the file on Karen's desk and flipped it open. "I was going through old witness statements, and I found one not taken seriously during the first investigation. A man reported seeing Sarah arguing with someone near York Minster late at night. It contradicts the original timeline we were working with."

"Any reason why it wasn't acted upon?"

"He was a local homeless fella. Often a bit pissed. They took his account as the ramblings of an old drunk."

"What else did the witness say?"

"Not much, unfortunately. He couldn't make out who

Sarah was arguing with, but he was certain it was her. The time he gave puts her at the Minster hours after she was last seen."

"Good work, Bel. Male or female?"

"The witness believed it was a man."

"I think it's time we spoke with Olivia Lockwood again. With this new information, she might remember something she thought unimportant."

"Definitely. And Izzy's post-mortem results on the journalist are in." Belinda waved a file.

Karen cycled her fingers for Belinda to continue. "What have we got?"

Belinda opened the file and summarised. "Cause of death was blunt force trauma to the head, consistent with being struck by a heavy object. Izzy estimates time of death between ten p.m. and midnight on the night before they found him."

Karen frowned as she added notes to her jotter pad. "Any signs of a struggle?"

"Some defensive wounds on his arms and hands," Belinda confirmed. "Izzy thinks he tried to fight off his attacker."

Karen shifted back in her chair, reflecting on the information. "What about the search of his apartment?"

Belinda grimaced. "That's where it gets interesting. The place had been ransacked by the time we got there. His laptop and desktop computer were both missing. Forensics didn't identify any prints other than the vic. No witnesses or CCTV either."

"Bollocks," Karen muttered. "Any signs of what they were looking for?"

"It's difficult to be certain, but we discovered numerous scattered notes about York Minster and its past.

His spare room, used as a study, was covered in printouts pinned to the walls."

"So, perhaps he asked too many questions to the wrong people? And he wasn't working with anyone?"

Belinda shrugged. "All signs point to him being a freelance journalist working alone. We found invoices for articles he'd written for various history and archaeology magazines."

"A keen amateur who stumbled on to something bigger than he realised and paid for it with his life."

"There's one more thing," Belinda added. "We found a business card for Marcus Brennan in Wheatley's wallet. It was pretty worn, like he'd been carrying it round for a while."

Karen's eyes narrowed. "Brennan. He must have approached Brennan."

"That's what we thought," Belinda agreed. "But with Wheatley's computers missing, it's going to be hard to prove the connection, and I doubt Brennan will blab if we approach him."

Karen sighed, frustration clear in her voice. "Alright. Well, we can't speak to him. It might scare him off and undo Preet's work."

Belinda nodded, standing to leave. "Will do. Want me to update the team?"

"Yes, please. And Bel? Good work on this. I know it's not the resolution we hoped for, but at least we can offer answers to Wheatley's family."

As Belinda left, Karen turned to stare out of her window. Her thoughts turned to the journalist who had lost his life in pursuit of the truth. It was a sobering reminder of the real-world consequences of the case.

A SHORT WHILE LATER, Karen stood outside the Lockwood residence. After pressing the buzzer once, when there was no reply, she pressed again, holding her finger in place for a few seconds.

Alistair Lockwood answered the door, his expression guarded. "Detective Heath," he said, his tone neutral. "What brings you here? Is something wrong?"

Before Karen could respond, she heard shuffling footsteps approaching. Olivia Lockwood appeared behind her son, looking frailer than Karen remembered. Her eyes stare softened at the sight of Karen.

"Please, come in," Alistair said, stepping aside.

He waited for Karen to pass before he helped his mother into the lounge, where Karen took a seat across from them.

"Mrs Lockwood," Karen began gently, "I know we've asked you about this before, but we've uncovered new information about the night Sarah disappeared. I was hoping you might help us."

Olivia's face twisted in confusion, her brow furrowing. "I've told the police everything I know," she said, her voice wavering. "So many times... and I've told you, too."

Alistair placed a comforting hand on his mother's arm. "It's alright, Mum. Let's hear what Detective Heath has to say."

Karen leaned forward, her voice soft but clear. "We've found a witness who saw Sarah having a heated exchange with someone near York Minster late on the night she disappeared. Does this ring any bells for you? Did she say she was meeting anyone?"

Olivia's eyes, previously bright and alert, clouded over with a sudden pensive stillness as Karen spoke. A flicker of recognition, perhaps even fear. The older woman's hands trembled.

"I... I don't know," Olivia said. "But there was something... I'd forgotten..."

With shaking hands, Olivia rose and reached for a small cabinet nearby. Alistair moved to help her, but she waved him off, determined to do it herself. From inside, she retrieved a little, ornate box.

"I found this after Sarah disappeared. I showed it to the police then but received no further follow-up."

Karen, leaning forward with bated breath, propped her elbows on her thighs, the faint creak of the box lid a prelude to what Olivia revealed. Inside was a crumpled piece of paper, yellowed with age. Olivia handed it to Karen.

Karen reached for her pocket and pulled out a pair of latex gloves, snapping them on, and unfolding the note. She recognised Sarah's handwriting. The message was brief but cryptic: "Midnight. North Transept. Don't tell anyone. This changes everything."

Karen's gaze sharpened, her eyes narrowed to slits as she reread the cryptic message, a frown furrowing her brow. She glanced at Olivia, who watched her.

"Do you know who she could have been meeting?"

"No."

"Mrs Lockwood," Karen said, "can you tell me about Sarah's involvement in the excavation? Did you notice any unusual behaviour in the days leading to her disappearance?"

Olivia's eyes filled with tears, but her voice was steadier now. "She was quieter than normal. Didn't say much when I asked about the progress at the dig, and if I pushed too hard, she'd have a hissy fit. I thought... she was being dramatic. She could be like that sometimes."

Alistair shifted in his seat. "I remember. She was

acting strange, secretive. I figured it was just typical Sarah, always chasing the next big discovery."

Karen nodded, making mental notes. "And you never knew why she was acting like that?"

Olivia shook her head. "No, she never said. But whatever it was, it must have been important. Important enough to..."

Karen reached out and squeezed Olivia's hand.

"Thank you, Mrs Lockwood. This information could be crucial to our investigation. I promise you, we're doing everything we can to find out what happened to Sarah."

Olivia's eyes, a mixture of dawning hope and lingering pain, held Karen captive for a moment as she stood to leave. It was a look she'd seen too many times in her career, the desperate need for closure warring with the fear of what closure might reveal.

Outside the Lockwood house, Karen paused on the pavement as she stared off into the distance. She pulled out her phone and dialled Belinda's number.

"Bel, it's me. I need you to chat with the team. New information has come to light."

As she drove back to the station, Karen knew they were closing in. They had the names, the motive, and add a potential smuggling operation spanning forty years.

## 42

Karen gathered her team in the incident room keen to share the new information from Olivia Lockwood.

"Alright, everyone." Karen pinned a scan of Sarah's note to the whiteboard. "We have a potential development. Sarah Lockwood left a cryptic message about a midnight meeting at York Minster's North Transept on the night she disappeared."

Ed stepped forward, adjusting his glasses to examine the note. "The language is vague," he mused. "It's possible Sarah was planning to meet someone involved in the artefact theft. The secrecy suggests she was aware of the risks."

Preet chimed in. "It could have been a black market deal she'd heard about, saw, or even been part of. I've seen similar setups in the antiquity's world. A private sale, away from prying eyes, but something went sideways."

The team mulled over this possibility, considering how it might tie into the broader conspiracy they'd uncovered. Belinda moved to the large screen, pulling up a detailed map of York Minster.

"Let's plot out potential meeting spots." Belinda zoomed in on the North Transept. "We need to cross-reference this with the witness statement about the argument."

Karen nodded in agreement. "Preet, reach out to your contacts in the antiquity's world. Can you see if you can gather any information about final destinations for the artefacts during 1987? Someone might recall whispers, even after all these years."

"I'll make calls right away."

With the team scattering, a murmur of voices fading, Karen gently pulled Ty away for a private word. "I've got a favour to ask of you. Could you please look into Alastair Lockwood's movements round the time of Sarah's disappearance? Something about him doesn't sit right with me. Call it a copper's nose."

Ty raised an eyebrow but nodded. "I'll be subtle," he assured her.

Karen then caught Preet before she left. "Are you sure you're okay to continue your undercover role?"

Preet's eyes lit up. "Absolutely. In fact, there's an important private auction in a few hours I'm planning to attend. Brennan will be there."

Karen squeezed Preet's arm. "Be careful and keep in touch. We need you safe."

With Preet gone, Karen found herself alone in front of the incident board, its surface covered in photographs and notes. She stared at the timeline they'd created, unable to shake the feeling they were missing something crucial. With a sigh, she headed back to her office and pulled out the original case files, hoping a fresh perspective might reveal overlooked details. With a can of Red Bull and a Twix bar she'd found at the back of one of her desk drawers, she settled in for the long haul.

Lost in the old reports, Karen barely noticed the hours passing, only the occasional rustle of papers breaking the stillness. The statements blurred into a monotonous stream, but as she read, a distinct pattern started to form, a repetitive rhythm in the chaos. Several members of the dig team had mentioned tensions between Sarah and one of the senior archaeologists, but the lead investigator at the time hadn't followed this lead.

She continued to scan the notes. Multiple dig team members mentioned conflicts between Sarah and a senior archaeologist, but it was never fully investigated. The name recorded in the notes was Terrance Chambers. Deceased.

Karen tutted. "Oh, dead end then. Literally."

## 43

Preet hovered at the back of the room in the exclusive auction house, her heart pounding with anticipation as she scanned the crowd. She recognised many faces, having been to a few meetings now, but several individuals were new and kept themselves occupied staring at their phones.

The elite of the antiquity world filled the room, their expensive suits and dresses contrasting with the ancient artefacts on display. Her gaze swept across the room until it locked on to her primary target: Marcus Brennan.

Brennan stood near the middle of the room, engaged in an animated conversation with a group of well-dressed individuals. His charismatic smile and easy manner belied the corrupt person Preet knew him to be. Her eyes followed him as he gestured enthusiastically, captivating his audience with every word.

Taking advantage of the opportunity, Preet moved towards Brennan. Navigating the bustling room, she overheard snippets of conversations—whispered speculations about rare artifacts and the hushed excitement of upcoming sales. She filed away each piece of information, knowing it could prove useful later.

"... heard there's a Viking piece coming up next month..."

"... private collection in Switzerland, absolutely stunning..."

"... rumour has it the provenance is questionable, but who cares at that price?"

Preet drew closer to Brennan's group. Brennan glanced in her direction. He nodded and waved her over with a welcoming smile. Preet's stomach tightened, but she maintained her composure, transitioning into her undercover persona.

"Ah, there you are!" Brennan exclaimed as she approached. "Everyone, I'd like you to meet a promising new collector in our midst." He introduced Preet to his associates.

His hand touching her back in a gesture of familiarity made her skin crawl.

Preet smiled, exchanging pleasantries with the group. She was aware of the hidden recording device, hoping it was capturing every word.

"I'm sure many will be keen to learn about your interests. They have pieces to blow your mind." Brennan lowered his voice and leaned into Preet. "A few pieces have to stay under the radar... a bit too hot to handle still."

"Thank you. I'm sure a conversation or two would be helpful. Price isn't an issue for me."

Brennan smiled and raised a brow before patting the small of her back. Preet wanted to punch him in between the eyes but settled for a clenched jaw and a tight smile.

The gavel banged, signaling the start of the auction; she settled into her seat, her gaze lingering on Brennan at the edge of her vision. She watched him exchange meaningful glances with Victoria Hartley who had slipped in at the last minute.

The auction proceeded, with rare and valuable artefacts changing hands for astronomical sums. Preet took part, enough to keep her cover as an interested collector. Her focus remained on Brennan and his interactions.

During a break in the bidding, Preet positioned herself closer to Brennan and the councillor. She pretended to examine a nearby artefact, a delicate Ming vase, while straining to overhear their hushed conversation.

"Sewers."

"... special item... Underground tunnel..." Brennan's voice was low, almost lost through the general chatter of the room.

Hartley leaned in closer. "... private buyer... plans to leave the country..."

"... smuggling operation can't afford another fuck up like last time..."

Preet's pulse quickened as she picked up on more fragments of conversation. The more she overheard, the more excited she became. This could be the breakthrough they'd been waiting for. Taking advantage of the opportunity, she inserted herself into their discussion.

"Excuse me," she said, her voice pitched low and conspiratorial, "I couldn't help but overhear. I'm always interested in... unique pieces." She let the implication linger, watching their responses.

Brennan and Hartley exchanged a look.

After a moment's hesitation, Brennan's face broke into a smile. "Well, my dear, maybe you'd be interested in a private showing later this evening?"

"I'd be delighted. Let me know the details, and I'll be there."

As the auction continued, Preet messaged Craig. She

updated him on the invitation and requested backup for the evening. The risk was increasing, but this could be their chance to gather crucial evidence.

The final gavel fell not long after, signalling the end of the auction. As the crowd dispersed, a commotion near the back of the room caught Preet's attention. Brennan was engaged in an intense argument with a man she soon recognised from the photos pinned to the whiteboards back in the SCU. David Pearson Jnr, who they'd been unable to locate... until now. Anger flushed Pearson Jnr's face as he squared up to Brennan, their noses almost touching.

Preet edged closer, trying to catch what was being said, but the men were too far away. Pearson Jnr stormed off, pushing past other attendees in his haste to leave. Brennan stood there for a moment, shaken. He ran a hand through his hair, composing himself, before disappearing through a side door.

Without hesitation, Preet followed. She skirted round the remaining attendees, making her way to the side door without drawing attention. She entered a dimly lit corridor, the rough stone walls cold beneath her fingertips, a musty odor hanging in the air. There was no sign of Brennan.

Preet hurried along the corridor, which led to an open fire exit door. She pushed it open and stepped out into the cool air.

The sound of screeching tyres filled the night. She stood there, frustration welling inside her as Brennan's vehicle vanished into the distance. She'd lost him, at least for now.

## 44

Karen sat at her desk surrounded by stacks of reports and evidence files. She'd arrived before dawn; the early morning quiet allowed her to focus without distraction. She preferred this peaceful time to do her best thinking.

Preet arrived a few hours later, her face etched with a mix of excitement and exhaustion. Karen sensed the urgency in Preet's demeanour.

"Karen, I've got more information. Shit, this stuff is gold dust," Preet said, closing the door behind her. She briefed Karen on Councillor Hartley's attendance at the auction, along with David Pearson Jnr, both of whom had spoken at length with Brennan.

The revelation left Karen speechless for a minute before further pieces of the puzzle slotted together. "Fuck. This is what we've been waiting for."

With excitement, Preet carried on and spoke about what she believed were the smugglers' methods, revealing their use of underground sewer tunnels to move artefacts undetected.

"Cheeky bastards. They've been using the old sewer system?" Karen said in surprise.

She relaxed in her chair, her fatigue forgotten as she absorbed this new information. They now had further proof Brennan was one of the key players behind the black-market trade in stolen artefacts, with Hartley and Pearson Jnr involved.

Preet delved into the details of the alleged smuggling operation. "Brennan's planning to move a significant artefact through the sewers."

Karen listened. "We need to catch them in the act."

Preet nodded. "I've already spoken with Sergeant Craig Roberts from Covert Ops. He's on board for an operation. He wants to meet with you tomorrow morning to go over the logistics."

Karen's eyes widened. "Great work, Preet."

Without hesitation, Karen reached for her phone and dialled Belinda's number. "Bel, I need you in my office if you have a moment. Preet is with me, and you *need* to hear the latest."

Karen hung up and looked back at Preet. "Walk me through everything you've learned."

Belinda rushed into Karen's office, out of breath.

Preet continued her debrief, her voice laced with a sense of urgency. "The smugglers are planning to move the artefacts through the Roman tunnels. It might even happen tomorrow. They're doing everything last minute to avoid detection. A buyer is lined up, someone with international connections. Morocco, I think."

A jolt of adrenaline tingled Karen's skin as the implications sank in. "Tomorrow? That doesn't give us much time to prepare."

"Do we know which artefacts they're planning to move?" Bel asked.

Preet shook her head. "Not specifically, but from what I overheard, it's something big. Something they think will fetch a high price on the black market."

Karen's mind raced. "We can't let that happen. We have the advantage because they don't know we're on to them."

Karen, Preet, and Belinda gathered round a large map of York spread across Karen's desk. Preet pointed to various locations, her finger tracing potential routes through the ancient Roman sewers.

"Based on what I overheard, they'll likely enter here." Preet pointed to a spot near the Minster.

Karen marked it with a red pin. "And where do you think they'll emerge?"

Belinda studied the map. "Given the layout of the old sewer system, there are three exit points." She placed blue pins at each location.

Karen frowned. "We'll need to cover all of them."

With each plotted route, Karen's certainty grew, pushing aside the pressure from higher-ups; they were undeniably closer to proving the brass wrong. They'd need to be careful not to tip off the smugglers while still being near to their movements.

"What about here?" Preet pointed to a spot on the outskirts of the city. "It's isolated enough for a discreet handoff."

Karen nodded, adding another pin to the map. The web of potential routes was complex, but with each addition, their plan became clearer.

"We'll need three units here, here, and here." Karen identified key points along the sewer route. "Sergeant Roberts and I will lead the main interception team at the most likely exit point."

Belinda added notes, her brow furrowed in concentration. Preet stood nearby, adding details about the smugglers' usual tactics.

"I know this is risky," Karen acknowledged, her voice calm. "But I need them in possession of the goods. Any questions?"

The room fell silent for a moment before Belinda spoke. "What about backup? If things go south, we'll need reinforcements fast."

Karen appreciated the foresight. "We'll coordinate with uniform to have more units on standby."

She strode into the incident room.

"Right, everyone," Karen began, her voice cutting through the murmurs. "We've got progress."

She scanned the faces before her. Belinda suppressed a yawn while Ed blinked and rubbed his eyes, trying to focus. Ty leaned back in his chair with his arms crossed, a look of intense concentration on his face. Despite their clear fatigue, Karen saw the spark of anticipation in their eyes.

"Thanks to Preet's undercover work, we've uncovered the smugglers' potential next move." Karen pinned a map to the board. "They're planning to shift a significant artefact through the old Roman sewers. As soon as tomorrow."

A ripple of excitement passed through the team.

"We have little time," Karen said. "But this could be our chance to catch them red-handed and get a result."

The team stood round the incident board as they debated various strategies.

"What if we organise surveillance at all potential exit points?" Ty proposed, his finger tracing the map. "We could track their movements without tipping our hand."

Karen shook her head. "Too resource intensive. We

don't have enough manpower to cover every route. We have to stick to the main ones."

The discussion dragged on, the team's frustration simmering to a boil, evident in the strained silence and tightened shoulders. Each proposed plan seemed to have a fatal flaw, and time was running short. Karen noticed the strain and tiredness on her team's faces as they grappled with the complexity of the situation.

"Let's hope Craig and his team have other ideas," Karen said, her voice cutting through the debate. "I'm meeting with him tomorrow and will see what he can bring to the table."

The team dispersed, leaving Karen and Preet alone in a quiet corner of the incident room; the low hum of computers and murmured conversations faded into the background.

"I know this undercover work can be taxing. You okay to continue?"

Preet offered a tired smile. "I'm managing. It's intense, but I can handle it."

"You're doing an excellent job, but don't push yourself too hard. We need you at your best."

"I'm fine," Preet insisted. "Sergeant Craig Roberts has been brilliant. His support makes all the difference."

Karen raised a brow. "That's good. Craig's one of the best in Covert Ops from what I've heard."

Preet's posture relaxed a bit. "He's been invaluable. I feel much safer knowing he's backing me up. I also like the fact he's good-looking, with smouldering eyes you find on the cover of a hot romance novel!" She puckered her lips. "Reminds me of Liam Neeson in *Taken*. Very rugged and tough."

Karen laughed. "Keep your eyes on the job, not him!" She squeezed Preet's shoulder.

"Can't promise that," Preet teased.

"Thank you for all your hard work. I'll catch you later after I've met with Craig."

After Preet left, Karen stared at the evidence board. Sarah Lockwood's face seemed to watch her. The young archaeologist's smile beamed from faded photographs, contrasting the grim crime scene images pinned beside them.

Councillor Hartley's association and presence only added weight to Kelly's discoveries. There was no way Hartley could come out of this smelling like roses. Her career was over.

Karen traced the web of connections and evidence they'd uncovered so far. At the centre of it all was Sarah, her disappearance the catalyst for a decades-long conspiracy.

She saw the truth—not just of Sarah's death, but of the long-held secrets buried right along with her.

## 45

With her body exhausted, Karen unlocked the front door. As she stepped into the hallway, a soft meow greeted her. Manky, her British Shorthair cat, padded towards her, his bright copper eyes sparkling.

"Hello, you." Karen bent to scratch behind Manky's ears.

Manky arched into her touch, purring contentedly.

Karen slipped off her shoes, grateful for the quiet welcome. Manky wound himself round her ankles as she hung her coat on the hook, almost tripping her in his eagerness for attention.

"Alright, alright," she chuckled, careful not to wake Zac or Summer. She scooped up the cat, his plush grey fur soft against her cheek.

Manky settled into her arms, his purring intensifying.

For a moment, Karen stood in the lit hallway, holding Manky close. The stress seemed to lift as she focused on the simple comfort of his presence. She took a deep breath, enjoying the familiar scent of home, before carrying him towards the kitchen.

With Manky cradled in her arms, Karen felt the soft fur against her skin as she entered; to her surprise, Zac was waiting by the counter. Two steaming mugs of tea in front of him.

"You're up late." Karen set Manky on the floor.

The cat wound himself round Zac's legs, meowing for attention.

"Couldn't sleep. Thought I'd wait for you." He pushed one mug towards her. "Figured you could use this. I'm on my third."

Karen accepted the tea and wrapped her hands round the warm mug. "Thanks. Summer asleep?"

"She's staying the night at Michelle's," His eyes searched Karen's face, concern clear in his expression. "Rough day?"

Karen nodded, taking a sip of her tea. The familiar taste was comforting, and grounded her after the long, intense day. "You could say that. The case is... complicated."

Zac reached out and squeezed her shoulder. "Want to talk about it?"

Karen set her mug on the counter and stepped closer to Zac. She noticed the worry lines round his eyes and hunched shoulders. With her hand in his, she said, "Zac, I know you're concerned, but we're safe. All of us."

She held his gaze, her voice steady and reassuring. "The security measures we've put in place are top-notch. The gated community, the guards, the panic buttons—they're all there to protect us. And my team at work is vigilant."

Zac smiled but doubt still lingered in his eyes.

Karen continued. "I promise you, I'm taking every precaution. We've learned from what happened before, and we're better prepared now."

She squeezed his arm. "You, Summer, and I—we're all safe. I wouldn't risk our family for anything. Not again."

Zac's expression softened at Karen's words. He smiled, seeming to gather his thoughts before speaking.

"I've been making progress," he said, a hint of pride in his voice. "Today, I went for a walk round the grounds. The gardening team were about, so I stopped to talk to them."

Karen's eyes widened in surprise and delight. "You did? That's fantastic, Zac!"

He nodded, a slight smile playing on his lips. "It wasn't easy at first. I kept looking over my shoulder, expecting... something. Don't ask me what. But after a while, it got better. I even chatted with one of the security guards for a bit. Clive, old fella, former para. He's a Falklands vet. Fascinating hearing about the Battle of Goose Green. He lost a good buddy when they came under heavy fire. The scrapes he'd been in while serving make my... well, nothing compared to what he and the boys went through. Clive put the kettle on at the guard box, and we had a cuppa. Hearing his countless stories and how he coped with what he'd witnessed..." Zac shook his head. "Incredible man. Kind of gave me a perspective shift as we talked about what I'd been through."

Zac stared at the wall behind Karen for a moment, lost in thought. "He said the SAS are the best in the business. Best in the world. He'd been on exercise with them on Pen-y-Fan in the Brecon Beacons. 'Hard as nails,' was how he described them."

This was a significant step for Zac, who had been struggling to leave the house since his abduction.

"I'm so proud of you." She reached out to squeeze his hand. "How did it feel?"

"Odd at first," Zac admitted. "But then... freeing. It felt

good to be outside, to move round without walls closing in on me."

Karen sensed the positive change in Zac's demeanour as he spoke about his experience. He looked relaxed, his eyes brighter than they had been in weeks.

"Won't be long till you're back to your old self again." She kissed him on the cheek and excused herself to take a shower, wanting to wash away the stress of the day.

The warm water cascaded over her, easing the tension in her muscles. She closed her eyes, letting her mind drift away from the case for a few precious moments.

After drying off and changing into her pyjamas, Karen headed back to the bedroom. Zac was already in bed, propped against the headboard, his face illuminated by the light of his phone screen.

As Karen slipped beneath the soft, cool cotton sheets, Zac silenced his phone with a click and turned to face her. The familiar scent of her shampoo filled the air between them.

"Feeling better?" Zac asked, tucking a damp strand of hair behind her ear.

"Yes. It's amazing what a hot shower can do."

Warmth radiated from Zac's body, a comforting presence in the darkness of their room. Despite the lingering worries about the case, Karen felt a sense of calmness wrap round her. Here, in this moment, with Zac beside her, she could let her guard down.

Karen shifted closer to Zac, grateful for the warmth of his body against hers. Without a word, he wrapped his arm round her, pulling her into a gentle embrace. She nestled her head on his chest, listening to the steady rhythm of his heartbeat. It was the closest they'd been in months.

The quiet of the night enveloped them, broken only by

the soft purring of Manky, who had curled up at the foot of the bed. Karen let out a soft sigh as the stresses of the day melted away.

Zac's fingers traced lazy patterns on her back, a soothing gesture that made Karen's eyelids grow heavy. She sensed his breathing slowing, matching her own as they both drifted towards sleep.

When sleep claimed them, Karen and Zac remained entwined, drawing strength and comfort from their closeness. Karen smiled when Zac's snores broke the silence.

## 46

Karen arrived at a nondescript building on the outskirts of York, its grey facade blending in with its neighbours and the overcast sky. She double-checked the address on her phone before stepping out of her car, scanning the surroundings for any signs of surveillance. After recent events, she'd become overcautious, or a touch paranoid.

When Karen approached the entrance, the door opened, and a figure emerged from the darkened hallway beyond. Sergeant Craig Roberts, his broad shoulders filling out his grey NYC hoodie, nodded in greeting. She agreed with Preet's assessment. A rugged-looking Liam Neeson but with shorter hair.

"DCI Heath," he said, his voice gravelly. "Glad you could make it."

Karen shook his hand, noting the firm grip and the calluses which spoke of years of fieldwork. "Sergeant Roberts. I appreciate you meeting me."

Craig gestured towards the building. "Let's head inside. We've got a lot to discuss, and these walls don't have ears."

"You here a lot?"

"It's a base away from too many prying eyes. Covert officers often come here for briefings and debriefs. It's secure and keeps our officers safe."

They entered the building, Craig leading the way through a series of corridors. The interior was as unremarkable as the exterior, but Karen sensed the purposeful design behind its bland appearance. They had similar units in the Met, and the more unremarkable the building, the better.

Craig stopped at a heavy metal door, punching in a code on a keypad. The door clicked open, revealing a sparse room with several tables, a couple of laptops, and makeshift camp beds.

Once inside, Craig Roberts stood hunched over a large table, his eyes fixed on detailed maps of York's underground tunnel system. Karen joined him, taking in the intricate network of passages and chambers spread out before them.

"This is what we have to contend with," Craig said, his finger tracing a path through the labyrinth. "From the intelligence we have, the smugglers have been using these tunnels to move artefacts undetected for many years. We've identified several key points where they're likely to emerge."

Karen leaned in, studying the map. She saw markers showing potential exit points and areas of high risk. A few appeared to correlate with what she'd discussed with her own team.

"How recent is this intel?" she asked.

Craig tapped a section of the map. "We've had eyes on these tunnels for the past few days. Our surveillance team has identified increased activity in this area here. We believe they're planning the move soon."

Karen nodded, absorbing the information. The complexity of the tunnel system was daunting, but she could see the strategic advantage it offered for their operation. A natural self-containment to eliminate the risk to members of the public.

Craig pointed to a convoluted section of the map. "This area here is our biggest concern. The tunnels date back to Roman times, and they're not modern safety standards. They crisscross at certain points and lead off into tunnels not in use anymore."

Karen frowned and studied the intricate network. "What are we looking at in terms of structural integrity?"

"It's a mixed bag," Craig replied, his voice grim. "Certain sections have held up well, but others are prone to flooding and cave-ins. We've had to rule out certain routes because of the risk."

"What happens if they take one of those routes? We follow?"

He shook his head. "No. We can't jeopardise the safety of our officers. We'd have to intercept them when they emerge."

"And visibility?"

"Not great," Craig said. "Non-existent. We'll be relying on night-vision equipment to give us the element of surprise."

"What about air quality?" Karen recalled horror stories of sewer gases from her early days on the force.

Craig's expression darkened. "That's another major concern. We'll need to monitor oxygen levels. There are pockets where toxic gases can accumulate without warning. The last thing I want is officers being overcome by hydrogen sulphide, methane, or ammonia."

Karen grimaced at the challenges ahead for the officers. But the smugglers had managed it, so it was doable with the right precautions. "It won't be easy?"

Craig shrugged. "No. But it's our best shot at catching these bastards red-handed."

He moved to a nearby desk where a laptop sat open. He gestured for Karen to join him.

"I've got something else to show you." He tapped a few keys.

The screen came to life, displaying a detailed 3D model of the underground network. Karen leaned in, her eyes widening as she took in the intricate visualisation.

Craig manipulated the model, rotating it and zooming in on specific areas. "This gives us a better idea of the vertical challenges we're facing." He highlighted a steep section. "A few of these drops are over thirty feet. We have to avoid them. The smugglers have used a few routes, so we do not know which one they'll choose when we move in."

Karen watched Craig navigate through the virtual tunnels, noting the narrow passages and sudden turns. The model provided a visceral sense of the claustrophobic conditions they would be facing. She swallowed hard. An uneasy feeling settled in the pit of her stomach when she remembered her earlier encounter with the London sewers.

"We've mapped out potential choke points here, here, and here." Craig marked several spots on the model. "These are areas where we could trap the smugglers, but they're also risky for our team."

Karen agreed, her mind already planning strategies based on this new information. The 3D model brought home the reality of the operation in a way the flat maps couldn't.

Craig led Karen to a secure storage area within the

room. He unlocked a heavy metal cabinet, revealing an array of specialised equipment.

"This is cutting-edge tech." Craig lifted out a sleek, compact device. "State-of-the-art air quality monitors. They'll give us real-time data on oxygen levels and detect any toxic gases."

He handed Karen a pair of night-vision goggles, lighter than the standard issue she was familiar with. "These have an enhanced infrared ability. They'll let us see in near-total darkness without compromising our presence."

Craig then pulled out a set of compact radios. "These radios were designed for underground use," he explained. "They'll keep communication even through the densest rock formations."

Karen examined each piece of equipment, impressed by the level of technology at their disposal. She could see how these tools would increase their chances of success in the challenging underground environment.

"This is all fab. I need to head back, but I'll be in touch. Oh, and I appreciate how you've looked after Preet."

"Preet's great. So good in fact, I might poach her for my own ops team."

Karen pointed a finger in his direction. "Hands off. Don't you dare."

Craig laughed.

"Thanks for your time," she said.

"No problem, I'll see you out. Good meeting you," Craig said as he led the way to the main door.

## 47

Karen headed back to the station, her mind still processing the details from her meeting with Craig. As she navigated the streets of York, she noticed ominous clouds gathering overhead. The air seemed heavy with the promise of rain as the sky had darkened since she had left for the meeting.

She frowned, hoping the weather would hold off. Rain could complicate their operation, causing flooding in the already treacherous tunnels. It was one more variable they didn't need.

As Karen pulled into the station's car park, the first fat drops of rain splattered against her windscreen, a rhythmic drumming sound accompanying her arrival. "Bollocks." She parked, grabbed her coat, and hurried towards her building. The wind had picked up, whipping her hair round her face as she made her way to the entrance.

Inside, she shook off the dampness, nodding at the two officers deep in discussion as she passed. The building buzzed with activity, a stark contrast to the gloomy atmosphere outside. Karen headed towards the stairs, her thoughts already turning to the next steps in their investigation.

Karen found Preet in the prep room, surrounded by maps and equipment. The officer looked at Karen as she entered.

"All good?" Karen placed a chair beside her.

Preet straightened, pushing a stray lock of hair behind her ear. "I'm fine. Just going over the tunnel layouts again and what I need to do."

Karen nodded and studied Preet's face. "It's been a tough assignment. You've done exceptional work, and Craig was singing your praises."

Preet raised a brow and smiled. "Bit of a dish, right? He was in the army before joining the force. We had a chat. Specialised in forward surveillance. Divorced. Wife got fed up with never seeing him."

"Oh, really? Seems you know a bit too much!"

Preet placed a hand over her mouth and laughed before changing the topic.

"I won't lie. It's been intense. Brennan and his lot... they're not pleasant company. But I can handle it. I'll be pleased to see the back of them."

"You've nothing to prove, Preet. If you need to step back, no one will think less of you."

"I appreciate it, Karen." Preet met her gaze. "But I'm good. If Brennan is going in the tunnels, then so am I."

Karen and Preet settled into a corner of the prep room, away from the bustle of the other officers. The low hum of conversation and shuffling papers from the main area provided a muted backdrop as they found a secluded spot near the back wall. Karen pulled out two chairs from beneath a cluttered desk, gesturing for Preet to take a seat. The fluorescent lights flickered overhead, casting a harsh glow on the floor as they sat to discuss the case in relative privacy.

Karen leaned back in her chair. "Tell me about your last meeting with Brennan. Any recent developments?"

Preet nodded. "He's getting nervous. The auction didn't go as planned—someone outbid him on a key piece. I think it's thrown off their timeline."

Karen's brow furrowed. "That could help us. Did he mention any changes to their plans?"

"Not explicitly," Preet replied, "but he was on the phone a lot afterwards. I overheard him mention 'accelerating the schedule'. They're spooked, Karen, and ready to go today."

"Good work, Preet. We'll need to adjust our strategy. Did you notice anything else out of the ordinary?"

Preet hesitated, then leaned closer. "There was something else. A name I hadn't heard before. Brennan mentioned someone called 'The Curator'. It seemed important, but I couldn't get any more details without raising suspicion."

Karen's eyes narrowed. "The Curator? Interesting. We'll need to look into that. Good catch. Keep your ears open for any more mentions of this person."

Karen and Preet continued their discussion, delving deeper into the intricacies of Brennan's operation.

"This 'Curator' could be a missing link." Karen tapped her fingers on the desk. "It might explain how they've stayed under the radar for so long."

Preet agreed. "I'll try to get more information about their identity during the next meeting. Brennan seems to trust me more now, so I might push harder without raising suspicion. He thinks I have money to burn and the right connections."

"Be careful. We're close, but Brennan's unpredictable. Your safety comes first."

As they continued to strategise, the sound of rain intensified. Karen looked towards the window as rivulets of water streaked down the glass. The worsening weather added another headache for her.

Karen turned to Preet, her expression serious. "I need you to stick with Brennan as much as possible. If there's an exchange taking place, we need to be there. Let's go over the extraction protocols one more time if things go sideways. You need to head for here." She pointed to a marked location. "There'll be a plainclothes officer stationed nearby. They'll be able to get you away sharpish."

Karen then outlined the secondary and tertiary extraction points if Preet was elsewhere in the city and needed to leave. "If you can't make it to any of these points, find a public place with CCTV coverage. We'll have eyes on the city's camera network."

She moved on to discuss communication protocols, making sure Preet was following them. "Preet, if at any point you feel your cover is blown or you're in immediate danger, get out of there. Don't hesitate. We'll be there in minutes."

After Karen finished briefing Preet on the extraction protocols, Preet's phone buzzed in her pocket. She pulled the phone from her pocket, frowning at the unfamiliar number displayed on the screen.

Karen noticed Preet's expression shift from curiosity to concern. The DC's knuckles whitened as she gripped the phone tighter, her free hand clenching into a fist on the table.

"Sounds good. I'll be there to have a look. I have a contact in India who would be very interested in taking it off my hands for the right price." Preet ended the call. She turned to Karen, her eyes blazing with urgency.

"Brennan. There's a rare piece exchanging hands, and it might be of interest to me. If I don't want it once I've seen it, they have another buyer lined up who will take the artefact out of the country tonight, as we thought."

Karen's eyes widened. "Great. We need to ready ourselves now. Get your gear and meet me in the briefing room in ten minutes. I'll alert the rest of the team."

Preet hurried off. Karen dialled Craig Roberts' number again.

## 48

Knowing the next hour would be the most crucial to her covert ops, Preet stepped into the dimly lit private club. Her eyes adjusted to the luxurious surroundings. The soft jazz playing in the background mingled with the low murmur of conversations from the well-heeled patrons. She scanned the room, her gaze settling on the bar where Marcus Brennan sat nursing a drink.

Preet smoothed her dress and made her way towards him. With practiced ease, she moved round the small clusters of people, her footsteps barely disturbing the quiet murmur of conversation. A few nodded in her direction as they stepped to one side. As she approached, Brennan's lips curved into a slight, almost imperceptible smile.

"Ah, Ms Daman," he said. "I'm glad you could join us this evening."

Preet smiled and chose the seat next to him at the bar. "I wouldn't miss it, Mr Brennan. I hear you've got something quite special to show me tonight?"

Brennan's eyes glinted with interest as he signalled the

bartender. "Indeed, I do. But first, let me get you a drink. What's your poison?"

"A glass of Prosecco would be nice."

Brennan placed the order and smiled, checking her over. "I must say, you look stunning this evening. Perhaps I could take you to dinner when you're free?"

Preet stood her ground and smiled even though she found the man repulsive and arrogant. "I'd like that very much. I must warn you I have expensive taste."

Brennan smirked, his eyes glistening. "Shall we step away from this crowd? I'm sure you'll be intrigued when you see what I have for you."

Preet nodded as Brennan slipped off his chair.

Brennan led Preet through a hidden door behind a floor-to-ceiling black velour curtain, revealing a narrow corridor. They walked in silence, their footsteps muffled by the plush carpet. At the end of the hallway, Brennan produced a key and unlocked an ornate wooden door.

The room they entered was small but opulent, with dark wood panelling and leather chairs surrounding a polished table. A single briefcase sat in the centre.

"Please, take a seat." Brennan gestured to one chair.

Preet dropped into a seat, her heart racing beneath her calm exterior. Brennan took the chair opposite her and placed his hand on the briefcase.

"What I'm about to show you is extremely rare and, shall we say, not above board. It's moved in certain circles, and recently acquired from a museum in Portugal," he said. "I trust you understand the need for discretion."

*Acquired, my arse. Stolen to order.*

Preet nodded, leaning forward. "Of course, Mr Brennan. You can count on my absolute confidentiality."

Brennan studied her face for a moment, then seemed satisfied. He clicked open the briefcase and removed a small object wrapped in velvet. With reverence, he unwrapped it, revealing an intricately carved Viking artefact.

"This," he said, his eyes gleaming, "is what all the fuss is about. A piece with a rather interesting provenance, I might add."

With a frown, Preet carefully traced the strange symbols etched into the artefact, causing Brennan's demeanor to change, his usual calm replaced by a nervous fidgeting. His eyes darted between her and the door, his fingers tapping an erratic rhythm on the table.

"You seem quite knowledgeable about these pieces," he said, his voice tight. "More so than most collectors I've encountered."

Preet forced a smile. "Viking history has always fascinated me. It's a passion of mine."

Brennan's gaze intensified. "And yet, with your immense wealth, I don't recall seeing you holding the winning bid at any major auctions, nor have I seen you before until a few days ago. I know most, if not all the collectors round the world, and other than knowing you're from one of the wealthiest families in India, I've not seen you on the 'circuit'. Funny how you've suddenly appeared on the scene."

Preet's pulse quickened. "I've turned my passion into collecting. I prefer to keep a low profile and I'm very fussy."

"Is that so?" Brennan's tone was sharp. He stood, moving to the door and checking the lock. "You know, I've been in this business a long time. I've developed a sense for when things aren't quite right."

He turned back to Preet, his eyes narrowed. "I've reached out to a few people, and, well, my contacts are not aware of you. Who are you, Ms Daman? Because I'm thinking you're not who you claim to be. I checked your car reg. It's registered to a car hire company. You might have your reasons, but it's made me somewhat wary."

Preet maintained her composure, but she could feel the situation slipping out of her control. Brennan's suspicion was real, as he stared at her through narrowed lids.

"I understand the need for discretion and secrecy on your part. Your attention to detail has kept you alive in a dangerous occupation. But I don't appreciate your tone. I don't have a car here because I'm not in the UK often, and when I am, it's only for a few days, perhaps a week or two at most. A rental from the airport makes things easier."

Prett reached into her bag and pulled out her phone. She searched through her contacts. "Alexander Ainscough. Malik Quereshi. Calvin Choi. All dealers I've conducted business with round the globe. I'll forward their numbers to you. Call them. Check them out. Do what you need to. I'll even give you a score out of ten for what Malik was like in bed if you want?" She raised a brow as her face hardened.

Brennan paused as he took her in, a sly smile spreading.

Preet steeled her spine. "I suggest you stop pissing around."

Brennan's face twisted into a grimace, his jaw clenching as he took a step towards her. "I'm wondering if we should postpone any future meetings until I've made the calls and checks," he spat, his hand reaching towards the inside of his jacket.

Preet's heart raced as she watched Brennan's movements, her mind searching for what to do next. Her wire tap was recording all of this, and a simple word would bring officers here in minutes. She rose from her chair, keeping him in her sights.

"Mr Brennan, I assure you there's been a misunderstanding," she said, her voice steady despite the fear coursing through her veins. "I'm a very private collector, as I've told you. You won't find me at most auctions or 'meetings'."

Brennan's hands closed into fists. "A collector? I think not. You're asking too many questions, showing too much interest in things you shouldn't know about. Now," he said, his voice deep and menacing, "you're going to tell me who you are and who sent you. And don't even think about lying to me again."

Preet's mind raced. She drew in a breath to calm the swirling in her stomach. Perhaps he was testing her? Roberts said he might.

"Mr Brennan," she said, her voice steady, "I think you're misunderstanding the situation. I'm not the one who should explain myself here."

Brennan's brow furrowed, but he didn't waver. "What are you talking about?"

Preet took a small step forward, her posture relaxed despite the tension in the room. "You're Marcus Brennan, the renowned collector and fixer with contacts across the globe. You've built a reputation on discretion and exclusivity. And yet, here you are, behaving like I'm a common thief or something, and yet I'm a potential client in a secret room. Is this how you conduct business?" She locked eyes with him, her bravado growing by the minute. "My family could buy everything you offer and still not make a dent in our wealth. If you choose not to work with me, I'll take my business elsewhere. I only deal with professionals."

Brennan glared at her.

Unperturbed, she carried on, scrolling through her image gallery until she found what she was looking for.

Preet turned the phone for Brennan to see. It took a few seconds before he gasped, wide-eyed. His eyes shifted to her.

Preet nodded. "Yes, that's me at home with the Marble Group of Leda and the Swan, as you know, circa 2nd Century AD. Sold at Sotheby's New York, for 23.5 million dollars to a private buyer... My family has it now. So, Mr Brennan, I'm happy to take my business elsewhere."

She saw a flicker of uncertainty cross Brennan's face. Preet pressed on, her voice taking on a hint of disappointment as she showed him the purchase and banking receipts. "Enough evidence for you? I came here expecting to deal with a professional, someone at the top of their game. Instead, I find paranoia and pathetic threats. It makes me wonder what you're hiding, Mr Brennan. Why, exactly, are you so worried about this transaction?"

Brennan wavered, confusion replacing some of the anger in his eyes. "I don't understand. You're the one who's been asking suspicious questions."

"Suspicious?" Preet raised an eyebrow. "Or simply thorough? A true connoisseur would appreciate such attention to detail. Unless, of course, you have something to hide. Something detrimental to you and your business if it were uncovered."

Brennan's shoulders dropped as he considered Preet's words. After a tense moment, he agreed.

"Perhaps I've been too hasty," he said, his voice still tight with suspicion. "But in this business, one can never be too careful."

"I understand. Shall we return to the matter at hand?"

Brennan hesitated, then gestured towards the briefcase. "Very well. I'll show you the rest of the collection."

With Brennan's back turned, Preet returned to her

seat, the cool air soothing her flushed skin as she focused on slow, steady breaths to calm her racing heart.

Brennan returned to the table, laying out a series of small, intricately carved objects. "These pieces are part of a set, which experts believe were created for a Viking chieftain," he explained, pride replacing his earlier hostility.

Preet leaned in, feigning intense interest while ensuring she maintained a dialogue. Her dark eyes widened with a look of wonder as she studied the intricate carvings. "Fascinating," she murmured, her gaze flicking between the pieces and Brennan's face, searching for any telltale signs of suspicion.

"And you say these all came from the same source?" she enquired, her voice laced with a hint of awe. She allowed her fingers to hover just above the surface of one ornate piece, as if drawn to its beauty, all the while aware of Brennan's watchful presence beside her.

"Yes. I've already sold a few pieces, and they're going abroad tonight. Well, as soon as I'm finished here, I'm meeting my contact for the handover. It's part of a private collection in Malaysia. These pieces are still available," Brennan added, pointing to a few. "A twenty-five grand price tag each. Interested?"

"That's very tempting." Preet stalled for a few moments. "I'll take two of them. They'll be perfect."

Brennan smiled. "Perfect, indeed. I'll keep them for safekeeping until you send the money. In the meantime, I need to leave. My contact is waiting for the handover. Shall we meet tomorrow evening at my house? We can have dinner together and finish our business?"

"The exchange needs to happen simultaneously. You'll get the money and I'll take my items. Agreed?"

Brennan hesitated before agreeing.

"I need help to get them out of the country. Do you have a contact?"

"I do. I'm meeting him. He's trustworthy."

"I would prefer to meet him myself," Preet pushed.

Brennan shook his head. "Not possible. He only liaises with me."

Preet folded her arms across her chest and raised a brow in defiance.

Brennan faltered. "I'll make a call. This room is secure. Wait here, and I'll bring him back to meet you before he leaves. He won't like it because he doesn't hang around once he's in possession of the goods."

Preet watched Brennan stow away the artefacts and leave. With him gone, she reached for her phone and sent Karen a text.

## 49

Karen stood at the entrance to a section of the ancient Roman sewers now not in use, her team and the Covert Operations Unit gathered round her. Tension hung heavy in the air, along with the musty scent of centuries-old stonework. Flashlights pierced the darkness, illuminating the damp walls and uneven ground ahead.

Craig Roberts approached Karen. "My team's in position. We've got eyes on all the major exit points."

Karen scanned the faces of her officers. Despite the short notice, they looked ready, determination etched on their features. She saw Belinda double-checking her gear, while Ed conferred with one of Craig's tech specialists.

"Remember," Karen addressed the group, "we're dealing with a sophisticated operation. They know these tunnels better than we do. Stay alert, stick to the plan, and watch each other's backs."

She paused, meeting each officer's gaze. "This isn't just about recovering stolen historic pieces. We're here for Sarah Lockwood, too. Let's bring her family the closure they deserve. They killed her for this reason."

With a last nod, Karen signalled to Craig. He raised his hand, and as one, the team moved into the yawning darkness of the sewer entrance.

Their footsteps echoed off the ancient stone walls. Karen led with Craig, her torch beam sweeping the path ahead. The air grew thicker as they descended, the musty scent of damp earth and decay filling their nostrils.

Belinda followed close behind, searching from shadow to shadow, alert for any sign of movement. Ed followed to the rear, his usual confident demeanour replaced by a tense vigilance.

They progressed, each step placed to avoid loose stones or unexpected drops. The tunnel forked and branched, a labyrinth of possibilities stretching out before them. Karen consulted the map on her wrist-mounted display, confirming their route with a quick nod to Craig.

Water dripped from the roof of the tunnel, the steady *plink-plink* adding to the oppressive atmosphere. Rats scurried for cover, diving into gaps between the brickwork. Karen shuddered as she checked round her feet for any of the large, hairy monsters. The further they progressed, the more claustrophobic the tunnels felt. She checked her watch. They'd been on the move for twenty minutes, and the tunnels kept going.

A sudden flicker of light, brighter than the ambient darkness, caught her attention as they turned the corner.

Karen raised her hand, signalling the team to halt as they reached a dimly lit junction in the tunnels. The sound of rushing water echoed from one passageway, adding to the eerie atmosphere. She turned to face her officers, keeping her expression serious in the flickering light of their torches.

"Right, this is where we split up and switch to the night-vision goggles," Karen said in a hushed tone.

"Belinda, you'll take Ed and go with two of Craig's team through the eastern tunnel. I'll go with Craig and the rest through the western passage."

Karen nodded and placed a hand on Bel's shoulder, leaning in close.

"Remember, if you meet any resistance, don't engage unless necessary. Our priority is to locate the artefacts and secure any evidence of the smuggling operation. Leave the fisticuffs to Craig's officers."

Belinda gave a curt nod. "Understood. We'll be careful."

Karen squeezed Belinda's arm before turning to address both groups. "Stay in radio contact. Any sign of trouble, you call for backup. No heroics, understand?"

Karen and Craig's group moved through the western passage, their night-vision goggles casting the tunnel in an eerie green glow. The air grew thicker, laden with the scent of damp earth and decay. Suddenly, Craig stopped, signalling the team to halt.

"Bloody hell." He muttered as he gestured ahead.

Karen edged forward, out of breath, and saw the obstacle ahead. A section of the tunnel had partially collapsed, leaving a jumble of fallen stones and debris blocking their path. Water trickled through the gaps, forming a shallow pool at their feet.

"This wasn't on any of the maps," Karen said. She turned to Craig, who was already assessing the situation.

"We might clear enough to squeeze through." He ran a hand over the rough stone. "But it'll take time we might not have."

Karen nodded, weighing up their options. Intel from Craig's team had already confirmed Brennan was meeting with Preet, and every second counted. She tapped her radio, preparing to update Belinda's team and consider alternatives. But there were none. The only way forward was through the fallen stonework. With all hands on deck, they began the task of finding a way through.

Karen and Craig's team reached their designated position after navigating the collapsed tunnel. They crouched in a small alcove, hidden from view but with a clear line of sight to the main passageway.

Karen checked her phone, the time glowing in the darkness. The steady drip of water echoed through the tunnels, punctuated by the occasional creak of ancient stonework settling. Her team remained still. Now it was a waiting game.

## 50

Karen crouched in the dank, musty darkness, her back pressed against the cold stone wall. She read the message on her phone and stuffed it back into her pocket. The air smelt of decay and stagnant water. From somewhere close, the sound of running water from a current sewer tunnel filled the air. As long as it didn't rain, they'd be okay. The soft breathing of her team members nearby only added to the tension.

Sergeant Craig Roberts knelt beside her. He scanned the tunnel ahead through his night-vision goggles.

"Any movement? According to Preet, Brennan is on his way," Karen whispered.

Craig shook his head. "Nothing."

Karen checked her watch, the luminous dial showing the time a little past midnight. She thought of Preet and the sterling work she'd done.

They'd been waiting an hour since Preet's text, and Karen wondered if Brennan had changed his plans. Had the location of the meeting changed? Had something scared him off? Bel reported nothing as well. Karen's muscles ached from holding her position, but she didn't dare move. And now she needed a wee! Great timing! Every sound echoed in the tunnel, and she knew the slightest noise could alert the smugglers to their presence.

Craig raised a hand, signalling for absolute silence and vigilance. In the distance, the faint sound of footsteps splashed through shallow water. Karen's body tensed as she realised the moment they'd been waiting for had arrived.

The echoes of footsteps grew louder, accompanied by the occasional splash of water. Karen exchanged a quick glance with Craig, who nodded and signalled to the rest of the team. They readied themselves as they bunched together, ready to move forward.

As the sounds drew nearer, Karen made out hushed voices. The smugglers were talking amongst themselves, unaware of the trap they were walking into. She strained to hear their conversation, hoping to glean any last-minute intelligence.

Craig tapped Karen's shoulder and pointed to a junction ahead. The smugglers would have to pass through there, giving the team the perfect opportunity to spring their trap. Karen nodded in understanding and relayed the information to the rest of her team through hand signals.

Karen's heart pounded, the rush of adrenaline sharpening her senses.

A beam of light cut through the darkness, dancing along the sewer walls. Karen and her team pressed themselves further into the shadows, not daring to move a muscle.

The first of the smugglers came into view, a burly man carrying a large, waterproof bag. Behind him, two more figures emerged from the gloom, each burdened with similar bags. Karen's eyes narrowed as she recognised Marcus Brennan among them.

Craig raised his hand, ready to give the signal. Karen tightened her grip on her torch. Her thigh muscles twitched, a silent scream of exertion as she held firm, gritting her teeth against the strain.

Seconds after Craig's hand dropped, signalling the team to move, chaos erupted in the narrow tunnel. Karen lunged forward, shouting, "Police! Don't move!"

The smugglers scattered, their panicked shouts echoing off the stone walls. Marcus Brennan, his contorted face caught in the halo of light, shoved one of his accomplices towards the officers and bolted into a side passage.

"Brennan, stop!" Karen yelled.

She raced after Brennan, her torch beam bouncing off the shiny walls. The tunnel twisted and turned, branching off in multiple directions. Karen heard Brennan's laboured breathing ahead.

"Craig, we need to cut him off!" she shouted.

"Roger that," he replied before barking into his radio. "Team Two, move to intercept at Junction C!"

Brennan glanced back, his eyes wide with fear. He stumbled, losing his footing on the slippery stones.

Karen turned the corner into the dimly lit cistern, the rough-hewn stones cold beneath her fingers, and there she saw Marcus Brennan cornered by Craig and two other officers. Brennan's chest heaved as he looked frantically for an escape route but found none.

"It's over, Brennan," Karen called out, her voice echoing in the cavernous space. "Put your hands where we can see them."

Brennan slumped in defeat. He raised his hands, the

fight draining out of him. Craig stepped in, securing Brennan's wrists with handcuffs.

"Marcus Brennan, you're under arrest for theft and smuggling of historical artefacts," Karen stated, her voice firm and clear.

As Craig led Brennan away, Karen's radio crackled. Belinda's voice came through, slightly breathless but triumphant. "We've got the others, Karen. Two in custody, and we've recovered all the artefacts."

"Who have you got?" Karen asked.

"David Pearson Jnr and Ross Marshall."

Karen let out a sigh of relief. With the suspects identified, it made sense now. The original sponsors were stealing the artefacts for personal gain, and their sons were carrying on with the illegal activity. The connection between the two generations was Marcus Brennan. "Good work, everyone," she responded, allowing herself a small smile.

The team regrouped at the entrance to the sewers, their suspects in tow. Karen watched as the team loaded Brennan and his associates into waiting police vans. The night air felt crisp and clean after the dank tunnels.

As the team talked in huddles about the operation, Karen noticed several large, waterproof bags being carried by Craig's officers. She approached Craig, who was overseeing the collection of evidence.

"What do we have?" Karen asked.

Craig unzipped one of them, revealing its contents. Karen peered in and saw the array of ancient artefacts nestled inside. The collection featured intricate carvings on Viking pendants, delicate gold filigree work, and what appeared to be an ornate dagger with runic inscriptions on its blade.

"This is just the start," Craig said. "There's more in the

other bags. Brennan was carrying a fortune in historical pieces."

Karen glanced at Brennan, who sat in the back of a police van, his head bowed. She approached him, her footsteps echoing in the quiet night air.

"Marcus Brennan," she said, her voice steady. "It will take us a bit of time to trace their origins and ownership, but to save the time, can you explain where these artefacts came from?"

Brennan's face showed defeat. "You wouldn't understand," he whispered.

Karen pressed on. "We have concrete evidence of your involvement in a smuggling operation. At least one of these pieces is identical to the description of one missing from the York Minster dig. How do you explain that?"

Brennan remained silent, but his eyes darted to the bags of artefacts being catalogued by the team.

Karen walked away and joined Craig. "This is the evidence we needed to tie everything together. The smuggling operation, the connection to the 1987 dig, Sarah Lockwood's disappearance—it's all here."

## 51

An officer's voice came through on Karen's radio. She stepped away from the evidence collection.

"DCI Heath. Control. We've received word from Preet. She's safe."

Karen closed her eyes for a moment. "Thank you, Control. Any details on her status?"

"Officers report Preet is unharmed and waited for the club to be secured before leaving. She's en route to the station now."

Karen nodded. "Understood. I'll meet her there."

She turned to Craig, who had been listening. "Preet's safe."

Craig's face broke into a grin. "That's fantastic news. She did a hell of a job."

Karen smiled back. With Brennan in custody, the artefacts recovered, and Preet's undercover work yielding results, they were closer to closing the case.

"Let's wrap this up," Karen called out to her team. "We've got a lot of work ahead of us. Preet will be at the station soon with more evidence. Good job, everyone."

The team filed into the SCU, their faces a mix of exhaustion and triumph. Karen watched as they settled round a large table to the rear, now covered with evidence bags containing the seized items. The air buzzed with anticipation as they prepared to sift through the haul.

Belinda spread out documents relating to the 1987 dig and the statement provided by Father O'Brien, her keen eye already picking out details. "A few descriptions of items unearthed but then disappeared match markings on a few of these pieces," she said, pointing to an ornate brooch.

Ed leafed through a stack of documents recovered from Brennan's possession. "And these papers... they're encrypted, but I'm certain they're records of black-market sales."

Karen skimmed the papers. "Good catch, Ed. We'll need to cross-reference these with known collectors and dealers, but if they're black-market sales, we'll struggle to pin down identities or names."

Preet, still looking jaded, joined them at the table. "Brennan mentioned a 'special buyer' during the auction. Someone with plans to move a significant piece out of the country."

"It tracks with what we found on Brennan." Ty gestured to a map he'd pinned to the evidence board. "A piece of paper with 'Rufforth' scribbled in it. Not far and there is an airfield. Twenty minutes by car. Perhaps an exchange point?" he suggested. "It has a glider base there, and often used by microlights, but a useful spot for light aircraft. A simple route out of the country."

Karen nodded in agreement. "Alright, let's connect the dots. Bel, I want you to work with the forensics team to identify and catalogue every recovered item. Ed, dig deeper into those financial records. Ty, I know it's the middle of the night, but wake someone and coordinate with the airfield, and see if we can trace any flights in recent months. Get a unit over there. For all we know, Brennan's contact might be there waiting and unaware we've made arrests. If we don't act, we might lose them. Then I want you and Dan to interview Brennan."

With the team scattering to their duties, Karen turned to Preet. "You did excellent work out there. Write your report, then rest. We'll need your insights as we piece this together."

---

KAREN STOOD behind the one-way glass, watching as Ty and Dan interrogated Marcus Brennan. The smuggler sat with an air of arrogance, his expensive suit now replaced with a grey police-issue tracksuit.

Ty's voice remained calm but firm. "Mr Brennan, we have you on multiple charges. Cooperation now might help you."

Brennan smirked; his eyes darted to the mirror as if he knew Karen was on the other side. "You have no idea what you're dealing with, Detective. This goes far beyond a few trinkets."

Karen's eyes narrowed, her attention sharpening at Brennan's words.

Ty pressed on. "Why don't you enlighten us, then?"

Brennan leaned back in his chair, a smug smile playing on his lips. "Have you looked at York Minster, Detective? I mean truly looked?"

A vein throbbed in Karen's temple as she listened to

Brennan; her jaw clenched, a silent scream building inside.

"There are treasures hidden in plain sight, right under your noses. The Minster holds unimaginable secrets and is all there for the taking."

Ty glanced at the mirror, aware Karen would share his intrigue. "What treasures are we talking about, Mr Brennan?"

Brennan chuckled and shook his head. "Oh no, Detective, that's not how you play this game. But I will say this—what you found in those tunnels? It's the tip of the iceberg."

Karen's mind raced, considering the implications of Brennan's cryptic comments. What could he mean by treasures hidden in plain sight? And how did it connect to their investigation of Sarah Lockwood's murder?

Karen's brow furrowed as she listened to Brennan's cryptic words through the live feed. She stepped away from the observation room and walked back to her office, a nagging thought taking shape.

Staring at her PC screen, she scanned the inventory lists, cross-referencing them with the photographs and notes from the excavation. Something didn't make sense.

Karen called out to Belinda, who was passing by. "Bel, can you grab the records of what we recovered from Brennan?"

Belinda fetched the documents while Karen continued her scrutiny of the old reports. When Belinda returned, they laid out the other evidence alongside the historical records.

"Look at this." Karen pointed to a series of entries in the 1987 inventory. "Someone listed these items as 'catalogued and stored', but there's no mention of where they stored them or who stored them."

Belinda leaned in, her eyes narrowing as she saw the discrepancies. "And two match what we found on Brennan, but they're not listed in any official museum or university collections."

Karen nodded as her suspicions grew. "It's as if someone recorded these items and intended to store them on a shelf in a basement somewhere, but instead, they vanished from official records with no one knowing... or checking."

She turned to the computer and retrieved the digital archive of York Minster's renovation history. "The Minster has undergone several minor restorations and repairs since 1987. What if Brennan or his associates removed and hid a few 'missing' artefacts during one of these projects, only to recover them later?"

Belinda caught on. "Hidden in plain sight, like Brennan stated."

Karen stood, energy coursing through her. "We need to re-examine every inch of the Minster. There might be more to find."

While Karen mulled over the connections between the artefacts and the Minster, a memory surfaced. She recalled a detail from Sarah Lockwood's diary which seemed insignificant at the time but carried a new meaning.

"Bel, do you remember Sarah's diary? There was a mention of a 'secret space' in the Minster."

Belinda's eyes widened with recognition. "You're right. I believe it was in one of the later entries, right before she vanished."

Karen searched for and opened the digital copy of Sarah's diary on her computer. She scrolled through the entries until she found the relevant passage.

Sarah had written: *I think I've found something*

*extraordinary. I believe there's a hidden space in the Minster. If my suspicions are correct, it's being used to hide things.*

"This might be what Brennan was suggesting. A secret space, containing artefacts never recorded, or recorded and then hidden."

"And if Sarah discovered it just before she disappeared..." Bel added.

"Her death may have been because of this secret space," Karen concluded. She stood and yawned. It had been a long night, but sleep would have to wait. "We need to get back to the Minster. Whatever this secret space is, we need to find it."

Belinda nodded. "I'll grab Ed and Claire."

---

DRIVING through York's early morning streets, the weight of the gloom pressed down on them, the silence broken only by the hum of the engine. Karen had an urgency to act. A need to get there as time wasn't on their side. The Undercroft, with its layers of history stretching back to Roman times, could hide secrets that had remained buried for decades.

They arrived at York Minster as the first glimmers of daylight were touching the ancient stonework. Karen had called in extra uniformed officers to support her and her team.

"Right," Karen said gathering the team at the entrance. "We're looking for anything out of place, any signs of recent disturbance, or areas not in keeping with the rest of the structure." She then split the officers in small groups and assigned them areas to search, each taking a different section of the Minster, from the Undercroft to the storerooms.

Her team made their way into the Undercroft, the air growing cooler and damper with each step. The space was a maze of stone pillars and arches, remnants of Roman and Norman construction intermingling with more recent additions. She felt a connection to the site as she stood near where Sarah's remains had been found. It felt like the investigation had gone full circle and they were back to where it had all started.

## 52

Karen and her team focused their search, torchlights casting long shadows across the ancient stonework. Three hours of searching offered nothing more than aching backs, dusty hands, and waning resolution. Karen was about to call time for a break and refreshments when her hand caught an imperfection, a lack of uniformity in the stonework.

"Bel," Karen called.

Belinda joined Karen at the spot where she'd noticed a difference. Together, they ran their hands over the rough surface, searching for any irregularities. Belinda's fingers caught on something.

"Here! There's a slight indentation."

Karen took a look, her eyes narrowing as she examined the area. It was almost imperceptible, but there was indeed a faint outline of what could be a change in the original stonework.

"Ed," Karen called. "Bring the thermal imaging camera over here."

Ed hurried over. He powered on the camera and waved it across the wall.

The team huddled round Ed. As he moved the camera over the area Karen and Belinda had been examining, a distinct temperature difference became visible; the thermal image showed a clear, cool patch where they had been standing.

"There's something behind this wall. A void perhaps," Ed murmured, adjusting the settings for a clearer image.

Karen nodded. "Alright, let's see if we can open this. Ed, get on the phone to the Minster's preservation team. We need their help to make sure we damage nothing of historical value."

Ed stepped away, the sound of his footsteps echoing slightly as he went to make the call; meanwhile, the team continued their examination of the wall, hoping to find the secret space Sarah Lockwood's diary described.

A little over an hour later, as the preservation team removed the stonework, a collective gasp echoed through the Undercroft. A small chamber, untouched for years, lay revealed before them. Air rushed out, carrying the musty scent of long-buried secrets.

Karen stepped forward, her torch illuminating the interior. Shelves lined the walls, each bearing an array of artefacts that glinted in the dusty beam of light. Viking jewellery with intricate designs, carved bone combs, and fragments of decorated pottery.

"This is incredible," Belinda said.

Ed moved in for a closer look. "These must be the missing artefacts from the dig." He examined each item without touching them.

Karen agreed. "This explains the discrepancies in the records. Someone went to great lengths to hide these. They were kept hidden until needed for buyers."

While examining the contents of the chamber, Ed noticed something tucked away in a corner. "Karen." He pointed to a small leather-bound book.

Karen put on a pair of blue nitrile gloves before handling the item with care. Inside, written in a neat hand, was a name: *Sarah Lockwood*.

"It's her notebook," Karen said. She recognised the discovery and its significance.

The team gathered round her as Karen opened it. The pages had yellowed with age, but the handwriting remained clear and legible. Karen scanned the entries until she came across a letter tucked between the pages, dated days before Sarah's disappearance.

With anticipation, Karen unfolded the letter and read aloud:

*To whom it may concern,*

*I fear what I've discovered may put me in danger. The dig at York Minster has unearthed artefacts far more valuable than anyone has admitted publicly. I've overheard conversations suggesting a plan to steal and sell these treasures on the black market.*

*Professor Fairfax and Councillor Matthew Hartley seem to be at the centre of this conspiracy. They've been meeting late at night, speaking in hushed tones about 'securing their future' and 'rewriting history'. I believe that along with others, they intend to falsify records and remove the most precious items before the dig concludes. A man called Marcus seems to turn up a lot and has taken a keen interest in what we're doing.*

*I've tried to gather evidence and question them, but it's challenging without arousing suspicion. If anything happens to me, please investigate these men and their connections to the antiquities trade.*

*I hope I'm wrong about all of this, but I feel I'm in over my head. Even Al has told me to stop snooping. He says it's putting my life in danger, but he's just as bad. Always hanging round Fairfax and doing anything for him. And I saw Fairfax pass over a cardboard box. No idea what was in it. I asked when we were home, but he said it was rubbish.*

*Something isn't right.*
*Sarah Lockwood*

The team exchanged shocked glances as Karen finished reading. The letter provided the missing link they'd been searching for, connecting Sarah's disappearance to the theft of the artefacts.

"That's revealing," Belinda said.

Karen agreed. "It does reveal a lot. Sarah must have confronted them about her suspicions, and they silenced her to protect their plan."

After Karen finished reading the letter, Ed's eyes widened with a realisation. He stepped closer, peering at the document in Karen's hands.

"Councillor Victoria Hartley knew all along what was going on. She's been trying to protect her dad's name... and her reputation."

Karen tutted. "You're right, Ed. And Fairfax has been lying to us since the beginning. I also believe Sarah's own brother was involved in this. He's never looked right to me. Now I know why."

Bel shook her head. "Alistar Lockwood... he's been playing us this whole time. Offering to help with the investigation when he was one of the prime suspects all along."

"This is a great find." Karen folded the letter and placing it in an evidence bag. "We need to bring both Alistair Lockwood and Councillor Hartley in for questioning. Can someone do that for me?"

Bel stepped away to make the call before returning to the search.

The team's search of the chamber revealed a cardboard box, and inside, amongst various items, Belinda found a weathered leather satchel; its musty smell and soft texture intriguing. She pulled it out, clearly itching to see what else they'd uncovered.

"Karen, you need to see this!" she called out.

Karen moved over, her torch beam illuminating the satchel as Belinda opened it. Inside, they found a collection of papers.

"These look like documents from the original dig," Karen said, her voice hushed with excitement.

The papers lay on the hastily assembled table, their texture rough beneath Ed's fingertips as he carefully positioned each one for his camera. The flash momentarily illuminated the room, capturing the detail of every creased, stained page before anyone could disturb them.

"Interesting." Ed pointed to a handwritten inventory list. "I don't recall seeing these items on the official records we have from the dig."

Karen scanned the document. "You're right. This seems to be an unofficial inventory. There are artefacts listed here never mentioned in the public reports."

Belinda picked out another sheet, this one filled with scribbled notes. "And this appears to be a plan for moving certain items. There are dates and locations mentioned."

As they examined the documents, a clearer picture of the conspiracy emerged. The unofficial inventories showed the true extent of the dig's findings, far more valuable and extensive than what had been reported.

"This is damning evidence," Karen said. "It proves there was a deliberate attempt to conceal and remove artefacts from the dig site for illicit financial gain."

Belinda's sharp eyes caught something unusual. She

pulled out a small stack of papers that looked newer than the rest.

"These are helpful." She handed them over.

Karen's brow furrowed as she realised their significance. "These are recent. Someone has been accessing the hidden space long after Sarah's disappearance and removing items."

Ed pushed his glasses further up his nose and peered at the papers. "The handwriting looks familiar," he mused.

He searched for an image on his phone of a document they'd received from the council earlier in the investigation. He held it against the newly discovered papers. "It's like Councillor Hartley's."

*The crafty cow*, Karen thought. Councillor Victoria Hartley, who had been so vocal about wrapping up the investigation, had been involved from the beginning. Preet's own observation of Hartley and Brennan together reinforced that suspicion. Their dubious professional and personal relationship had been a long-standing one.

"Hartley has a lot to answer for." Karen bagged the evidence. "Her involvement goes far beyond protecting her father's legacy."

They all agreed.

"They had sealed the entrance. We only just discovered it, so how were they gaining access?" Bel commented.

Karen stood back. Bel was right, of course. That meant one thing. There was another entrance to the chamber. "Check every shelf and exposed wall. There has to be another way in."

With renewed energy, the officers examined every square inch of space, and it wasn't long before Karen spotted dust on one of the lower shelves had been disturbed, and finger smudges trailed through the debris.

She dropped to her knees and shone her torch along the shelf until she saw what she was looking for.

"Over here," she shouted.

With Bel and Ed's help, the lower shelf was soon cleared of boxes; however, their efforts stirred up a cloud of fine dust that filled the air with a gritty smell. They coughed and spluttered fanning away most of it. And there it was, hidden from view, a small opening in the wall, chipped away and wide enough for someone to squeeze through.

"Shit," Bel exclaimed. "Cheeky fuckers."

## 53

It took a while to dismantle enough of the shelving to gain access, but Karen and Ed stood before the hidden gap in the wall, their torch beams illuminating the dusty opening. The musty scent of long-forgotten spaces wafted out.

"Ready?" Karen asked.

Ed nodded. "After you."

"Bel, you hang back here and get more bodies here to catalogue everything."

Karen took a deep breath and squeezed through the narrow opening, her shoulders scraping against the rough stone. Ed followed close behind, his larger frame making the gap more challenging.

Emerging on the other side, they found themselves in a dark, musty walkway, the air thick with the smell of damp earth and decaying leaves. Dust filled the air, and cobwebs hung from the corners. Their torch beams cut through the darkness, revealing weathered stone walls that seemed to absorb the light.

"Watch your step," Karen cautioned as they moved

forward. The floor was uneven, with loose stones and debris scattered about.

Their footsteps echoed in the confined space. The walkway seemed to stretch before them, curving to the left as it descended deeper.

"This must have been part of the original Minster structure," Ed suggested, his voice hushed with awe. "Imagine how many people have walked this path over the centuries."

"And how many might have used it for less than holy purposes?" she added.

The air grew noticeably cooler and damper, carrying the earthy smell of moss as they walked. Water droplets glistened on the walls, catching the light of their torches. The sound of their breathing seemed amplified in the enclosed space, mixing with the distant drip of water.

After what felt like an eternity, they reached a steel door. It stood out against the ancient stonework.

Karen exchanged a glance with Ed before reaching for the handle. It was cold to the touch, and for a moment, she hesitated. Then turned it. The door's metal hinges creaked in protest as it swung open, the sound echoing along the corridor. Karen winced at the noise, hoping it hadn't alerted anyone who might lurk in the depths below.

Beyond the door lay a series of metal steps, descending into inky blackness. The beam of Karen's torch couldn't penetrate the gloom at the bottom.

"Well, this is ominous," Ed muttered, a nervous chuckle escaping his lips.

Karen shot him a wry smile. "No turning back now. Let's see where this rabbit hole leads us."

They began their descent, the metal steps clanging under their feet. The sound seemed to reverberate through the shaft as Karen strained to hear any answering noises from below. Her torch beam danced across the walls, revealing patches of moss and lichen clinging to the damp stone. When they reached the bottom, they found another narrow walkway, the ceiling so low Ed stooped to avoid hitting his head.

"This way." Karen gestured along the passageway with her torch.

The narrow confines of the walkway opened into a much larger space. The beams of their torches couldn't reach the far walls or ceiling, suggesting they had stepped into a vast underground cavern.

Yet, the first thing they encountered was the odour—a strong mix of rotting sewage and decay made them both wrinkle their noses in disgust.

"Oh God." Ed gagged and covered his nose with his sleeve. "What is that?"

Karen's eyes widened as realisation dawned. "We're in the Roman sewers," she breathed, her voice a mix of awe and disgust.

With her eyes adjusting to the gloom, she made out the contours of the ancient sewer system. A central channel ran through the middle, filled with dark, sluggish water. Walkways lined either side, allowing access for maintenance—or, as Karen now suspected, for more nefarious purposes.

"This is how they've been doing it." She shook her head. "The smugglers have been using this route to move the artefacts out of the Minster without being detected."

"It's brilliant, really. Who would think to look here?"

"I reckon no one knows about it," she replied. "There was no reference to it on the maps Craig showed me.

They moved further into the sewer, their torches revealing centuries of built-up grime on the walls.

"Here!" Ed pointed his torch at the floor. "Footprints."

Karen crouched, examining the muddy tracks. They were fresh, the edges still sharp in the soft silt covering the walkway. "They can't be more than a few weeks old. We're on the right track."

They continued following the footprints. The sound of running water grew louder, and soon they could see where the sewer joined a larger channel, the water rushing past with considerable force.

"This must lead out to ground level," Karen said. "The perfect escape route."

Taking in the scene before them, a loud snap echoed from behind, causing them both to whirl, raising their torches high.

For a moment, the beams of light revealed nothing but an empty sewer stretching back the way they had come.

"Rats?" Karen said.

"I hope not, because I'll be running off in the opposite direction."

"Cheers, Ed. I knew I could rely on you for backup."

Karen's phone pinged. She pulled it out from her jacket pocket and checked the screen. "Let's head back," she said. "We have Lockwood at the station."

"You don't need to ask me twice." Ed raced off at speed.

## 54

Karen pushed open the door to interview room two to see Alistair Lockwood leaning forward, elbows resting on the table, hands cradling a paper cup.

"DCI Heath, why did you ask me to attend? Why did your officer refuse to answer my questions?" he said, his voice betraying a hint of nervousness.

"Alistair, I need to speak with you about fresh evidence in your sister's case," Karen replied as she pulled out a chair and sat opposite him.

He tapped the side of his cup. "New evidence?"

"I'm recording this interview," Karen said as she pressed the button on the recorder and provided the formal introduction and caution.

"What's this about?" he asked.

"How well do you know Professor Fairfax?"

The question threw him, and he stuttered in reply. "Um, he was the dig leader. We all knew him."

"I'm not interested in the others. How well did *you* know him?"

Lockwood shrugged and turned away, his lids flickering.

"It's a simple question."

"I... didn't know him well."

Karen studied Lockwood as he shifted in his seat.

"So you weren't friends, or business associates?"

Lockwood's eyes narrowed.

"I need an answer."

Alistair shook his head and remained tight-lipped.

Karen pulled out a copy of the letter they'd found in the hidden chamber. "We discovered this in a concealed room at York Minster. It's a letter from your sister, detailing her suspicions about artefact theft during the 1987 dig. A dig you were part of. There's a reference to a conversation she had with you."

Lockwood's face paled as he recognised the handwriting. His composure cracked; his hands trembled, cold and clammy, as he reached for the letter.

"How... where did you find this?" he stammered, his eyes darting between Karen and the damning evidence in her hands.

"I think it's time you told me the truth about what happened during the dig," Karen said.

Lockwood looked away, avoiding Karen's steady gaze. He ran a hand through his greying hair, his composure crumbling.

"I don't know what you're talking about," he said, his voice lacking conviction. "That dig was decades ago. How could I remember every detail?"

"Alistair, your sister knew something was wrong, didn't she? She confided in you, and you warned her off. Do you know what happened to her? Who harmed her? Was it Fairfax? Marcus Brennan? Matthew Hartley? Tell me."

Lockwood slumped into his chair. "You don't understand," he croaked. "It wasn't supposed to happen like that."

"Sarah said Professor Fairfax and Councillor Matthew Hartley were in the middle of it. You were close to Fairfax. Why?"

His vision blurred as he looked at Karen. "Sarah... she was so idealistic. She didn't understand the pressures we were under, the expectations from the university, the funders."

He sniffed and wiped his eyes with the back of his hands. "When she threatened to expose everything, I tried to reason with her. But she wouldn't listen. Things... things got out of hand."

"You were the person spotted arguing with her late at night?" Karen asked.

Lockwood pressed his face into his hands, his body shaking with suppressed sobs. "I never meant for her to get hurt. It was an accident, I swear."

Karen watched as the man before her crumbled, years of guilt and secrecy breaking through his constructed facade.

Alastair Lockwood's shoulders shook with barely suppressed sobs, his face pale and drawn. He sighed, his eyes meeting Karen's with a mixture of guilt and resignation.

"It was supposed to be simple," he replied. "We'd found artefacts of immense value, but the university wanted them catalogued and stored away. I... I saw an opportunity to secure financial security after Fairfax introduced me to Brennan. Brennan presented a foolproof plan."

Karen listened as Lockwood continued, his words coming faster now, as if a dam had broken.

"I arranged for pieces not to be catalogued. They

would disappear to be sold privately. Fairfax was friends with Marcus Brennan, and Brennan had the contacts. We would split the money between us, including our sponsors... Sarah stumbled upon our arrangements when she caught me discussing it with Brennan and Matthew Hartley. She was furious, threatened to expose everything."

Lockwood's voice cracked. "We argued that night outside the Minster. I tried to make her understand, but she wouldn't listen. She turned to leave, and I... I grabbed her arm and pushed her. She lost her balance, fell down the stairs."

Tears streamed down his face, hot and heavy, as he confessed, "I panicked. She wasn't moving. I couldn't think straight. The only thing I could think of was calling Brennan. He said he'd sort it. They hid her body in a sealed-off section of the Undercroft due to be filled in the next morning. She wasn't supposed to be found. Ever. I've lived with the guilt every day since."

Karen watched as the weight of his confession seemed to age Lockwood before her eyes. The truth she'd sought for so long was out, but it brought no satisfaction, only a deep sadness for the lives ruined by one man's misguided actions, and the growing realisation Olivia Lockwood had now lost both of her children.

Karen's phone buzzed in her pocket. She ended the interview and stepped outside, leaving the sobs from Lockwood behind her.

"Heath," she answered.

"Karen, it's Belinda. We've got a problem. Councillor Hartley's gone off the grid. We can't find her. Her office says she left for a meeting but never showed."

Karen's jaw clenched. "Any idea where she might be?"

"Nothing concrete, but the meeting was at an office close to Rufforth. I'm thinking..."

"Me, too. Good work, Bel. Head there now. I'm on my way. Lockwood has confessed to being responsible for Sarah's death," Karen said.

"No way," Bel exclaimed.

"Yep, says it was an accident. I'll get someone from the team to process him. I'll deal with him later."

With a breathless rush, Karen bolted from the interview suite; Hartley's vanishing act was as good as a confession, but they needed concrete proof, hence her arrest.

With time running out, she jumped into her car and raced from the station.

---

Karen's car sped through the narrow streets of Rufforth, and she scanned the road ahead for any sign of Hartley's vehicle. The radio crackled with updates from local units who had spotted the councillor's car driving erratically towards the airfield.

"All units, suspect vehicle heading east on Wetherby Road," a voice reported.

Karen's grip tightened on the steering wheel as she made a sharp turn, tyres screeching. She glimpsed Hartley's silver Mercedes in the distance, weaving through traffic.

"This is DCI Heath. I have visual on the suspect. In pursuit on Wetherby Road," Karen radioed in.

The chase intensified as Hartley's car swerved on to a side street, narrowly missing a parked van. Karen followed through tight corners. Further units tucked in behind her, their blue lights bouncing off the surrounding darkness.

Hartley's desperate attempt to escape was clear in her reckless driving. She flew through a junction, other drivers braking to avoid a collision.

Karen's heart pounded in her chest, a frantic drumbeat against her ribs, as she followed, keeping a safe distance while trying not to lose sight of the fleeing councillor. The airfield loomed ahead, its open spaces offering a potential escape route.

"Suspect approaching Rufforth Airfield," Karen updated the pursuing units as she slowed. "We need to box her in."

Hartley's Mercedes veered on to the airfield, Karen's instincts kicked in. She knew the soft, damp grass would make it difficult for Hartley to handle her car.

"All units, suspect has entered Rufforth Airfield," Karen radioed.

Hartley's car fishtailed violently as it hit the grass, showering the rear bumper with thick, dark mud. The vehicle's speed dropped as it struggled for traction on the slippery surface.

Further into the airfield, a small aircraft sat on the runway, its engine running in readiness to escape. Karen noticed the rudder and flaps moving as it inched forward. On seeing the approaching blue lights, the pilot taxied off, obviously not wanting to hang about any longer. Minutes later, its lights disappeared into the clouds.

Karen watched as Hartley's desperate bid for freedom unravelled before her eyes. The Mercedes slewed sideways, its wheels spinning on the sodden earth. With a final, sickening lurch, the car came to a halt, half buried in the mud.

Without hesitation, Karen brought her own vehicle to a stop and leapt out. Other units fanned out round the Mercedes, blocking any opportunity for escape. Karen approached Hartley's car, aware the cornered councillor might still be dangerous.

"Councillor Hartley, step out of the vehicle with your

hands where I can see them," Karen commanded, her voice carrying across the open field.

For a moment, there was nothing. Then the driver's door creaked open. Hartley emerged, her face a mask of defeat and fury.

Karen moved in, securing Hartley's hands behind her back. "Victoria Hartley, you're under arrest for conspiracy to pervert the course of justice and suspicion of involvement in the death of Sarah Lockwood."

## 55

With Hartley in custody and officers picking up Fairfax, Karen brought her team together in the incident room.

"Right, we need to trace every international connection," she said. "Ed, I want you to liaise with Interpol. See if they've got any similar cases on their radar."

Ed nodded, reaching for his notepad.

"Belinda, dig into the financial records we seized from Brennan. Can you look for any overseas transactions, shell companies, anything that might lead us to their international partners. Arrange for a search of his property, too."

Belinda was already at her computer, fingers flying over the keyboard.

"Ty, I need you to work with the ports and the Border Force. Check if any of our suspects have made recent trips abroad and see if we can track any movements linked to the operation. We also need to trace the flight plan of the small plane. Who owns it and what was its final destination? Victoria Hartley had made plans to leave the country. Where was she going?"

Karen turned to Claire. "Can you Liaise with Preet and go through her notes from the auction houses she attended. Any names, places, or dates with international connections. Even the smallest detail could be crucial."

The team set to work, the room buzzing with focused energy. They had figured out the local operation, but she knew there was much more to uncover. The international web of artefact smuggling was vast and complex, and they needed to unravel every thread.

As the team delved deeper, a breakthrough came from an unexpected source. Belinda, poring over financial records, identified a recurring pattern of payments to a Moroccan bank account.

"Karen, I think I've got something." Bel waved her over.

Karen slid between the desks and leaned in. "What am I looking at?"

"These transactions," Belinda pointed, "they're all to the same account in Marrakech linked to the Pearsons. And look at the dates—they align with our timeline of artefact movements we know of in Brennan's notes."

Ed, overhearing, chimed in from his desk. "My call to Interpol was interesting. They're keen to have a chat with you. Here's the number." Ed handed Karen a Post-it. "They've had their eye on a Moroccan dealer suspected of fencing stolen antiquities from sources in Europe to the Far East."

Karen's eyes narrowed. "Do we have a name?"

"Youssef El-Amrani," Ed replied. "He's been on their radar for years, but they've never been able to pin anything concrete on him."

Preet joined the huddle, refusing to go home, a notepad in hand. "I remember overhearing something at the auction about a 'Moroccan connection', and do you remember Brennan introduced me to a Professor Messaoudi from Morocco? At the time, I didn't think much of it because they didn't mention any other names and they never brought it up again, but..."

Karen's worry turned to relief as she saw it as a positive development. "So everything points to Morocco as the central point. Ty, can you see if any of our suspects have travelled to Morocco in recent months?"

"I'll do that now," he confirmed.

Karen reached for her phone and dialled the number for the Interpol contact. As she waited for the call to connect, she glanced at the evidence board, thinking ahead of what to do next.

"Officer Dubois? It's DCI Heath from York. We've uncovered a link to a Moroccan dealer named Youssef El-Amrani, and I understand he's a person of interest to you?"

She listened as the Interpol officer provided more details about their ongoing investigation into El-Amrani. Karen scribbled notes, her handwriting barely legible in her haste.

"We need to coordinate our efforts," Karen said. "Can you set up a secure video conference with the Moroccan authorities?"

Within the hour, Karen faced a screen filled with faces from various law enforcement agencies. She outlined their findings, emphasising the connection between the York smuggling operation and El-Amrani's activities in Marrakech.

The Moroccan police chief, a stern-faced man named Hamid Benali, raised a hand and cleared his throat. "We've been building a case against El-Amrani for months. Your information could be the key element. And we know Professor Messaoudi is a known associate of El-

Amrani, so it seems as if together, they are the Moroccan connection and middlemen to clients in the Far East."

Karen nodded. "We need to shut this down quickly. If El-Amrani gets wind of the arrests here, he might go to ground."

They spent the next hour hammering out a plan before ending the call. The Moroccan police would offer surveillance on El-Amrani's known locations, while Interpol coordinated with border control to prevent his escape. Karen's team would offer real-time intelligence as they continued to unravel the UK end of the operation.

Karen stood before the evidence board, studying Sarah's features. Soft skin, kind eyes, and a wholesome smile. The young archaeologist had stumbled upon evidence of the initial theft and had paid the price when she'd confided to her brother. The ultimate act of betrayal. Following his confession, he was charged with manslaughter and perverting the course of justice.

Councillor Hartley and Alastair Lockwood's involvement made sense in this broader context. They weren't only covering up a single crime but protecting a network.

## 56

Karen sat across the table from Councillor Victoria Hartley in the stark interview room. The woman's usually impeccable appearance was dishevelled, her designer suit wrinkled from her night in custody. Dark circles underlined her eyes, a stark contrast to her polished image.

"Interview beginning at nine fifteen a.m.," Karen stated for the record. "Present are myself, DCI Karen Heath, and Councillor Victoria Hartley. Also present is Councillor Hartley's solicitor, Mr James Black."

Hartley's gaze remained fixed on the table, her fingers drumming an erratic rhythm on its surface. Karen allowed the silence to stretch, observing the councillor's body language. Karen noticed Hartley was clearly rattled, her usually composed image gone, replaced with her chewing her bottom lip and clearing her throat.

"Councillor Hartley," Karen began, "we have arrested you on suspicion of conspiracy to pervert the course of justice and involvement in the smuggling of stolen artefacts. Do you understand these charges?"

Hartley's eyes flicked to meet Karen's, fear clear in her

gaze. "I understand the charges, yes," she replied, her voice hoarse. "But I maintain my innocence."

Karen nodded, acknowledging the statement. She opened a file in front of her, pulling out several documents. "Let's start with your connection to the 1987 dig at York Minster. Your father, Matthew Hartley, was a councillor, correct?"

"Yes, correct," Hartley replied, a hint of wariness creeping into her tone.

"We've uncovered financial records showing suspicious transactions linked to your father's accounts during and after the dig," Karen continued. "Your father moved large sums of money to offshore accounts. Can you explain these transactions?"

Hartley's solicitor leaned in, whispering something in her ear.

She nodded before responding. "I was not privy to my father's financial dealings at the time."

Karen pressed on. "But then, after your father's death, you closed these accounts and transferred the funds to an account in Spain under your name. How do you explain that?"

A flicker of unease crossed Hartley's face. "I... I inherited my father's estate. All legitimate."

"Was it?" Karen asked, her tone sharp. "Because our investigation suggests otherwise. We believe these funds were part of a long-running smuggling operation, one your father was involved in and you continued with after his death. We've traced the source of these payments to your father. They came from Marcus Brennan. Why would your father receive payments from Brennan, and if they were legitimate, why not have them deposited in his Barclays account in the UK?"

Hartley's composure cracked further. "You can't prove

any of this," she snapped, her voice rising. "This is nothing but speculation and conjecture."

Karen pulled out another document. "This is a record of a phone call between you and Marcus Brennan, made only days before we arrested him. Care to explain the nature of your relationship with Mr Brennan?"

The colour drained from Hartley's face. She turned to her solicitor, who nodded. "I... I've known Marcus for years. He's a respected antiquities dealer."

"A dealer now in custody for smuggling artefacts," Karen countered. "We believe some of those same artefacts were stolen from the 1987 dig. The dig your father showed a keen interest in."

Hartley's fingers clenched into fists. "You're twisting everything. My father was a respected councillor. He would never have been involved in anything illegal."

Karen smiled. "Then explain this." She slid a photograph across the table. It showed a young Victoria Hartley standing next to her father and Marcus Brennan, all three smiling at what appeared to be a private auction with Brennan holding an artefact Karen's team had identified as stolen. "They took this in 1988, just months after Sarah Lockwood disappeared. You were there, Councillor. You knew what was going on."

Hartley stared at the photograph, her breath coming in short gasps. "I... I don't remember this. It was a long time ago."

"And this." Karen placed a photo on the table of Matthew Hartley standing with others in Masonic robes. She tapped on each face and named them. "All involved in funding the dig and then stealing items, while your father turned a blind eye for financial reward."

Hartley swallowed hard and clenched her jaw.

"Let me refresh your memory," Karen said, her tone

unyielding. "We have visitor records from an auction house. You and your father attended private sales with Mr Brennan. Stolen items were sold to private collectors and fifty percent of the revenue landed in your dad's account."

The councillor's facade fractured. Tears welled in her eyes as she looked at her solicitor for a way out. The lawyer placed a hand on her arm, whispering in her ear.

Karen waited, watching the internal struggle play out on Hartley's face. After a moment, the councillor took a deep breath, seeming to decide.

"I want to make a deal," Hartley muttered.

Her solicitor interjected. "My client will provide information in return for consideration to any potential charges."

Karen settled back in her chair, her expression neutral. "That depends on the information, Councillor. We're not interested in half-truths or attempts to minimise your involvement. We want the full story, from the beginning."

Hartley nodded, wiping away a tear. "It started with my father," she began, her voice shaky. "Brennan approached him before the dig even started, and he knew about potential artefacts that might be found. He offered my father a cut of the profits if he could make sure certain items went... unrecorded and the council turned a blind eye."

As Hartley spoke, Karen took detailed notes.

"My father agreed," Hartley added. "He used his position on the council to influence the dig's funding and oversight. Brennan had a team ready to move the artefacts before they could be properly catalogued when they were found."

"And Sarah Lockwood?" Karen prompted.

Hartley's face tightened as she closed her eyes.

Karen's pen paused over her notepad. "What happened next, Councillor?"

"I don't know the full details," Hartley admitted. "My father never told me what happened. But I know Sarah confronted her brother and there was a struggle. Sarah fell… or she was pushed. Alistair panicked and called Brennan, who arranged for her body to be hidden in a part of the Undercroft scheduled to be sealed off."

The room fell silent as the weight of the confession settled over them. Karen took a moment to collect her thoughts.

"And your involvement? When did you become active in the operation?"

Hartley sniffed and wiped her nose with a tissue. "After my father died. Brennan approached me, said I needed to continue what my father had started. At first, I refused, but… he had evidence, photographs, documents implicating my father. He threatened to expose everything if I didn't cooperate."

"So you protected your father's legacy by carrying on his criminal activities."

Hartley nodded. "I told myself it was victimless. Just old artefacts that would sit in a museum basement otherwise. But deep down, I knew it was wrong. I didn't see a way out."

Karen closed her notebook, fixing Hartley with a penetrating stare. "Councillor Hartley, I hope you understand the seriousness of what you've just confessed to."

Hartley's solicitor spoke. "My client understands the gravity of the situation. We hope they will take her full cooperation into consideration."

Karen shrugged. "That will be up to the Crown Prosecution Service. For now, I have a few more questions about the specifics of your operation. I need names, dates, and locations of any sales or exchanges you were involved in or aware of."

For the next two hours, Karen probed Hartley, drawing out every detail of the operation. The councillor's initial reluctance gave way to a flood of information.

As the interview concluded, Karen gathered her papers, a slight ache in her back. With little sleep last night, she was running on fumes.

"Interview ended at eleven forty-seven a.m.," Karen stated for the record. As she stood to leave, she paused, looking at the broken figure of Victoria Hartley.

"One last question, Councillor," Karen said. "Was it worth it? All the lies, the cover-ups, the betrayal of public trust... was it worth it in the end?"

Hartley raised her eyes, red-rimmed and filled with regret. "No," she confessed. "God help me, it wasn't worth any of it."

Karen left the interview room, a whoop of joy escaping her lips as she pumped her fist in the air.

Hartley's confession was the beginning. But for now, Karen allowed herself a moment of quiet triumph. Karen knew justice would finally be served for Sarah Lockwood, and York's dark history would be revealed.

Her next visit this morning would be a painful one.

## 57

KAREN STOOD on the doorstep of the Lockwood family home, her hand poised to ring the doorbell. This wasn't a conversation she was looking forward to as she pressed the button.

Moments later, Olivia Lockwood appeared. "Detective Heath, what a surprise. Please, come in."

Following Olivia into the living room, she noticed how the older woman seemed more at peace than during their earlier visits. The constant tension lining her face had eased, replaced by a quiet serenity. It made what Karen had to do even more difficult.

"Can I get you a tea?" Olivia offered, gesturing for Karen to take a seat.

Karen shook her head. "No, thank you, Mrs Lockwood. I'm afraid this isn't a social call."

Olivia's smile faded as she registered the serious tone in Karen's voice. She sank into an armchair. "What is it? Has something happened?"

"Mrs Lockwood, I'm here about Alistair. We've uncovered fresh evidence in Sarah's case, and... I'm afraid it implicates your son."

The colour drained from Olivia's face. Her hands, which had been resting calmly in her lap, trembled. "What... what are you saying, Detective?"

Karen sighed. "Alistair has confessed to being involved in Sarah's death. He claims it was an accident, but he admitted to covering it up and being part of the artefact smuggling operation."

Olivia stared at Karen in disbelief, her mouth opening and closing without a sound. When she finally spoke, her voice cracked. "No... there must be some mistake. Alistair loved his sister. He would never..."

"I'm so sorry, Mrs Lockwood," Karen said. "I wish it wasn't true. But Alistair provided details only someone involved could have known."

The reality of the situation crashed over Olivia all at once. She doubled over, a heart-wrenching sob tearing from her throat. "My children," she wailed, "my babies..."

Karen moved to kneel beside Olivia's chair, placing a comforting hand on the older woman's arm. She remained silent, allowing Olivia to process the devastating news.

For several minutes, Olivia's grief echoed through the room. Karen's eyes burned with tears, the raw emotion of the moment overwhelming her professional detachment.

When Olivia's sobs subsided to quiet weeping, she looked at Karen, her eyes red and swollen. "How could this happen?"

Karen explained what Alistair had told them—about arguing with Sarah, the fall, and the later cover-up. She watched as Olivia absorbed each piece of information, her face a canvas of pain and disbelief.

"All these years," Olivia murmured, "he knew. He

knew what happened to Sarah, and he said nothing. He watched me grieve, watched me search for answers..."

Karen squeezed Olivia's hand. "I can't imagine how difficult this must be for you, Mrs Lockwood. Is there someone I can call to be with you and your husband? A friend or family member?"

Olivia shook her head, a bitter laugh escaping her lips. "Family? I thought I had two children. Now I learn one is dead and the other is responsible."

The stark reality of Olivia's words hung in the air.

"Mrs Lockwood, I know it might not seem like it now, but you're not alone. There are support services available, people who can help you both through this."

Olivia's gaze landed on a family photograph of a much younger Olivia with George, Sarah, and Alistair, all smiling at the camera. "We were happy once. Where did it all go wrong?"

"Sometimes people make choices they can't take back. But it doesn't negate the love that existed in your family. Sarah's memory doesn't need to be tainted by this."

Olivia turned back to Karen, her eyes shimmering with fresh tears. "What happens now? To Alistair, I mean."

Karen explained the legal process ahead—the formal charges, the likelihood of a trial. She was as honest as she could be about the potential consequences Alistair faced.

Olivia tensed as Karen spoke. The initial shock and grief were still there, but something else was emerging.

"I want to see him," Olivia said. "I need to hear it from him, to look into his eyes and understand why he did this."

Karen nodded. "I'll arrange it. It might take a day or two, but I'll make sure you get to see Alistair."

Olivia reached out and grasped Karen's hand. "Thank

you, Detective. For everything. For not giving up on Sarah, for uncovering the truth, even though it's not the truth I wanted to hear."

A lump formed in Karen's throat. "You don't need to thank me, Mrs Lockwood. I only wish I could bring you better news."

Olivia walked Karen to the door. The older woman appeared to age years since their conversation.

At the doorway, Olivia paused. "Detective Heath. I know you were simply doing your job, but you have given me something I never thought I'd get—the truth. It's a difficult truth, but it's better than the uncertainty I have lived with for so long."

Karen nodded, unable to find words adequate to respond. She reached out and squeezed Olivia's hand one last time before stepping out into the afternoon sun.

Exhausted, Karen walked back to her car. The raw grief she had witnessed in Olivia Lockwood's eyes would stay with her for a long time. It was moments like these which made her question the cost of uncovering the truth, even as she knew the importance of her work.

She had reached her car when her phone rang. Glancing at the screen, Belinda's name popped up.

"Bel, what's up?" Karen leaned against her car.

Belinda's voice came through, laced with excitement. "Karen, you will not believe this. We've had word from Interpol and the Moroccan authorities."

Karen straightened, her fatigue forgotten. "Go on."

"They've done it," Belinda said, her words tumbling out in a rush. "The operation was a complete success. They've arrested Youssef El-Amrani and his entire network, including Professor Messaoudi, as well as several of their top buyers in the country."

Karen let out a low whistle. "That's incredible, Bel. Any seized items?"

"They've found dozens of valuable pieces in a lock-up. Several look like items stolen from the York Minster dig and from museums and archaeological sites across Europe."

Belinda continued. "Interpol is calling it a very significant bust in the illegal antiquities trade in years. And, Karen, they're giving a lot of credit to the information we provided. Our case was the key."

Karen smiled. "This is fantastic news, Bel. It means we've brought everyone involved to justice, from the local players to the international smuggling ring."

"There's more," Belinda added, her voice now tinged with awe. "Some items they've recovered... Karen, they're priceless. There's talk of pieces historians thought were lost forever. It's going to take weeks to trace them back to their rightful owners."

"Blimey. Days like today make all the hard work worth it."

"Absolutely," Belinda agreed. "So, when are you coming back to the station? We're thinking of opening a bottle of fizz to celebrate."

Karen glanced back at Olivia Lockwood's house. "I'll be there soon. I need a few minutes."

Karen started her car, her mind already turning to the work ahead. There would be reports to file, press conferences to handle, and the painstaking process of returning the recovered artefacts to their rightful places. But for now, she allowed herself to feel a sense of accomplishment.

When she pushed open the station doors, a wave of quiet pride washed over her. This was why she did it—the long hours, the endless paperwork, the sleepless nights, the time away from Zac and Summer. Today, they hadn't just closed a case; they'd preserved history, protected its legacy, and struck a blow against those who sought to exploit it. For all the darkness she faced, moments like this reminded her why the fight was worth it.

Inside, Karen found her team gathered in the incident room, a buzz of excitement in the air. Detective Superintendent Kelly was there, too, a rare smile on her face.

"Alright, everyone." Karen drew their attention. "Before we celebrate, let's tie up the loose ends. We need to be clear on the status of all involved parties."

The room quietened as Karen took her place by the evidence board.

"Professor Fairfax has agreed to a plea deal." She moved a photo on the board. "He's providing key testimony for a reduced sentence. He might end up with five to seven years.

"Father O'Brien, given his limited involvement and full cooperation, is being charged with a lesser offense. He's facing a suspended sentence and community service. The church is also conducting its own internal investigation."

Kelly nodded. "The Dean of York Minster has issued a public statement condemning the actions of those involved and pledging full cooperation with ongoing investigations into any other potential irregularities."

Karen continued, "Pearson Jnr and Ross Marshall will also be charged. As for the other dig participants, most were unaware of the smuggling operation. They're being treated as witnesses rather than suspects. We'll be conducting follow-up interviews to ensure we haven't missed anything."

After Karen finished her summary, she blew out her cheeks.

"Excellent work, all of you." Kelly looked round the room. "This case has been a challenge from start to finish, but you've all shown exceptional dedication and skill."

Karen nodded in agreement. "Indeed. Now, let's make sure all our reports are in order. And someone get the fizz opened!"

A loud cheer erupted.

## 58

*One week later...*

Karen sat in the waiting room of Dr Laura Morales's office, her fingers drumming on her knee. She'd been putting this off for weeks, but after the intensity of the recent case, she knew she couldn't delay any longer.

Doctor Morales opened her office door, greeting Karen with a warm smile. "Karen, please come in."

Karen followed her into a cosy room filled with soft lighting and comfortable furniture. She sank into an armchair, aware of her vulnerability without her usual professional protection.

"So, Karen," Doctor Morales began, her voice gentle but firm, "it's good to see you today. It's been a while. I thought you were avoiding our sessions?"

Karen searched for the right words. "Sorry. I've been busy. Work, life, you know how it is."

As Karen spoke about the challenges she was facing, she found relief in voicing her difficulties. Doctor Morales listened, making notes but mostly maintaining eye contact, her expression one of understanding and empathy.

Karen reclined in the chair. "The pressure during the Lockwood case was... intense," she admitted. "It wasn't just about solving a decades-old murder. There were factors involved."

She paused, smoothing her hair. "It seemed like I was walking a tightrope. One wrong move and the entire case could have fallen apart. And all the while, I had Sarah's family watching, hoping for answers after all these years."

Doctor Morales nodded, prompting Karen to continue.

"Then there was the threat to my safety," Karen said, her voice catching. "Being followed, the note on my car... I thought I was being watched. But I couldn't let it show. I had to be strong for my team, for Zac and Summer. But I never found out who was behind it. I suspect Councillor Hartley and her cronies tried to intimidate me."

She drew a breath, her sweaty hands clasped in her lap. "And all the while, I was trying to balance my work with my home life. Zac was still struggling with his own trauma, and I felt like I was failing him every time I had to stay late at the office."

Karen's eyes met Doctor Morales's. "I kept telling myself solving the case would make it all worthwhile. But now it's over, I'm not sure the pressure has really lifted."

Doctor Morales nodded. "Let's talk about how this case might have brought up memories of your own abduction. Did you experience any flashbacks or heightened anxiety during the investigation?"

Karen's breath caught in her throat. She hadn't wanted to admit it, even to herself, but the parallels had been impossible to ignore. "There were moments," she mumbled, her gaze fixed on her hands. "Especially when we were in the tunnels. The darkness, the confined space… It all seemed too familiar.

She closed her eyes, remembering the suffocating fear she'd experienced. "I kept telling myself it was different, I was in control this time. But there were moments when I could almost feel the ropes on my wrists again."

"I see. It's natural for such a case to trigger those memories. How did you cope with these feelings during the investigation?"

"I tried to focus on the job. But sometimes I had to step away, just for a moment, to catch my breath. I didn't want the team to see how much it was affecting me."

Doctor Morales jotted a few points in her book. "What about coping strategies to help you manage these feelings? Have you considered any techniques to use when you feel overwhelmed?"

Karen hesitated, her brow furrowing. "I've tried deep breathing exercises, but sometimes it's hard to remember in the moment."

"That's understandable." Doctor Morales nodded. "Perhaps we could work on developing a more structured approach. Something you can recall and start when you're under pressure."

As they discussed various techniques, from mindfulness practices to grounding exercises, she felt a glimmer of hope. Doctor Morales then steered the conversation towards the future.

"Looking ahead, how do you see yourself balancing your work and personal life? Are there any changes you'd like to make?"

Karen considered the question. "I know I have to set better boundaries. Maybe delegate more at work. Make sure I'm home for dinner more often."

"That's a great start. Let's explore some specific strategies to help you achieve a better balance. How is your relationship with Zac? And how are things at home?"

Karen tensed, her gaze drifting to the window. "It's... complicated. Zac's still struggling with the aftermath of his abduction. Some days are better than others."

She ran a hand through her hair, a gesture of frustration. "He's making progress, but it's slow. At times, I glimpse the old Zac, but then something will trigger him —a loud noise, an unexpected visitor—and we're back to square one. We also have the added stress of Zac's ex-wife creating a fiction between us. Zac and I do our best to provide a stable home for Summer, but Michelle comes in like a wrecking ball, accusations flying, and undoes all our hard work. She has a drinking problem and is always spoiling for an argument. It's not healthy, or helpful."

Karen's voice softened as she continued, "At home, we're trying to establish a new normal. Summer's been amazing, but I can see the strain on her, too. She's caught between wanting to help Zac and being a typical teenager."

Doctor Morales nodded, prompting Karen to elaborate.

"The hardest part is the tension," Karen confessed. "Zac worries every time I leave for work. I can see the fear in his eyes, even though he tries to hide it. And I feel guilty, like I'm choosing my job over his recovery."

She paused and chewed on her bottom lip as she considered her predicament. "But at the same time, I know my work is important. It's who I am. I just don't know how to balance it all without someone getting hurt."

"Understandable. We can monitor it over the next few weeks."

They talked further until Karen's hour was up. She thanked the doctor for her time and said goodbye. The session had been intense, forcing her to confront emotions and fears she'd been pushing aside. But Doctor Morales's calm guidance and practical advice had given Karen hope.

As Karen drove through the bustling streets of York, her mind wandered to Zac and Summer. She felt determined to make changes, and to be more present for them. The idea of setting clearer boundaries at work no longer seemed like an impossible task.

Karen pulled into a nearby park, deciding to take a moment for herself. She found a quiet bench overlooking a small pond and grabbed a seat. Pulling out her phone, she opened her calendar and began blocking out specific times for family dinners and activities with Zac and Summer. A more pressing issue provided the driving force beside her desire to make those changes… planning for a wedding which could only happen once Zac was better.

It felt great as she made these small but significant changes. Karen realised that while the challenges ahead were still daunting, she now had a roadmap to navigate them.

## 59

Karen pulled into the driveway, the familiar sight of her home bringing a sense of comfort after her draining therapy session. As she approached the front door, a tantalising aroma wafted through the air, catching her by surprise.

She stepped inside, hanging her coat and slipping off her shoes before sliding her feet into a pair of goofy slippers Summer had given her for Christmas. The house was quiet, save for the soft clinking of dishes coming from the kitchen.

"Zac?" she called out, curiosity piquing her voice.

"In here," came the reply.

Karen made her way to the kitchen, her eyes widening at the sight before her. Zac stood by the stove, a proud smile on his face. He had set the table with their best, chip-free plates, and a bottle of wine chilled in an ice bucket nearby. Candles flickered, casting a warm glow over the room.

"What's all this?" Karen asked, a smile tugging at her lips.

Zac approached and wrapped his arms round her in a gentle embrace. "I thought you'd appreciate a nice dinner after your session, And... I wanted to do something special for you. To show you how much I appreciate everything you do for us."

Karen's throat tightened. She was touched by Zac's thoughtfulness. She appreciated the effort he'd put into this surprise, a clear sign of progress in his recovery.

Karen and Zac sat at the table, an awkward silence settling between them. They exchanged glances, both unsure how to begin. Zac poured the wine, his hand trembling as he filled Karen's glass.

"So, how was your session?" Zac asked, his voice hesitant.

Karen took a sip of wine before answering. "It was... intense. But good, I think."

Zac nodded and fidgeted with his napkin. "I'm glad you're going. I know it's difficult."

Another silence fell, broken only by the soft clink of cutlery against plates. Karen sensed Zac wanted to say more but was holding back.

After a long silence, Zac let out a sigh. "Karen, I... I've been thinking a lot about us. About everything we've been through."

Karen met his gaze. She saw vulnerability there, mixed with determination.

"Me, too," she admitted.

Encouraged by her response, Zac continued. "I know I haven't been easy to live with. But I want you to know I'm trying. And I'm so grateful for your patience."

Karen reached across the table and took his hand in hers. "We're in this together, Zac. Always."

The tension in the room eased, and they talked more openly about their fears, hopes, and the challenges they'd faced. As the conversation flowed, a warmth spread through Karen's chest, a renewed connection with the man she loved.

Zac's grip on Karen's hand tightened, their intertwined fingers. He took a shaky breath, struggling to find the right words.

"When you're not here, Karen... I feel so helpless," he confessed. "Every time you walk out of the door, I'm terrified it might be the last time I see you. This paranoia eats away at me, and I hate it."

Karen remained silent, giving him space to continue. Zac's gaze lifted to meet hers, his eyes brimming with tears.

"I know your job is important, and I'm proud of what you do. But after everything that's happened... I can't shake this fear something terrible will happen to you or us again."

He swallowed hard, his Adam's apple, bobbing. "Sometimes, I wake in the middle of the night, and for a moment, I forget where I am and the panic sets in. It's like I'm back in the cave, waiting for..."

Karen squeezed his hand, offering silent support.

"I'm annoyed with myself," he continued, frustration creeping into his tone. "I want to protect you, to keep you safe. But I can't even leave the house without feeling like I'm going to fall apart. And it leaves me more helpless."

Karen listened as Zac poured out his fears and frustrations. She saw the pain etched on his face, the struggle between his love for her and his anxiety about her safety.

"I understand, Zac. And I'm sorry I've put you through so much worry."

Zac shook his head. "It's not your fault. I know. I'm struggling to keep everything in order."

Karen sighed and considered her words. "Perhaps we

should look for a way to make you feel more involved, more connected to what I do. Would it help if I called you more often during the day, to check in?"

Zac nodded. "That might help. And maybe... Perhaps I will start visiting the station occasionally? Just to get used to being out again and be round people I know."

Karen smiled, encouraged by his suggestion. "I think it's a great idea. Perhaps we should begin by having lunch in the canteen once a week?"

They continued to discuss ways to bridge the gap between Karen's work life and their home life. Karen suggested setting clearer boundaries for work hours, while Zac proposed having a regular family night with Summer, where work talk was off-limits.

They discussed practical solutions to the challenges they faced.

Karen and Zac also focussed on finding ways to strengthen their relationship. They agreed communication was key and would set aside time each evening to talk about their day, sharing both the challenges and the positive moments.

Zac suggested they try a few activities together not revolving round work or their trauma. Karen agreed, realising how much they needed it for enjoyment and connection.

They also discussed the importance of individual self-care. Karen promised to be more consistent with her therapy sessions, while Zac committed to continuing his walks and joining a support group for survivors of trauma.

The couple agreed to revisit their wedding plans and not to rush into anything, but to have something positive to look forward to by perhaps finding venues or discussing potential guest lists.

Later that evening, Karen and Zac ended up on the

sofa, nestled close together. The warm glow of the living room lamp cast a warm light over them. Zac's arm draped round Karen's shoulders, while she savoured the moment. They sat in companionable silence for a while. The air between them seemed lighter, as if a dense fog consuming their lives had lifted.

Zac tilted Karen's chin up, meeting her gaze. His eyes, once clouded with fear and uncertainty, now held a renewed spark of determination and love. "Karen, I want you to know no matter what challenges we face, I'm in this with you. Always."

A warmth filled Karen's chest. She cupped his face with her hand. "And I'm with you, Zac. Through everything. We're stronger together."

Their lips met in a tender kiss, a physical affirmation of the commitment they'd renewed.

## 60

The next evening, Karen parked outside Jade's apartment, balancing a bag of fragrant takeaway and a bottle of wine in her arms. She rang the doorbell, her heart lightening at the prospect of spending time with her friend and colleague.

Jade opened the door, her face breaking into a warm smile at the sight of Karen. "You're a lifesaver," she said, ushering Karen indoors. "I couldn't face cooking tonight, so this is a result!"

They made their way to the living room, where Karen set out the containers of food on the coffee table. The aroma of spices filled the air as Jade fetched plates and glasses from the kitchen.

Settling onto the sofa, Karen poured the wine, offering a glass to Jade. "How's your day been?"

Jade sipped her wine before answering. "Better, I think." She paused, then added with a hint of her old spark, "But I'm going stir-crazy not being at work. Any chance you could smuggle me a few case files?"

Karen chuckled, relieved to see glimpses of the old

Jade emerging. "Nice try, but you know I can't do that. Besides, I don't want to be blamed for you having a meltdown at work!"

The conversation flowed between them. Karen filled Jade in on the latest developments in the Lockwood case, careful to avoid overwhelming her with details.

As they ate, the clinking of forks against plates mingled with Karen and Jade's laughter as they shared light hearted stories about their day. Jade recounted a humorous incident with her enthusiastic mum while Karen described Summer's latest school project.

The conversation shifted to more serious matters. Jade set her fork on her plate and looked at Karen. "I miss work. Miss being round people. I feel like I should be there, stuck in the middle of an investigation."

Karen sighed, understanding her friend's frustration. "I know it's been tough for you. I'd climb the walls, too. But these things take time, and you're making bloody brilliant progress. And you know your job is waiting for you when you're ready."

Jade nodded, her expression a mix of gratitude and impatience. "I know, it's just... I feel so useless sitting at home."

"You're not useless. You're healing."

They fell silent for a moment, each lost in thought.

Then Jade asked, "How's Zac coping? He's not sick of you yet?"

Karen laughed. "Not yet. Give it time. He has good and bad days. It's been hard on him, watching me dive back into work while he's still struggling."

Jade reached out and squeezed Karen's hand. "You're both incredibly strong. You'll get through this." She took a deep breath, her fingers tracing the rim of her wine glass. "The therapy's been... intense," she admitted. "Doctor

Morales's been great, but digging into everything is like reliving it sometimes."

Karen listened, giving Jade the space to speak at her own pace.

"The nightmares are the worst." Jade stared at a point on the wall. "I wake in a cold sweat, convinced I'm back there. It takes a while to remember I'm safe."

She paused and sipped her wine. "The mental side is a real challenge. Some days, I feel almost normal. Others, I can't get out of bed."

Jade's eyes met Karen's, a flicker of vulnerability in them. "I miss work. I miss feeling useful. But the thought of being back out there, in dangerous situations… it terrifies me. And I hate how it terrifies me."

Karen understood the conflict in Jade's mind.

"Doctor Morales says it's normal. Recovery goes through phases," Jade said, her voice tinged with frustration. "But I can't help feeling like I should be further along by now. Like I'm letting the team down by not being there."

Karen's fingers tightened round her wine glass. She knew it was time to share her own struggles with Jade.

"I've been carrying this weight," Karen began. "Every time I think about what happened to you, I feel this overwhelming guilt."

Jade protested, but Karen raised a hand, needing to continue.

"I know it wasn't my fault. But I should have done more, seen it coming." Karen's eyes glistened with unshed tears. "You were under my command, and I didn't protect you."

She paused, gathering her thoughts. "There are nights when I lie awake, replaying every decision I made leading to your abduction. I wonder if I'd done something differently, if you wouldn't have had to go through this ordeal.

"I need you to know I'm doing everything in my power to make sure nothing like this ever happens again. Your recovery matters to me, not only as your boss, but as your friend."

Karen had just finished speaking when James walked into the living room. He offered a warm smile.

"Evening, ladies," he said, shrugging off his jacket. "Hope I'm not interrupting."

Jade's face brightened at his arrival. "Not at all. We were just chatting. There's plenty of food if you're hungry."

James settled on the sofa next to Jade. He glanced between the two women, sensing he'd interrupted their chat.

"Everything alright?" he asked.

Jade leaned into him and tucked her legs on the sofa. "We were talking about the recovery process. It's been... challenging."

James nodded. "It has been. But you're making progress every day, even if it doesn't always feel like it. I've noticed big changes in you. More of the old you. You put the cap back on the toothpaste. You're using tons of anti-bac hand gel again, and you're farting in bed. The old Jade is back, Karen."

Karen roared with laughter as Jade playfully poked him in the ribs.

Karen watched the interaction between Jade and James, noting the easy comfort they seemed to find in each other's presence. James had been a steady support for Jade throughout her recovery.

James excused himself to attend to some unfinished work.

Karen reached out and took Jade's hand, giving it a gentle squeeze. "I'm here for you, always. Whatever you need, whenever you need it."

"I know, and it means more than I can say. You've been my rock through all of this."

"We're in this together. Your recovery, the case, all of it. We're a team, on and off the job."

Jade managed a watery smile. "Partners in crime-solving?"

Karen chuckled. "Always."

They embraced, holding on to each other.

"Thank you for tonight. For the food, the company, and for being you."

"Anytime, Jade. That's what friends are for."

## 61

SIX WEEKS after wrapping up the case, Karen, Zac, Jade, and Summer stood solemnly in York Minster for Sarah's memorial service. The historical Minster was filled with a mix of emotions—relief at the case's resolution, sadness for the life lost, and a sense of closure for those who had waited decades for answers.

Karen glanced round, noting the faces of those she knew through the investigation. Sarah's frail parents sat in the front row, their expressions solemn as they stared ahead.

Zac squeezed Karen's hand, offering silent support. She looked at him, grateful for his presence and the progress he'd made in his own recovery.

With the Dean of York's resonant voice booming through the cavernous cathedral, the scent of incense mingling with the aged stone, Karen felt an overwhelming sense of completion. The case had brought justice for Sarah. For Karen, it had also strengthened the bonds between her own team at work and her family at home.

Following the dean's speech, Olivia Lockwood made

her way to the lectern, her steps slow but determined. The Minster fell silent as she unfolded a piece of paper with trembling hands.

"Sarah was more than just my daughter," Olivia began. "She was a bright light, full of curiosity and passion."

Olivia shared memories of Sarah's childhood, her love for history blossoming early. She spoke of Sarah's excitement when she was accepted into the archaeology programme, and the pride she felt when Sarah joined the York Minster dig.

"I remember the day she came home, bursting with news about a significant find," Olivia said, her eyes misting. "She couldn't give me details, but her enthusiasm was contagious."

In the hushed grandeur of the Minster, Olivia's reading of Sarah's diary excerpts filled the space, the diary's words painting a vivid picture of Sarah's life and spirit. The entries spoke of Sarah's dedication to her work, her dreams for the future, leaving out her growing concerns about irregularities in the dig.

Karen felt Zac's hand tighten round hers as Olivia's voice broke while reading Sarah's final diary entry.

"Sarah may have been taken from us," Olivia concluded, her voice gaining strength, "but her spirit, her passion for truth and history, lives on. And now, thanks to the dedication of Detective Heath and her team, we finally have answers."

After the service, Karen and her group made their way through the crowd to where Olivia Lockwood and her husband stood, surrounded by well-wishers. As they approached, Olivia smiled with recognition.

"Detective Heath," Olivia said, her voice wavering slightly. "Thank you for coming."

Karen introduced Zac, Summer, and Jade to Olivia,

*The Bones of Deceit*

who greeted each of them warmly. As they talked, others connected to the case gathered round them.

The group stood in a loose circle, united by their connection to Sarah. Despite the sombre occasion, there was a sense of closure and shared understanding among them.

With a round of farewell hugs, Karen said her goodbyes to Sarah's family and left with her family.

Jade turned to Karen as they walked away. "Muffin at Cupcakery?"

"Thought you'd never ask!"

Printed in Great Britain
by Amazon